Yours, For Now

A fake dating, plus size romance

Leonor Soliz

Leonor Soliz

Book Cover by Leonor Soliz

Illustrations by Leonor Soliz

First Edition

Paperback ISBN: 978-1-7380562-0-0

Ebook ISBN: 978-1-7380562-1-7

To everyone who has had to toughen up:
keep reaching for your dreams

Contents

Author's Note

MY BOOKS ALWAYS END in a Happily Ever After. My stories are generally fluffy, with humor and light angst sprinkled in. Nevertheless, I believe it's important to give readers every chance to consent to reading my book. Although I write generally happy romance, if you'd like to access content warnings for this story, check **leonorsoliz.com/books/yours-for-now**, or use the QR code below:

Additionally, both main characters in this book are Latine. While I believe the Spanish spoken through the book should be understandable through context cues, I wrote a blog post on my website to help with other things. If you'd like a visual aid to keep track of all family and friends mentioned in the book, as well as some information on the many foods that make an appearance, then check **leonorsoliz.com/yfn-content**, or use the QR code below:

I hope you enjoy!

Chapter 1

Gabe

NOT EVEN AN OCEAN of people could stop me from searching for Lina at the Construction Cares Gala. The organization hosting the annual fundraising party seemed to be as dear to her as it was to me, and we spent some time checking in with each other every year— six straight times by my count. Relief coasted through my insides when all the faces around me parted like a biblical sea, and her eyes locked with mine through the crowd.

I smiled and made my way to her. People were jam-packed in the hall this year, and I strode among my well-dressed and deep-pocketed peers. I never let my connection to Lina waver. The theme for this year's party was *A Bright Future*, and everything was decorated to glow— several sparkling chandeliers hung from the tall ceilings, the walls and table linens had a subtle glitter effect, and tall extravagant centerpieces were filled with flowers shaped like stars. It made me feel like I walked on the arm of a galaxy towards Lina. I couldn't wait to see all the lights glimmering in her eyes.

Strolling toward her was my chance to admire her generous curves, but I tried to be discreet about it. This year, she'd chosen a deep amethyst dress, pinned and tucked and cut in such a way that my eyes wanted to feast on her breasts. The gown had an old Hollywood style to it, and the curls of her hair accentuated the look. The full skirt camouflaged her abundant hips, but I hid the disappointment of it. She looked wonderful regardless.

Lina waited for me with an arched eyebrow and a relatively familiar purse of her lips. Like facing me was mildly inconvenient, but she'd endure it without much of a fuss. Maybe just a little bit of fuss.

It was the same gesture that overtook her face every time we met at this event. And, like every year, it brought a teasing smirk to my lips.

"Catalina Martínez. I'm glad to see you." I was being honest, but I added a charming smile anyway.

She pulled her long hair to one side and over her shoulder. "Gabriel Sotomayor. Can't say I'm surprised to see you."

She looked so good that it triggered a wave of self-consciousness over my simple tuxedo, and made me regret that I had surreptitiously loosened my tie earlier. I patted down my stomach, my fingers catching on the single button keeping my jacket closed.

"Why, because we meet every year?" I asked. I should have tried a more daring suit this time.

"No, because you go out of your way to find me every year."

A cheeky gesture accompanied her statement, and it brought a laugh out of me.

I shrugged. "Maybe I do it for the irony. We live and work in the same city, and yet, we only meet at Construction Cares. In another city, far away from home."

As far as I knew, Lina had started working at her family's company a couple of years after I had started at mine. We didn't quite move in the same circles, and we rarely saw each other. This party was it for us.

Lina squinted at me, and studied me from under the ridge of her eyebrows. "Eh. I think you just wanted to see a familiar face. Then you can jump back on your private jet and go home knowing you said hi to me. Another task crossed off your list."

That stole another smirk out of me. She liked to keep me on my toes, direct as always. "Did you know I come to this gala with my friends every year? I have plenty of familiar faces at this event. They're all around schmoozing and starting deals and having fun."

She gazed around, looking for proof that my friends were working the room around us, or maybe like she doubted they were even real. I smiled. What lived under such a self-assured and slightly defiant personality? I'd wager she used it as a shield. Meeting me with a challenge was part of our annual ritual, but I had seen enough to know there was a softer side to her somewhere inside. I'd peeked at it before, too.

"Deals?" She arched an eyebrow. "I thought we're meant to be buying ridiculously overpriced tables, and bidding for things we don't need, to raise money for underprivileged folks."

Sometimes I wondered why I didn't seek her out, during all those months from one gala to the next. Not only did I appreciate the way she looked, I also found her intriguing. I wanted to know *more*. Understand. Maybe even test if she'd soften for me. Then I remembered my business goals and realized, all over again, that it would be the wrong way to derail my plans.

I gave her my best smile, to show her I wasn't intimidated by her challenge. "That's happening, too. We make sure to do our part— we got five tables and brought a bunch of people as well. I promise I'll be giving away lots of money tonight."

"Your own, or the company's?"

I grinned. "Both."

Now that I thought about it, that was probably why I sought her out every year. I enjoyed the way she challenged me.

She sipped from her tall glass, her eyes steady on me. "As long as you do."

"We do. It's the right thing to do."

She gave me a small nod. Someone walked past her and she stepped toward me to make room for them. I didn't move, so we ended up standing closer.

"I have to admit I was hoping to see you this year, too," she said. "I have a project I'd like to discuss with you."

The surprise of her words pulled a small jerk out of my head. "A... business deal?"

Lina frowned. She watched the crowd around us, then lifted her eyes at one of the big chandeliers hanging from the ceiling near us. "Yes."

This was big. Technically, we didn't have much of an over-lap. Her family's company was in construction, and focused on public deals across the country. The Sotomayor Group was a big name in private construction, but those projects were larger than what Martínez and Associates usually dealt in. We typically worked in different areas and kept to ourselves; if it weren't for this gala and the fact the Martínez family were Latine, too, I didn't think I would have ever exchanged words with Lina. The possibility of a business opportunity sparked a curious tingle behind my sternum.

"Interesting." I inspected her face. "How do you feel about grabbing lunch sometime? We could talk more."

"Well..." she gazed at me as she considered. "I'd like it to be a bit more formal than a casual conversation over a meal. I've been preparing a presentation."

My eyebrows went up. "Okay. Intriguing. I can ask my dad to be there."

"I would love that. Hearing what Don Raúl has to say would be helpful. Can I reach out to your assistant to schedule some-thing?"

I had barely started to nod when we were interrupted by a booming voice.

"Pero si no es Gabriel, how are you? How's your dad? That's a good man, Raúl."

"Buenas noches, Don Miguel. How are you?"

I shook his hand while Miguel dropped heavy slaps on my shoulder. He grinned. "Good, good. I hope our Lina here isn't talking your ear off about a telenovela or something? I don't know what women see in those shows, I swear."

Miguel's smile was confident and wide, the kind that only a man with no concerns could feature.

His comment and lack of awareness built disgust in my gut, but I hid it. "I'm the one who approached her to talk, actually."

"We were talking about work, Tío," Lina said.

Miguel smirked, a teasing look on his face. He didn't respond to her, and talked to me instead. "Sometimes I think work is all she can think about. What about marriage? And kids? She's thirty, you know?"

He didn't seem to notice or care that this statement was a total contradiction to his previous comment on Lina's interests, nor that it was completely misogynistic. And this was Lina's uncle. And boss.

I stopped myself from rolling my eyes, but was pleased to see Lina didn't.

"And you?" Miguel continued, still engaging me. "Getting married soon?"

"Nope. Single." I crossed my arms. "And I'm thirty-two."

"Young people." He shook his head like those words said it all, but his smile never wavered. "Well, you're a man. But if you ever change your mind, you may consider dating my niece—"

"Tío!" Lina exclaimed and her uncle laughed.

Miguel shook a hand in the air. "It's just a joke, relax. Anyway, it was good to see you, Gabe. Tell your dad we should go out for drinks sometime. Just because we said no to his acquisition attempt years ago, doesn't mean we can't be friends. Lina, I wanted to introduce you to someone. Come with me?"

I nodded in goodbye. Lina and her uncle turned and walked away; I let my face contort in a scowl as they disappeared among the crowd.

I didn't like Miguel and his machismo. Nor how he treated Lina. It sucked that so many Latine men still thought that way... and I was protected from it, being a man. Lina had to live with it every day.

I wasn't sure if I'd see her again at the gala, but when she came to my dad and I with her proposal, I'd keep an open mind.

Chapter 2

Lina

THE STRATEGIC MEETING AT Martínez and Associates was well underway and, as always, boring. I sipped from my life-saving coffee and watched Tío Miguel and my dad discuss the projections for the next quarter.

Although eight people filled the boardroom, the two brothers mostly listened to each other. They'd made me the Chief of Staff, after I diligently climbed the ladder in the family business. I was in charge of client relations, basically. Keeping the people paying us happy, and helping close deals. But the two ran the company, and everyone knew it. The other officers were used to keeping their mouths shut while they made decisions, unless my dad or uncle asked them a direct question. I was the only one who dared add my two cents to their conversation.

Such small business minds. Still running the company like we were the tiny family venture they'd begun.

Despite my skills and hopes, I hated that when they looked at me they didn't see possibilities.

Oh, how I wanted to prove them wrong.

I tapped my fingers on the table and waited for my moment. Dad opened the final folder to be discussed. "This is the Municipal bid in Richmond. Thomson is running it. Same kind of requirements as usual, but this time they have more proposals, from what I was able to find out. We have a bit more competition this time. Thoughts?"

I opened my mouth to respond but tío Miguel beat me to it. "It's fine. Thomson likes us. This one should be in the bag."

"The fact that we've won bids with them before doesn't guarantee—" I tried, but Tío Miguel interrupted.

"— I can call my friend that works there, confirm the parameters, and we're set."

I continued without taking a breath and without waiting a beat. "They'll do due diligence. They can't just award an RFP based on friendship—"

"— No, no, no. Lina, you don't know the industry—" Tío Miguel's voice got louder than mine.

"I've been in the industry for twelve years, I think I know it well by now—" I insisted.

"— But not as well as I do!" His hand turned into a fist.

"The industry's changing!" I hid my hand under the boardroom table. That way no one would see me doing the same in irritation.

"What do you know about that?!"

"Okay, okay, let's calm down." Dad put two hands up, each one facing one of us, me and my uncle. "We can do both. You can contact your friend, Miguel, and we can hear what Lina has to say. You have something to say, right?"

He cast his eyes at me, and the unaffected face didn't conceal the hint of doubt in his eyes. The rest of the people around us remained silent as usual, ignoring the loud voices or the way the light changed in the room, now that a building blocked the sun on its way down to the horizon.

I dug my nails into the flesh of my palm. "We need to find ways to stand out. We could do that by pushing accessibility goals for all infrastructure projects starting next year. I want to position us as leaders in that space. We can start with a smaller project like Thomson's."

Tío Miguel scoffed. "You and your obsession with finding a new niche. I've told you before, we need to cast a wide net. Infrastructure is niche enough."

"But how do we get people to notice us above other companies? What makes us special?" I wanted to drink more coffee, to soothe my throat and stop it from tightening up any further, but I didn't reach for my cup. Any lull would give mi tío a chance to overtake the conversation. "And you know I hope to expand to commercial infrastructure. Big projects included. We *need* something to make us more noticeable."

Tío Miguel shook his head. "It doesn't make sense. We've incorporated ramps in several of our semi-commercial designs. How can that be a niche?"

Temptation coated my tongue, and I almost talked about the importance of inclusivity, call him out for his ignorance, but I knew from experience that it would make us fight. If I wanted to effectively get my point across and get us closer to my goals, I needed to speak a language he understood. One he cared about. I allowed myself a sip of coffee, this time.

I unclenched my jaw to respond. "Accessibility is more complex than adding a ramp out of the way and out of sight. We can make sure to make it part of the design and architecture of the place, make it *belong* in the space, like it's on purpose. We can scale that expertise to bigger projects, too. Our clients could capitalize on that as a marketing point."

"We don't need a niche," Tio Miguel said. "We have a reputation."

"And yet our income has declined." I glared at my dad's brother. "We've lost more projects than we ever have."

Tío Miguel's brown skin darkened, the effect of an angry blush on him. He didn't like it when I pointed out our current financial stress. I knew this, and yet I wouldn't skirt around the issue. Tío Miguel could keep up his hopes that his son would one day decide to take over the business, but I wouldn't give up that easily. I needed to protect the company as much as I wanted to prove I was the right person for the job.

If there was one thing I had learned growing up in my family and working in this business, it was to be strong. To endure my family's machismo and remain standing. His explosion wouldn't make me back down. I steeled myself in preparation for his outburst, turning my veins into rebar.

My dad had to have noticed the building eruption of Tío Miguel's anger. He pushed a hand forward between Tío and I as if to grab our attention, like we were two kids about to fight over a toy. He locked eyes with me. "Bueno, bueno, there's no need to go there. We're still doing fine. Why don't you put it all on paper, create a proposal, and show us what that would look like?"

This time, when I reached for my coffee, I did so to drown my own rage. This is what they did when they wanted to shut me up, they told me to write it down and they'd look at it later. My last proposal still gathered dust on my dad's desk. Two shots of espresso and water wouldn't suffocate the gunpowder building in my gut, but I had to try. Or I'd burn all bridges and leave in the glory of fire.

I nodded, if only so he would point his pitying eyes away from me.

If only my father believed enough in me to leave me his share in the company. He had the majority of them in the family business, and the only reason Tío Miguel had more power was because he was older, louder, and owned the remaining minority. And every time Dad tried to pacify his brother, he ended up dismissing me. Like he had every time he said he'd read my proposals.

This time it would be different. I would take it a step further. I had reached out to Gabriel's assistant earlier in the day, and had scheduled a meeting with him for the following week.

If I couldn't shake my dad— and uncle— out of this pattern of ours with this proposal, involving a whole other company, then I might have to ask myself some hard questions about my future that I'd rather not face.

Chapter 3

Gabe

"THERE YOU GO, GABE." Jake entered my office in all his imposing size, two cups in hand.

My best friend since childhood left a mug full of steaming coffee on my desk, and dropped his big Scottish body into one of the chairs in front of my desk.

"Thanks." I grabbed the mug without looking and almost burnt my fingers. I hissed.

Jake chuckled. "Beware, Gabe. Coffee's hot."

"Har har." I turned the mug on the wooden surface until I could grab it from its handle. "Is the coffee machine not working properly, or what?"

"Maybe the lack of manual labor is making your skin too soft?"

I didn't bother answering. I rolled my eyes and took a deep breath, filling my lungs with the smell of high quality beans. "Thanks again."

Jake nodded and took a sip of his own drink. "So. Is Tío Raúl coming to this unexpected meeting today?"

"Yeah. He's also very curious about what Lina wants to discuss."

"So you have no idea what that's about?"

Jake, almost like a second son to my parents and the COO to my VP role, knew all the intricacies of our company. His question didn't shock me; I expected him to want to know.

I shook my head. "Nope. And you know what's the most intriguing thing? She's coming alone. No uncle or dad, that I could gather."

He ran his fingers through his red-blond beard. "Huh. I heard through the grapevine that they might be trying to restructure the company."

"*I* told you that, you jackass."

Jake laughed. "Right. After you analyzed their business in preparation for the meeting. But what if she'd like to discuss an acquisition? It could be something to help convince the board to make you CEO when your dad retires in a year."

"I don't know. I don't think that's it." I checked my watch. It would be another hour until the meeting. The idea that I'd be seeing Lina soon took a few detours in my brain, one road where I wanted to know what she planned for the meeting, and another where I was excited to see her again so soon after the charity event. "My dad tried to buy them out a few years ago and they said no. Unless things have changed radically, I don't think that's it."

A frown appeared on my best friend's face. "Are you going to suggest it again, though? With all their experience in running commercial-public infrastructure deals, it could be a great asset to the portfolio. It would strengthen that branch of the Group."

My stomach bubbled nervously at the idea that Lina's proposal could solve this little problem of mine; that it could offer something to present to the Board and help me prove that I have what it takes to become the new CEO once my dad retires.

I bit the inside of my lips. "We'll see. I'll hear what she has to say, then I'll consult with Dad, you, and Violeta."

As usual, a soft blush appeared on Jake's white face at the mention of my sister and, as usual, I ignored it.

"Sounds good," he said. "We have some time until we figure out the best plan."

The glass walls separating my office from the rest of the space were clear— I could make them opaque at the push of a button— and I watched as a couple of people walked by.

"But not too much time." I drank more of my coffee. "I need to present a strong plan, and an even stronger initiative. I need to focus on this; being the CEO's son won't be enough to get appointed as his replacement, and you know that."

"Of course. And you know you can count on me." Jake smiled. "I want you to be the new boss."

We all did— my parents, sister, Jake and I. It would take every minute of the year ahead of me, to plan and prepare the vision I wanted to share with the board, and manage to do so on top of my current responsibilities. If successful, they might confirm me as CEO. That would only be the start of an even busier period, working extra hard to figure out the transition with my dad; likely another year to fully settle in my new role. Only after that would I allow myself a break, maybe two weeks on a private beach somewhere, wearing nothing but shorts and sleeping under the shade of palm trees, before I came right back to it. But until then, work would be all I knew.

"And I want you to replace me as VP of Operations," I added. "Working together on this will help make the transition easier for you, too."

"As long as my promotion isn't nepotism, either."

"C'mon. You know you're here because you earned it, too." I smiled, and hoped it contained the long story of how we'd all made it here, at the helm of an international conglomerate. "You helped us build all of this."

He raised an eyebrow. "And I'm also your best friend."

"That you are. Will you be my best man, too?"

That made him laugh again. "Since when are you getting married?"

"Don't have a bride yet, but I thought I'd book you in advance." I grinned. "I'll probably start looking into that in three to four years, if you want to put it on your calendar."

"Asshole." His blush deepened, a sign he may fight it, but he still liked all our reassurances, even twenty five years later. "You don't even have a girlfriend, do you?"

"Nope. That's penciled-in for two years in the future."

"Until after the transition, I gather?"

I nodded. "Can't see getting a girlfriend while going through it all."

"So strict. What if someone surprises you?"

"Nah," I shrugged. "Can't see it happening. I'm too focused on this—" I waved around my office— "to even find someone."

Jake smirked. "We'll see, I guess."

"Please. Don't tell me you think it's easy to find someone? You don't have a girlfriend."

He sipped from his mug. "But I'm not the one asking you to be my best man."

"I'd still say yes if you asked."

"Shut up. Of course I'll ask you when— if— the day ever comes."

"You better. I didn't ask you to have lunch with me in third grade for nothing."

Jake rolled his eyes and got up, unfurling his long and wide body. "I should go. I need to prep for a meeting myself. We'll talk later, and you can tell me what the hell the meeting with Lina was about."

I nodded as he stepped out of the office, and I put my head down to work.

―――

Lina

The head offices for the Sotomayor Group were located on five floors at the top of a skyscraper. Apparently, the offices in Chicago, New York, and Toronto were only three floors. From the research I had done, in every other city, the offices were only two floors... but they had thirty-eight workplace locations throughout the world. That's how the conglomerate ran their international businesses in style.

The elevator zoomed up to the top-most level; when the doors opened, I was greeted by a pretty woman I had only met a couple of times before.

"Lina?" she asked, a half-surprised, half-confused look on her face.

"Violeta! Hola!" I stepped out of the elevator, and we moved to the side to not block the doors for anyone else.

"It's been ages!" she said. Her long, wavy hair was up in a half ponytail, and the cream blouse she wore contrasted beautifully with her plum-colored skirt. Both made her light brown skin shine with a warm undertone.

I was glad I'd chosen a blue power suit, with pretty piping on the blazer. If we'd had the time, I would have loved to share notes, to see where she found— or got tailored— her clothes to fit bodies like ours, with plenty of volume and curves. As it was, I hoped she'd feel the same kind of silent camaraderie that I felt, knowing we both seemed to be the kind of people who wanted to decorate our bodies and be okay standing out, despite what most fashion designers thought of fat bodies.

Not to say anything about my admiration for her, considering how high up she was in such a large company, with enough power for her voice to matter in every decision. Just like I wished I could do, on the much smaller scale of my family's company.

"We met at the Construction Cares gala a few years ago, right?" I asked. "I think Gabe introduced us."

"That's right! That's the year he took Jake and I as well."

I grinned. "You make it sound like Gabe doesn't like to take you to it."

"Oh, no, he'd love it if we went. We tend to avoid it." The smile that stretched her face was so brilliant, it was like it illuminated all of the floor by itself. Yes, she was gorgeous. "So what are you doing here?"

"I have a meeting with your brother, actually. I guess he didn't mention it?"

"Oh, I'm the head of the legal department. I was on my way to a meeting elsewhere. He likely didn't think I needed to be involved yet. Was he wrong?"

I chuckled. "Well, I wouldn't want to say anything that could incriminate me."

"Perfect answer." Violeta laughed. "I have to get going though. Can I help you find Gabe?"

"Yes, if you can show me the way."

"I'll text him and he'll come find you. More welcoming that way, right?" She took her phone from her bag and typed on it.

"Aaaaand I'm sending him and his assistant a quick email, too. You never know if maybe he's distracted on a call or something."

"Thank you, Violeta."

"Call me Vi." She said it in a way that sounded like *Vee* and I took note of it; she lifted her eyes back to me, but cast them to the side in a quick glance at someone approaching us. "Yes, Cynthia?"

The woman by our side smiled at both of us. "I got a message from Solange— Gabriel's assistant. I can take Miss Martínez to his office."

"Thanks, Cynthia. Well, I'm going." Vi gave me a single kiss on the cheek and pressed on the elevator's button. "I hope to see you sometime soon, and that it's not another few years until we cross paths again."

I grinned. "I'd love to make that happen."

"Then I'll see you around!" The door to the lift opened and Vi stepped into the car. "Take care."

"Bye, Vi." Once the elevator started its journey down, I turned back to Cynthia. "Hi. Which way do we go?"

"Please follow me."

Cynthia guided me through the wide hallways deep into the offices. White walls gave structure to the place; they had a sheen to them, like they weren't made of painted drywall, but some other, more fashionable material. Most offices were walled in glass, and the design boasted copper metallics and dark wood. Overall, the modern look balanced organic and futuristic elements. By the blueprint and details alone, it made me feel like I knew what the Sotomayor Group was all about.

I concealed a sigh. Even if this business proposal didn't end up happening, my gut was still certain I had made the right choice to approach Gabe first.

We entered a larger open space, with a few offices flanking the corner area of the building. Just as Cynthia appeared to choose a specific desk to walk toward, a door opened and Gabe appeared behind it.

His eyes connected with mine, the smile on his face reminding me of Vi. I pressed my lips together, not to let his gorgeous face affect me. I was a woman on a mission— not just today, but every day for the past ten years— and an attractive man was not in my business domination plans.

"Lina! Glad to see you, though I feel like we should be surrounded by tons of people at a fancy party."

"I know what you mean. It's weird to be meeting with you in our actual hometown."

And with him wearing a navy suit rather than a tuxedo, but looking just as good.

"Isn't that right?" He grinned. "Would you like a coffee? We can get you some before we go to my dad's office for the meeting. And if you mention how good it is, you'll immediately fall into his good graces."

My smile was reluctant, mostly because I've always been adamant about not showing any inkling of how my hormones reacted around him. It was already a miracle he wasn't an egotistical asshole with the way he looked, or with the size of his wallet, but I still didn't want him suspecting he had an effect on me.

"Thanks for the tip," I said. "I'm sure it'll come in handy."

"Ready to go? Dad's waiting."

I nodded and followed Gabe to a break room with two wonderful espresso machines and multiple types of snacks. He made me a coffee himself, and then showed me the way to Don Raúl's office.

I'd practiced this presentation to the bone. I could recite and quote numbers in my sleep. The rest was up to the Sotomayor Group.

Chapter 4

Gabe

LINA'S PRESENTATION MESMERIZED ME. She entered the room, greeted my dad, complimented the coffee, and set up her slideshow with a confident arch to her eyebrow. She cast her computer to the big TV in the office, and we all sat in the comfortable sofas set in front of it. For the next half hour, light shining on Lina from the large windows framing the office, my dad and I remained quiet as she took us on a journey through an alternate universe... one that led us to a prime-time bid on an upcoming sports stadium capable of hosting major events and a hundred thousand guests.

"To reference my earlier point," Lina said, her eyes taking turns between the TV screen, my dad, and I, "a project like this can strengthen the construction branch of your business, expanding it into major bids in the public sector, while significantly expanding our capacity— without straining yours. Both companies can become stronger thanks to the other and, thus, we can better compete with the most powerful players in the industry. Billion dollar projects in the commercial-public domain situate both our businesses as leaders, pushing for an important expansion with great potential to all of us."

She held my eyes for a moment, then my dad's. A small smile appeared on her lips. "I hope what I've shown you today aligns with your goals, while fueling ambition into your projections. Any questions?"

I blinked a few times. Lina painted a picture so good that I had trouble processing the full realm of possibilities. A project like this had the potential to dazzle the board and secure my transition to CEO. My gut had made its mind, twirling already with enthusiasm, but my brain was slow to catch up and form words.

"Wow, Lina, what can I say?" My dad shook his head with a grin on his face. I didn't often notice his accent, but I did so clearly this time. "This is impressive. You obviously put so much work into it!"

I tried not to gawk. "You never talked about any of this with me at the gala. I would have never known you'd been thinking about this."

"I didn't choose this company for this proposal based on a few passing talks at a party, you know." Lina gave me a teasing look. "Though knowing you certainly got me through the door, I'm sure."

Her eyes shined in what seemed like pride, and I smiled. I had always enjoyed the look of confidence on a woman, and I would have let myself enjoy it on Lina, if my business brain weren't so tickled by her proposal.

"What did Miguel say about this?" Dad asked. "And your dad?"

That seemed to make her satisfied look falter. "They wanted to hear a proposal from me. I thought that it would be stronger if I already had a company in line and willing to get involved with us this way. If you cosigned the documents with me."

I raised my eyebrow at Lina's words and mulled them over. "So this isn't a done deal. If we say yes, we still need to ask your family for approval."

She closed her laptop with a slap, a determined slant to her mouth. "I don't plan to let them say no."

This time, both my eyebrows went up. Brave of her to approach the business this way, and to enlist the Sotomayor Group as bait for the executive team of her family's smaller company.

Good thing my dad was more likely to focus on the opportunity, rather than the optics.

"Well, I certainly appreciate your ambition, Lina." He nodded in her direction.

That was the gentlest comment possible with which to respond, and much better than what I could offer at the moment. Aside from the possibility of turning this into my Board project, all I had was that I found ambition sexy, but I didn't share that with anyone. I barely knew Lina, but she came across like a self-protected person, and flirting with her in a situation like this seemed like a douchey thing to do. My dick might want me to do something about my general attraction to her, but my brain overrode it easily. Having my dad in the room helped. He wouldn't be proud of me if he knew the kind of thoughts I was having. And anything sexy-related with Lina or anyone would be completely out of the agenda.

Better to focus on her proposal and all it could do for my family's business goals.

My dad continued, "if we decided to move forward with this, do we have time to put everything together in time for the stadium negotiations?"

"I understand that deals take time to progress in large corporations. Based on my research, the bid will start in a year, but there's a shortlist deadline approaching in a few weeks. I've prepared a large portion of that application document, so we should be okay timewise. For everything else, I also have everything set up and documented to a tee; I'd be happy to share it all with your legal and development heads. Regarding how long it might take us to sign on the line, I'm sure we can follow your schedule. As long as we can submit the shortlist document and close that deal in two to three months, we should have enough time to build a strong proposal for the stadium bid."

It sounded really, really good, even if it meant adding work to guide the project with the other VPs. With my dad's help, I might just be able to run this deal, and use it to prove to the board that I was CEO material.

My dad and I exchanged a look. He gave me a sign we'd been using for years for business situations like this. He appeared to be thinking along the same lines.

I responded to Dad and turned to Lina. I gazed at her for a second, studying the way her eyes focused on me and enjoying it a bit too much for my own good.

A single nod carried my answer. "You'll hear from us within a week."

―――

Lina

The offices for my family's construction company were different from the Sotomayors'. Ours lived in a renovated three story building in a business district near downtown. It wasn't as design-forward or expensive looking, but we owned it, and it served our needs well. The soft gray walls and array of windows illuminated the many people making big projects happen, with reception, a break room, and two boardrooms on the main floor; a big open working space taking up the entire second floor, and the directors' offices on the top-most level, with a smaller meeting room tucked to the side.

My office was one door away from my dad and my uncle's. The door in the middle belonged to Enrique, Tío Miguel's son, who he dreamed would eventually take over the company. It remained empty, but Tío Miguel refused to repurpose it. Its perma-closed door haunted me, because if it were ever used by my cousin in any consistent manner, my dreams might disintegrate. Luckily, I hadn't seen anyone in it for over a year now.

Enrique's sister, Lucía, worked in an admin role on the first floor, and it was her phone line that lit up my phone.

"Hey Luce. What's up?" I asked as I answered the call.

"Gabriel Sotomayor is here to see you. He said he's not on your agenda but would like to talk."

Gabe and I didn't have each other's personal numbers. Chances were, Gabe was here to tell me what he and his dad had decided. He could have called the office, but it seemed he'd chosen a different way to reach me.

A flutter interrupted the normal pattern of my breathing. "Tell him to come up. Thanks!"

I ran my fingers through my hair and fluffed it up, as if how I looked could help convince Gabe to say yes. With a smirk at myself, I got out from behind my desk and went to find him... but Tío Miguel found him first.

"Gabriel Sotomayor! This is a surprise," Tío Miguel said, standing in the middle of the shared space among all of our offices.

Gabe sported a small smile and a sexy as hell suit. No tie, because when you were at his level, the quality of the fabrics clothing his body were enough to tell you he could make all deals happen. He could afford to leave the top button open, even.

"Hello, Don Miguel." Gabe shook my uncle's hand. "Is Lina around?"

"Lina, huh?" His smile turned teasing, like he wanted to say more.

"Hey, Gabe," I interrupted before Tío Miguel could try. "You wanted to see me?"

Gabe nodded. He gazed around our offices, until his eyes landed on me. "Can I take you out for lunch?"

I thanked the heavens that I had felt flirty that morning, and had chosen to wear a belted sweater dress that I loved. Not because I hoped Gabe would notice how it wrapped my body, but because I liked feeling attractive when negotiating my future. It made me feel stronger, somehow.

I nodded. "Sure. Let me grab my bag."

Fearing that my uncle would ask too many questions if left alone with Gabe, I rushed to the office, took my bag, and left with the young Sotomayor. We got in a sleek car, and he asked his driver to take us to a nice restaurant nearby.

The restaurant's light was warm and dim, the modern furniture was solid wood in dark colors, and the waiters wore elegant waistcoats as they moved silently and efficiently. I hadn't been there before, but I guessed Gabe had, because the maître d' greeted him by name.

"Do you mind if we order Chilean wine? They have a really good one here."

"I don't mind. Your family is Chilean, right?"

"Yeah. It feels like a betrayal to my ancestors to order anything else."

I chuckled as he took charge of that, and we ordered our meal.

"I'd like to start by thanking you." I crossed my legs and prepared for the conversation. "I'm not sure how you knew I didn't want my uncle hearing anything yet, but I appreciate it."

He lifted a shoulder, his eyes roaming over my face. I resisted the urge to do the same with him, and stared at his eyes instead.

"I don't know. I know he's your uncle but..." He didn't finish his sentence, and sipped from his water instead. "Well, you said the other day he doesn't know yet about your proposal to us. I wasn't sure if that had changed. And a restaurant seemed like a great excuse to find neutral territory."

I squinted at him. Whatever he'd chosen not to say about my uncle teased my curiosity, but this wasn't the time. Hearing Gabe's opinion on Tío Miguel wasn't my priority.

"No, he doesn't know about any of that yet. Like I said, I'm hoping that having you backing up my proposal would help."

Gabe nodded, a glint in his eye. "I see what you did there. Nice. Subtle."

My smile was unapologetic. "What do you think I did?"

"You're both putting pressure on us to accept, telling me why we should at a personal level, and asking me where we're at."

My grin stretched wide. "And?"

He chuckled but didn't respond right away. The sommelier brought the wine, and Gabe tasted it, eyes closing as he savored it. He approved it, and after making sure I liked it too, we settled to wait for our food.

He sipped more of his wine. "I won't play around. My dad and I reviewed everything you shared with us and talked. We looked at the numbers, did our own projections." He leaned back on his chair, a relaxed curve to his torso. A couple walked past us and he watched them go by, and I resisted the urge to rush him. He cast his eyes back at me, and the brown clarity of them stilled my heart beat for a second. "It's solid, Lina. The numbers, the organization, the division of labor and admin... It makes me wish I'd made more of an effort to get to know you earlier."

When my heart returned to action, it did so like it was trying to make up for lost time.

I managed to speak around its fast beating. "I put a lot of work into the proposal. I'm glad it shows."

"It shows. My dad and I had a meeting with Jake, our COO, and my sister and mom, of course. We'd love to be a part of this."

If we weren't in such an elegant place, I would have broken down and pumped the air with my fist. As it was, I let out a small but assertive, "yes!" escape my lips.

I must have shown my reaction in my body, too, somehow. He smiled. He licked his lower lip; I tore my eyes away from it and focused on the hand he lifted for me to high five. If he could high-five in this place, so could I. I gave his hand a symbolic slap with mine, letting him see just how happy the news made me but not so forceful people would stare at us.

"I'm excited about this," he said. "I don't know how your dad and uncle could say no."

"They can't. Not if they truly listen to what we have to say. I just need to plan; meet with your representatives to practice. Do you know who will come do the presentation to my family with me?"

"I will. I want to head this project."

We stopped our conversation while the servers brought our food and topped up our wine glasses.

A frown threatened to appear on my brow, but I smoothed it. I hadn't expected to work closely with Gabe for this. There were potential pros and cons to having him be an integral part of this plan, and the idea that his power and reputation could help sway my family's decision twinkled with promise. I could always resist the temptation to admire his looks; I had experience hiding how my body responded to him.

"To be honest, I'm excited to hear that." I grabbed my fork in preparation to taste the wonderful meal in front of me, its smell already teasing me: a creamy pasta dish with sea urchin and spices. "I thought you would assign the project to someone else, but your involvement can really strengthen the presentation."

Gabe had chosen a duck and greens dish that looked as divine as mine. He took a bite, studying me as he tasted the food. "No. This project is major, and could turn out to be great for me personally, too. I'm looking forward to it, Lina."

I didn't answer but gave him a winning smile. I drank some wine and we discussed plans to present the deal to my family, brainstorming with Gabe in the hope that we'd build a bridge to the future I wanted.

Chapter 5

Lina

DURING THE FOLLOWING WEEK, Gabe visited me in the office twice for a quick meeting. Each time, we rushed through it, trying to make the most of the time we had together. I had offered to go to him to save some time, but he said he wanted to be seen in the Martínez offices, to get people wondering about his presence. He said that despite his packed schedule, getting people interested could help us when we presented to my family. We mostly exchanged emails to get everything else ready and studied on our own, until the day came to come clean to my dad and uncle.

After our receptionist announced his arrival, I waited for Gabe by the elevator to guide him to the small top-floor boardroom. Nerves shook up my legs with every step I took, but I hid it. If I straightened my back and squared my shoulders hard enough, no one would notice the tremors at the end of my fingers.

I had everything set up in the meeting room; folders with relevant documents in front of each place, water for each of us, as well as a computer and slides cast to the TV.

Gabe unbuttoned his blazer and we sat side-by-side, settling in to wait for my dad and uncle to arrive. The work day was about to end, and the four of us would be free to discuss the potential journey ahead.

"So, how are you feeling?" Gabe asked. He'd worn a tie today, and even though he looked spectacular as always, I missed the hint of brown, smooth skin I'd seen the last few times, when the top button had been loose. "Ready?"

I stared at him with as much aplomb as I could muster. "I can be put on trial to answer anything and everything about this project and presentation. But I have that anticipatory excitement thing happening, know what I mean?"

If he happened to notice any of my nervous tells, I wanted him to have a reason for them. I would rather he thought it was excitement than worry.

A smirk danced on his lips. "Yeah. I would never know from looking at you, though."

"That's good, right?"

"Very good. Would you guess my stomach is doing somersaults?"

That stole a smile from me. "No. Never."

"It is." He chuckled. "I really want this to work out. It could really help me on a couple of plans of mine."

His ready confession softened the iron in my shoulders.

I flicked the clip on my pen's cap. "You're not alone in wanting this to work out. This could change my future in this company."

"No pressure then. Only our future in the balance."

I laughed. "Exactly. At least, in your case, you get to make decisions as to how to move forward regardless of what happens. I completely depend on my dad and uncle's support."

The light in the room turned a beautiful mix of gold and rose, sparkling off every shiny surface. I took a long, deep breath, and gazed at the many shades coloring the clouds in the sky. A hint of calm eased the pressure in my chest.

Gabe tapped two fingers on the wooden boardroom table. "If, for some reason, this doesn't work out, we'll figure it out. I could ask my dad to call, or do something else to try and change their minds. We won't go out without a fight."

It was easy to believe him, when his eyes gazed at me with intense certainty.

The iron in my shoulders melted into my blood, and I relaxed against my chair. "Thank you. It's good to know we can be a team in this. That this helps you as much as it helps me. Because I really, really need to fight for this."

He grinned at me, and our thighs touched. "I will fight for it, too."

"Wonderful." I checked the time on my phone and casually moved a bit away from him. "They'll be here any second now. We're about to do it, Gabe."

"It'll be great, I'm sure. We can do it." He lifted his hand for a high five and, when I clapped it with mine, he interlocked our fingers in a victory shake in the air.

"Stop." I laughed and took away my hand. "You're going to jinx us."

"Impossible." He grinned at me and gazed with humor in his eyes. "Any plans for later? We could go celebrate a job well done."

"Stop flirting with my daughter."

I turned to my dad as he entered the boardroom, his voice surprising me and kicking my nerves into gear again.

Tío Miguel followed behind. "Did I hear that right? Gabriel was flirting with our Lina?"

Gabe pushed his chair back with an audible scratch on the floor. "Good evening. Hello, Mr. Martínez. Don Miguel." He shook both their hands.

Both of us ignored their teasing.

"I asked Lucía to bring us all coffee. She'll be here in a minute, then we can start," Tío Miguel said. "What's this meeting about, again?"

"The email said *business meeting* only," my dad added.

They sat next to each other at the table, in front of Gabe and I.

"You'll see." I pointed at the folders in front of them. "Gabe and I have a plan."

Luce came into the boardroom balancing a tray with cups and a carafe. We served drinks and settled into the meeting.

When I checked with Gabe, he was already looking at me. He lifted an eyebrow as if asking, *ready?* I smiled, nodded, and started our presentation.

"First," I said, "Thank you both for giving us a chance to tell you about a great opportunity for both our companies..."

Gabe

As planned, Lina started the last slide twenty three minutes after we'd begun. Her eyes glittered as she wrapped up the presentation, engaging with her dad and uncle like they were a concert hall worth of people, and she had them all hypnotized with her charm and smarts.

My share of the slides was over, offering an opportunity to focus on Lina. With her eyes on her family, I studied how her face moved, just like I had wanted to do while preparing for this meeting over the last week. With her focus elsewhere, I gazed at her, uninterrupted, truly settling into it.

Increíble, the seed of awe at the bottom of my stomach, seeing just how fascinating Lina was. Every time I'd seen her at the gala, I'd known she was attractive, and that I wouldn't do anything about it. Over the past couple of weeks, an inkling had started to scratch my brain, etches made in the shape of wanting to uncover who Lina was beneath this drive. Seeing her confidence and light shining through as she delivered a flawless presentation, it became much harder to ignore that I wanted to learn what her body might feel like in my hands, too.

Pity that my chance to pursue that desire was way in the future, after I'd gotten the CEO role, and had completed the transition. My present couldn't involve scratching an itch. I wouldn't be able to live with myself if I messed everything up, so I had to wait. I could only hope the gods would see it well to make our futures line up, and that Lina would be single at the time.

Thoughts of all the potential paths I could follow a couple of years down the line stopped, when Lina finished the presentation.

Lina gave me a smile and a glance, before she returned to her dad and uncle. "I hope that what we've shared today illustrates the opportunity in front of us. The Sotomayor Group and I believe we can do great things together, and we can't wait to move ahead toward a brighter future. Any questions?"

I glanced at Miguel and Edgardo, Lina's dad. They both stared at Lina, then at me, then back at Lina, with a smile on their face. The corner of my lips stitched up; this looked promising.

"Well, well," Don Miguel said. "Very interesting proposal."

"What are your first thoughts?" I asked.

He gave me a winning smile. "That I knew you two would come up with great things together."

I stopped a frown from showing on my face. That was a weird way to say it.

"As much as I'd like to share the glory," I said, "this was Lina's idea. She created and planned it and invited us to join this project. I'm grateful, because I truly believe this has great potential for both our companies."

"I'm glad to hear she's already taking care of you!" Don Miguel laughed and wiggled his eyebrows as if that made perfect sense and it was hilarious. "We taught her well, right?"

He continued to chuckle and Lina's dad joined him. "A man is always a bit worried about the day this happens for his daughter, but I'm happy with the look of this. Don't mess it up, kids!"

I glanced at Lina, searching for answers, but the look she gave me held as many questions as I had at the tip of my tongue.

She turned to her dad. "Does that mean you're giving us the green light to start with the project?"

"Oh, bueno, no need to rush. We need to think about that. Check that everything is planned as it should be."

"I'm glad you're bringing Gabriel into the fold." Miguel continued to nod, appearing satisfied. "This project wouldn't work without a man like him. Or the power behind his last name. He can help guide you."

I cringed. I opened my mouth to say something, but Lina beat me to it.

"I didn't choose the Sotomayors based on Gabe's gender, or hoping he'd guide me. I am perfectly capable of running our share of a project like this one."

"Ay, don't get so sensitive." Don Miguel stood and began collecting his things. Edgardo joined him. "You know what I mean."

"No, I don't." Lina stood as well and placed both hands on the table.

I got on my feet, and watched the situation evolve. I didn't want to step in and talk for her, but I wasn't okay with what was happening, either.

Folders under an arm, Miguel started out of the office. Lina's dad held his folder in one hand and, with the other, he made a pacifying sign toward Lina.

"It's okay, hija. It was a good presentation. I'll look at everything with Miguel and let you and Gabriel know in a week."

Miguel turned in place at the door and gazed at us. "Like I said, it looked good. And with your new boyfriend involved in it, I'm hopeful."

He hadn't mentioned thinking it looked good, but I didn't get a chance to think about that much.

"What do you mean, my boyfriend?" Lina zeroed in on the same part I did.

"Oh, don't play coy." Miguel softened the words with a smile. It seemed genuine. "I was here when he invited you for a date. I even suggested it, right? At the gala?" He added a laugh. "I knew the two of you together would be great. Didn't expect a good idea like this stadium deal, though! Maybe it will be worth it, huh? Bringing our families together. Making sure you can keep him interested."

He patted the folder against his chest, then used it for a salute, and left the place.

"Dad—" Lina's word clipped, like she was as in shock as I was— "I don't know why Tío Miguel thinks that Gabe and I—"

He put a hand on Lina's shoulder. "It's okay. I'm proud. No need to be shy." He turned to me. My stomach turned into a knot. "The Sotomayors are good people. Known for their integrity. I'm glad you're dating my daughter. If we decide to go ahead with this, at least we know she's gotta listen to her man, right? Our Lina is smart but she needs a firm hand."

"That's not okay—" I tried. But the thoughts jumbled on the way out, when Lina grabbed my sleeve and squeezed.

Edgardo's eyes switched between us. "We love our Lina, but she has so much to learn. You're your dad's right hand, you know what it's like to properly run a company already. You'll see what we mean as you get to know her better."

With that, he squeezed her shoulder and left.

I blinked into the open space in front of Lina and I. A chill went down my spine. What the hell had just happened?

I turned to Lina. Her eyes shone with unshed tears. My stomach dropped at the sight... and her dad hadn't even seemed to notice. Or had chosen to ignore it

"Lina—" the words dried up on my tongue, and I could do nothing but shake my head, my mouth still open like I would eventually find what to say.

"Shit." She lifted both hands and tapped at her face as if tears had fallen; she ran her fingers below her eyes. "I hate that you had to see that."

I shifted on my feet, uncomfortable. My instinct was to soothe, maybe rub a hand on her back, but we weren't anywhere near a place where that felt okay. Especially when she avoided my eyes and gave me a cold shoulder.

"Are they always like that?" I ran my hand through my hair.

Light had mostly gone for the day, and lights shone in the other small buildings nearby.

She shrugged, still not looking at me. "Yeah. I should be used to it by now, but I just— I can't— I still hate it."

"Of course you do! Why would they treat you that way?"

She finally gave me her eyes, but I hadn't been prepared for the glare she sent my way. "Don't act so shocked. You're Latino. If this is the first time you've seen machistas in action then I have news for you."

"I— I've seen it, for sure." I scoffed. "But I don't live surrounded by it the way you do."

"I suppose I shouldn't be asking you." She turned to me and crossed her arms. "I should be asking your mom and your sister."

Irritation tensed my lips. "Yeah, ask them. They will both tell you exactly what they think, just like they do with me. If you ever see me acting machista, please call me out on it. Both my mom and my sister would and, you might not believe this, but I would listen."

She shook her head and looked at the ceiling, wetting her lips. "I guess we'll see about that."

She didn't seem inclined to want to follow through. I shook my head and leaned on the table, palms flat on the cold surface, my head hanging from my shoulders.

"Now what?" I let out a humorless chuckle. "Do we risk telling them that we're not dating before they look at the documents, or after? Based on their reaction, they might decide against it solely on the basis of that."

Her face hardened as she gazed at me. She pressed her lips into a thin line. "I guess we can't tell them."

A hint of sadness permeated the laugh that escaped my lips. Her family had put us in an awkward position with their assumptions and ill favor of Lina.

My folder was still on the table and I grabbed it. "Can you imagine?"

The silence that followed my question hung heavy with tension. I lifted my eyes to Lina; she looked back at me with a calculating gaze. The folder grew colder in my hands.

"I was joking." My body stilled as I tracked her face.

"No, what you were was *right*. They might say no to the project if they realize we're not together."

"If that changes their mind, then they're even worse than I thought." I jumped to continue when she remained silent. "I'm sorry, I know I'm talking about your dad but—"

It seemed that I had gotten it wrong. She fisted her hands at her sides and squared her shoulders.

"That's not the point of this conversation." Her body stiff, she turned back to the table and closed the laptop, staring at me the entire time. "The point is that they are worse than you think, and they will think I am the problem, that somehow it's because of something I did that we're not dating."

"Oh, c'mon—"

"Did you hear them just now?" She grabbed the remote and turned the TV off, pressing hard on the plastic device like she wanted to suffocate it. She threw it back on the table. "They didn't have to say it in as many words, but the only reason they're doing this is because they think you'll keep me in line. As if. Fuck!"

She grabbed the back of a chair, her knuckles white as she squeezed the top edge of it.

Shock at the absurdity of the situation slowed my senses. The only part of me that seemed to be working were my lungs, which went into overdrive.

"Okay, let's talk this out," I said when I could use the air in my chest for something other than hyperventilating. "I'm not saying you're wrong about your dad and uncle, but I *was* joking. We have to tell them we're not dating."

"They'll think we're lying— or were lying at some point— either way, they'll take it poorly. And they'll blame me for it."

"They'd be wrong to blame you. But if we don't tell them the truth and let them believe we're together, then we're actually lying. Then they would have something real to blame us for."

"Omission is a negotiation tactic." Her voice deepened, a certain hoarseness to it.

"A dirty one." I could see my dad in my head as I said that. I could see my mom judging me for choosing to lie, if we did what Lina was suggesting.

"I know!" She turned back to me, and her light brown skin seemed a bit gray. "I don't want to lie! But I also don't want them to dismiss my idea because it's mine, because I'm a woman, or because I'm single."

"They shouldn't!"

"But they *will*. Gabe, I invited your company to this project because I know what it can do for us. That included the power to help convince my family that this is the right way to go, to grow. I've tried so many times, but— they dismiss me. I've written and planned so many ways to make this happen and you know what they've done each time? Pat me on the head, told me to find a boyfriend, and sent me back to do follow up calls to deal with clients. They have let my words and my plans rot on their desks. I thought—" her voice broke, but when she spoke again she'd firmed it up. "I thought that if a bigger company came to support my idea, they'd finally listen. It's so close. I want this so badly. And I can't have it because I'm a single woman. God."

She closed her eyes and the frustration on her face dropped a ton of lead on my chest. My lungs went from overworking to shallow attempts.

I bit the inside of my lips. "There has to be another way. Lying about this— it's preposterous. Lying about it won't change how unfair the situation is to you, but we won't be honest throughout the process. Do you even realize how it would damage the trust people have in me and in my family's company if it came out that we were lying about being together?"

"Honesty is getting me nowhere!" She slapped the air with the back of her hand, half shaking her hand to the sky. "I've built my career in this industry that I actually like. I love this, Gabe. I want to work here. I want to grow this company. But I've worked at it for twelve long years, biding my time, trusting my cousin won't come back, banking on my dad and uncle being too tired to keep denying me one day, and this is what I get?!"

I crossed my arms and stared at her, torn.

"We need to expand." She pursed her lips. "It's the next logical step in making this company succeed. Recover from—" she shook her head. "Do something to sustain the business beyond small deficits and once in a while exceptional profits."

"That I understand." I tapped my fingers against my arms. "It's the right move for a company like yours. Much better than doing it alone. And it's a good plan for me, too. It would help me secure the steps I'm taking. The issue isn't with that at all, or I wouldn't be here."

"I don't know why you're here. You could have sent someone several levels below yours in the company, but you chose to be the one involved. I hope it means this matters enough to you to reconsider, because I don't see any other options. I wanted your company to back me up as a business. My dad and uncle want you to back me up as a person. Fundamentally, they don't trust me because I'm a woman, while you get implicit trust because you're a man. And they think because we're together, I'm going to be the woman they want me to be and I'll put my head down and listen to you." She stopped in the middle of her tirade, the gray intensifying on her skin. "I'm gonna be sick."

"No, no." I stepped in closer and put my hands on her shoulders. I squeezed and rubbed and did my best to give her a breath of support, even if we weren't close enough for the friendly gesture. "There's gotta be a way. Maybe if I bring my dad and we talk to your dad and uncle... explain why they should..."

Even as I said the words I could imagine their response. Two machista Latino men, being told by a larger company that they're doing business wrong. The same company that had tried to buy them out in years past, and could acquire them in a heartbeat. It didn't bode well.

Lina looked at me with sad eyes. She'd likely reached the same conclusion. "They'll say no, if only out of pride. Just like they say no to me, just because I'm a woman." She scoffed and dropped her head.

She crossed her arms and I released her; I ran my fingers through my hair.

I closed my eyes, and dug my fingers into the back of my skull. "You honestly think that anything that disappoints them at this time... including the fact we're not together... could make them say no?"

"Anything could spook them and leave me in the same place for the foreseeable future. If I don't get this company moving in the right direction somehow, I'll have a stagnant business when my dad retires. As long as I have permission to run this project, I can use it as a proof of concept and grow from there. But I have to get them to say yes first."

She searched my face, and I could see the request building in her mind.

"Lina... I don't know. Lying to them now means lying to them for a while. When would we stop? After they agree? They still could say no. And no one could ever know we lied. No one. Not my parents, not our employees, not even a random barista."

"If we were to do this... then I think we'd have to do it until the contracts between our companies are signed. Then my family can't backtrack."

"I..." my sentence died before I could start it. She looked at me with bright eyes, and despite her strength and drive, I could see the vulnerability behind it.

Memories of the times my mom told me about how she was treated by her family came up; how she explained, as I grew up, that it was why she was raising me the way she was. So I could be a man like she wished she'd had around.

Lying would be wrong, and not lying would leave her stuck with her family and looking for options. If this decision were easy for me, then I wouldn't be the kind of man my parents wanted me to be.

No sounds disrupted the quiet that followed. It seemed we were alone on the floor, people's working hours over. I stared at Lina, my brain jumping through possible scenarios. There had to be a way out of this, where we got what we wanted, without lying.

I spoke the first one that made any kind of sense. "Look, Lina. If this doesn't work out for you, I'll find something for you at the Sotomayor Group. Someone with your ambition and smarts shouldn't be treated like this. You'd be great in our construction division."

She gave me an incomprehensible look. "That... that's really generous, Gabe. But I have to try to make this work. For me, and all of the work I've put into this. I won't give up yet. Besides, I can see my family berating me for it. Then I would still have to deal with all of it at home."

"I understand." I pressed my lips together. "But the offer stands."

Silence continued to surround us, no obvious solution in sight for Lina's dilemma.

"Gabe... I hate myself for saying this, but I don't see any other way. You could undo me. If you say no, my chances of moving forward with this— ever— go almost down to zero. I'd have to wait for a miracle. But you? I gave you everything on a silver platter. You could go and find another comparable company and do it with them, leaving me in the dust."

I frowned. "I know you don't know me well enough to believe me, but I would never do that."

"I hoped you wouldn't, even when I didn't know that I would have to ask you to pretend to be my boyfriend, to have a better chance at my career goals."

A scoff escaped me. "When you say it that way..."

"I'm depending on you."

I groaned. "Pulling at my heartstrings?"

She gave me a small smile and nodded once. "And I'm hoping that trying to help me will win over your scruples."

"Wow. You're really pushing it." I smirked.

"Only because of how much this matters to me. Just lie for a little bit and pretend to date me, so my future doesn't crumble right before I can touch it."

"Stop."

"I'm serious. I would never beg for things but for this... if you asked me to beg..."

"Enough." I shook my head. I jammed my hands in my pants pockets and gazed at her. Her eyes were soft on me, the deep brown of them open and raw. "No one could know. Ever. There'll be gossip either way now, about us. But..."

"We'll both get something good out of it, I know you will too." Lina reached for my arm, her fingers clinging to the rich fabric of my blazer.

We both stared at the point of contact.

I sighed. "Let me sit with it for tonight, okay?"

She pulled away from the fabric around my arm. "Thanks, Gabe. I know I'm asking for a lot."

I smiled; she did the same. She closed the offices and we walked out of the building together. I got into my car and asked Josué to drive straight to my parents' house, my mind cleanly split in two.

Chapter 6

Gabe

MY PARENTS BOUGHT THE three storey estate home five years before, at about the same time that the family company had grown from a multinational to a conglomerate. Even though they had residences in several large cosmopolitan cities, this was their home base.

The car slowed down on the long gravel driveway, pointing toward the stone and white stucco structure, the black trim of its windows merging with the night. Most lights seemed to be off, except for the room I knew to be my sister's, and the subdued shine coming through the formal dining room window.

Even after the company reached every expansion goal we'd set for it, and our bank accounts grew beyond our dreams, my parents remained down to earth. The dim light told me that, as usual, they were in the kitchen, putting away the results of whatever my mom had cooked— cazuela or charquicán, maybe. Even though they had a private chef make some of their meals, my mom still liked to make things that reminded her of home.

The four-car garage attached to the home out of sight, at the end of the gravel road extending to the side of the house. Josué parked outside of it, next to the porch connected to the kitchen entrance. The door was unlocked, like I knew it would be. My dad filled up the dishwasher while Mom sat at the kitchen table with a coffee; the chatter I had just caught between them stopped once I crossed the opening.

"Hola, Gabriel." My mom got up from the table and came to me, a smile on her face. She'd said my name in Spanish, which always gave me a feeling of home. "We weren't expecting you, but I'm so happy to see you."

I hugged her, squeezing her close for a couple of seconds. "Yeah, I was hoping to chat about something with you both."

I had thought about this conversation non-stop during the drive home.

She put a hand on my shoulder and the other on my face, and took a good look at me. "Claro. Come sit."

"I'll be there in a sec, but I'm listening." Dad closed the dishwasher and ran it, and focused on cleaning up the sink and other surfaces. "I'm going to make myself a coffee. You want one?"

"Sure." I followed my mom and sat next to her at the breakfast nook. The window overlooked the patio terrace, with plants mostly free to grow naturally rather than manicured. The relaxed style fit my parents much better, despite their wealth.

"¿Qué pasó?" She took a sip of his coffee. "You look like something is bothering you."

"I need your advice."

My dad dried his hands on the kitchen towel and studied my face from across the kitchen island; I let him. When he went to make coffee, I turned back to my mom.

I looked into her big, brown eyes, wrinkles left by her smiles spiking out of the corner of them.

"Something happened to a friend." I'd planned how I'd present this to them carefully. "They're in a shitty situation and I could help them but... helping them could put me in a bad position."

The sound of the coffee machine filled the space as I chose my next words. I wasn't surprised they were mostly silent; they usually let me spill my thoughts and worries before they said anything. What stood out to me was how comfortable this was for me; to just arrive after dinner and interrupt them because I could trust they'd be there to listen. That they'd want to.

Warmth spread through my chest with love for them. Making them proud was important to me for many reasons, a crucial one being that it felt right to thank them for everything they'd done, and everything they still did, this way.

I gulped to soften my emotions, and continued sharing some of the thoughts that had plagued my head for the past hour. "I want to help my friend. I don't like the situation they're in, and the whole thing could help me, too, but... I'd have to go against my integrity."

"Hmm." My mom took another sip of her coffee and continued to study me.

My dad brought my drink and set out to make his own. "Do you have any other options?"

I bit the inside of my lips as I went through the events of the evening again. "I think walking away would make things easier for me, but would make things worse for them."

"And we've raised you to care about how you impact other people." Mom wrapped her hand around my forearm and squeezed.

I drank some of my coffee, its warmth hitting me right in that magical first sip. "Yeah. The situation reminds me of things that are incredibly unfair, and to think I could do something about it and choose not to? I don't like how that feels."

My dad sat down with his coffee to the other side of my mom. "But it also feels bad to do things against your morals."

"Exactly. And if I do it, it could put me at a slight risk... and it would mean lying to you guys, too. For a while."

My voice didn't come out clean as I said that. Even admitting as much settled on my stomach heavy and dense.

Mom and Dad exchanged a look.

"Not that lying is a small thing," Mom said, "but aside from that, could this hurt us? Is it breaking any laws, or could it create financial risk?"

"Not at all." I released a hard gust of air through my nose. "And it can't hurt us at all if I'm careful."

Mom gave me another long look, before she finished her coffee, set the mug down. She gazed at my dad again, and they shared one of those conversations that happened in an instant through a look.

"So let me see if I got this right." She pushed the mug away from her. "You're in a shitty situation because someone else is in a shitty situation. If you help them, you'll go against your values and will lie to us about something but, if you're careful, it won't hurt us or others. If you decided against it to act according to your values, you're still not because it means not helping someone who could really use your help, and potentially making their already bad situation even worse."

I gulped and tried to loosen the tightness in my throat with coffee. It didn't work. "Yes."

For a moment, the only sound in the kitchen was the low hum of the dishwasher.

My dad leaned back against his chair; he drank more coffee and instead of putting his mug down on the table, he held it up close to his mouth. "I see why you wanted to talk this through. It's like you have to choose between different values, all of them important."

"Yeah. And I don't want to lie to you guys."

"That's the part that worries me the least." Dad lifted a shoulder. "You've never been a liar. If you could tell us the truth you would. The part that worries me is what happens if, no matter how careful you are, things go wrong and bad things happen as a result of this."

"And what about this person who's in a bad position?" Mom interjected. "In a way, this is about choosing himself over other people."

My dad studied me with a long gaze. "How much of this is about you getting something good out of it?"

I took a deep breath. "Probably a fair share. Except I wouldn't want to do it this way. I'd rather find alternatives first... but it would mean leaving my friend hanging."

This was the part that could make my dad connect the dots, but I hoped he didn't. I counted on him taking me at my word, which he typically did, and there was no way he would ever imagine that the issue I was talking about was faking a relationship with Lina. If he suspected anything, my parents would guess it was one of the guys in my friend group. Since my parents had pseudo-adopted them all, that's who they would think about when I talked about a friend.

"Here is what I think." My dad finished his coffee in one big gulp and put the mug down on the table. "Not helping this person is for sure going to leave them without support. If you help them, it's not assured it'll go wrong— it could go well. Then you'd have helped them without negative consequences."

Mom nodded. "One is certain— the other is a game of probability."

Seemed like their trust in me was enough to veil the situation, and I'm glad I'd chosen to rely on them. Because hearing them frame things this way really helped me make up my mind.

I gazed from one to the other, relief spreading through me. "One is already true— the other is a gamble."

I still didn't like the idea of lying, nor the risk to my name and integrity if this were to come out and people around us learned it had all been a lie. But how could they know? It wouldn't be hard to fake liking Lina, pretending to be really into her in front of other people. Who could doubt that, after spending all this time together, we'd gotten interested in each other this way? Then, in a couple of months, we could amicably break up and everyone would accept it didn't work out, as simple as that.

And I would be helping her— now. And we'd likely get this project going, and achieve our goals.

Ironic, that I might end up pretending to date Lina now, when I'd spent so much time reminding myself this couldn't happen. Who knew how things would turn out; maybe faking things would help me test what could happen in two or three years, and see if it was worth the wait.

If nothing else, it made the chances higher to reach everything I wanted for the Sotomayor Group, and help me succeed my dad as the CEO.

———

Gabe and his best friends

Tres Amigos + Jake Chat Group

Jake: roll call. Where's everybody?

Max: London. And isn't Gabe usually the one asking for a check in?

Jake: he was busy, so I'm taking over for a sec. It's been a while since we all talked

Javier: you're such a great guy, Jake. I'm glad you're our token white friend

Max: LOL

Gabe: back off or he'll get his claymore out of the closet

Max: only if he's also wearing a kilt

Javier: Jake wouldn't hurt a bug

Gabe: well, you've never seen him angry, but claymores would be too much of an overkill for a bug

Javier: have you seen him angry

Gabe: never, of course

Jake: I don't know why I miss you all, when I'm treated this way

Max: Ha! There's the real reason why you wrote. You miss us

Jake: Gabe is really extra busy though

Javier: cuéntanos, Gabriel. Do tell us

Gabe: So, Max. Found a wife, yet?

Max: shush and don't evade

Gabe: you're the one evading, my friend

Max: why are you busy?

Javier: if you don't tell us, we can always put pressure on Jake. He'll tell us

Gabe: fine. I think I found the project I want to present to the board. But it's not a done deal yet

Max: when will you know?

Gabe: I have to figure some things out in the next couple of days, then I should hear the final word next week

Max: let me know if it's a deal I can invest in. You know I'm always looking

Gabe: for sure.

Javier: do not let me know about any investing opportunities, thanks

Max: we won't. Gabe and I are new money and know our place. We don't have transgenerational wealth like a Pendleton does

Javier: terrible joke. stop it

Jake: we all appreciate your philanthropic nature, Javi. Where are you, by the way?

Javier: NYC

Max: of course. You're always there

Gabe: we should set a date for a weekend at the lake house. We're all so busy we need to plan months in advance

Jake: unless we do a spontaneous one. It's not like you guys need to book a plane ticket

Max: let's do it. Let's schedule something but also keep an eye out for a spontaneous weekend

Javier: deal

Gabe: it'd be great to see you all so soon after the gala. I'm in

Jake: perfect

Chapter 7

Lina

SLEEP ESCAPED ME MOST of the night, after the request I'd made of Gabe. I tossed and turned, a pit in my stomach every time I thought of something I'd revealed and wished I hadn't. The blame rested sorely on my emotional state; the pain of witnessing so clearly how little my dad and uncle thought of me. It had left me in a spiral and my filters had come down, and I'd ended up telling Gabe I'd beg if he wanted me to. I'd even teared up in front of him. Groan.

Little tremors plagued my hands as I worked the next morning. I dropped my pencil ten times before I gave up manually editing proposals for some of our smaller accounts. I kept staring at my phone, knowing Gabe didn't have my personal phone number and wishing he'd text me anyway. Waiting for his response occupied most of my mind, getting in the way of my to-do list. Why focus on managerial tasks for a company that could betray me and leave me bereft? If Gabe said no it was a near certainty but, even if he said yes, it could still be the case.

If he said yes, though...

I gulped. The gesture rasped through my dry throat, so I drank half my water bottle instead. It did not help. When the phone rang from Lucía's line, I startled and dribbled some water onto my blouse.

"Shit." I grabbed the phone. "Yeah?"

"Gabriel Sotomayor is here."

Shit shit shit. I both needed to see him and dreaded it, and I would have to do it with a wet spot on my white top. I checked— my mauve bra showed. Faint, but it showed.

"Oop—" Luce added before I could say anything. "Your dad is taking him upstairs."

I held back a sigh. "Thanks, Luce."

I hung up, jumped off my chair, dabbed a tissue on the wet spot with the speed of a machine gun, and prayed.

"Lina!" My dad called from the common area. "Look who's here to see you."

The balled-up piece of paper made no sound as it fell neatly into the garbage can. I squared up my shoulders and walked into the common area.

Gabe stood with his hands in his pockets, a relaxed gesture on his face. His eyes dipped to the wet spot on my shirt, but I didn't check the state of it. I pretended nothing was wrong and approached them.

My dad put a hand on Gabe's shoulder, heavy on the blue fabric of his suit jacket. "I caught your boyfriend loitering downstairs. But don't worry, he wasn't flirting with Lucía!"

He laughed, while Gabe gave him the slightest side eye. "I'd been there for less than a minute when you arrived. Lucía was on the phone letting Lina know I was there."

Dad slapped Gabe's shoulder again, a smile still on his face. "Yes, yes, don't worry. I was just teasing."

Like what I thought of it all was inconsequential.

I ignored the way my stomach dropped. "Hola, Gabriel."

He raised an eyebrow, maybe in response to my use of Spanish and my saying his name in that language's pronunciation. He opened his mouth to say something, but my dad's phone rang and interrupted the moment.

"Ajj, don't mind me." Dad left us and stepped into his office. He grabbed his phone and started talking into it.

I gazed back at Gabe. "You came to see me? Should we go into my office?"

"Can we go out for lunch, actually?"

I stole a glance at my father, who was stealing glances right back at us.

Gabe noticed and did the same. He took a step closer to me and leaned even closer, his mouth dropping next to my ear. My heart did a weird thing, where it seemed to stop for a beat and resume at double the pace, like my brain had forgotten what it was doing in the middle of it.

He took a breath; it moved the tiny hairs on my neck like wind on water. Everything in me stopped and waited; even the tremors plaguing my hands stopped to see what he planned to do. Why he stood so close, and why he affected my bodily functions like this.

"I'd like to chat with you about last night." He retreated for a second, barely gaining distance from me beyond what was absolutely necessary to check my reaction.

I nodded, and studied his long eyelashes for the second it took him to read my face.

He returned to the general area of my ear, the tiny hairs now standing at attention, and whatever had gone cold before now turned aflame.

"Is it okay if I touch you?" A second went by. "I'm sorry it's awkward but... for show. I want to put my hand on your lower back."

A chill built at my nape and began its descent down my spine, but even the shiver I did my best to control receded to the background. Gabe's words implied he might have agreed to help me.

He'd seen an opportunity to start the pretense, with my dad watching and people around us to witness the intimacy of his gesture. If I was right, this was him jump-starting the farce, as much a yes as all the words we still had to say.

The impulse that sparked inside of me this time was to hug him and thank him. I stopped myself; he was waiting for my answer. All details would have to be left for later.

Gabe retreated again to watch my reaction and, when I nodded this time, he responded with one of his own. Something vibrated in the air between us, and we stared at each other for a second too long.

"Hey, you two." Dad called from the doorway to his office. "Shoo. Go have lunch. The grown ups will run the shop as usual."

I didn't respond to my father's smile, and breathed through the papercut of his comment. I went into my office and grabbed my bag. As we walked past my dad, I glanced at Gabe and he gave me a nod; his hand rested big and warm on my lower back and, again, I wished he didn't get to see this side of my every day.

Gabe

My stomach hurt as we made our way out of Lina's office and got in my car, before I gave Josué the green light to start driving. If someone had asked me earlier why I thought that might be the case, I would have said it was because I was nervous about this plan we were about to embark on. The truth was, hearing Edgardo's casual insult to Lina's capabilities had stung.

If my dad had made a comment like that about me, I would have laughed. But I couldn't imagine what it was like to live with that every day. When it reflected a deeper negative idea of who you were, each time.

We arrived at a restaurant I liked and asked to sit on the patio. The host took us to a great table in their private garden, with a water feature surrounded by greenery and flowers, and ornate lamps hanging from the modern-looking pergola.

Food ordered, the sommelier approached us to discuss options. A few minutes later, Cabernet Sauvignon in our glasses, I smiled at Lina, whose eyes were steady on me.

"Thanks for taking me out for lunch." Lina sipped from her wine. "Very... boyfriend of you, I'd say."

The sparkle in her eyes brought a smile to my face, but I camouflaged it by licking my lower lip. "Maybe I'm the kind of person who loves to discuss business over lunch."

She took another sip and left the glass on the table, her sight never straying away from me. It dared me to— *something*, and it brought a tingle into my chest that I enjoyed.

She squinted at me like she didn't believe me. "But this is only tangentially about business, isn't it? I thought lunch was a sign that you'd decided to help me. Another sign, really— after what happened in front of my dad."

The food arrived and we fell into silence, while the servers set everything up for us.

It hadn't only been the harsh comment from her dad that had caught my attention back at Martínez and Associates; the subtle peek of her bra— light purple, maybe?— had caused a feeling very different from compassion. The way she'd gasped and held her breath when I asked her for permission to touch her had added to it, too. But maybe that wasn't what she was talking about.

I took a bite of my gnocchi. A delicious mixture of herbs and cheese exploded in my mouth. "What signs are those? At the office."

"You didn't correct my dad when he said you're my boyfriend. Then you said you wanted to fake it and put your hand on my back."

That stole a full smile out of me. "This is how you discover I'm not good at lying. Do you still want me to do this with you?"

Lina put two fingers on the table and walked them a few steps towards me. She smiled. "You see, it's not like I have a choice."

I laughed and she chuckled, before cutting into her chicken.

We took a few bites of our lunch. I looked for a way to explain myself.

"I talked to my parents about this, you know."

She stopped chewing and stared at me, her eyes opened wide. It seemed she didn't like my confession, and her shock looked funny enough that I stopped myself from continuing.

She spoke through the food in her mouth, a hand covering the view. "Why did you do that?! No one can know!"

I grinned. "I fully agree. That's why I didn't tell them what—or who I was talking about."

"What?" She pulled back in her chair, leaning against the backrest. A ray of sunlight shone on her dark brown hair, stealing red and blonde streaks from it. "How...?"

"I went for advice. Told them of my dilemma without any names or details. I just said I was in a position to help someone and lie, going against my beliefs, or..." A sudden cascade of vulnerability opened in my chest. I hesitated, but she gave me time, her eyes steady on me, questioning yet patient. I continued. "Or fail to help someone, and fail myself anyway."

At first, her face didn't shift, nor did the way she leaned back in the chair. She watched me for a second, another, until she finally leaned forward. "What did they say?"

Two kids ran past our table and sat nearby, calling for Mamma and Mommy. Two elegant women walked toward them, making quieting gestures with their hands. The children began chattering with each other in a low voice.

"I told them there was risk in helping this person. I didn't explain it to them, but I need you to know... If anyone ever learns, for any reason, that we're faking this... people in my company won't trust me the same, Lina. And I will disappoint my parents. That cannot happen."

She drank more wine, her eyes serious on me. "Understood. I will do everything in my power to make everyone believe this is a real relationship."

"I *am* going against my values here, no matter what I do. But the risk of someone finding out— if we do a good job of it, I don't see why anyone would ever suspect it's not real. We're both single, have things in common..."

I stopped myself from sharing that I had entertained one day inviting her out, even before all of this had happened. It could only complicate things, not to say anything of revealing the part of me who looked at Lina and knew she was my type.

"You don't think it's that much of a stretch." She cut a piece of asparagus and put it in her mouth. She studied me, her gaze intense.

I frowned. She didn't show much on her face, and I didn't quite get her tone, so I answered directly. "It isn't. On the other hand... if I don't do this, I know for a fact that I left you to deal with all of this by yourself."

"And, somehow... in your mind... lying versus leaving me alone weigh the same."

My insides went still. "Yeah. What kind of person leaves someone else in a shitty situation and doesn't care enough to even regret it?"

Her face softened, and this time her eyes gazed at me with warmth. Getting that from her for the first time convinced me that I had made the right decision.

But it was brief. A breeze blew a strand of her hair in front of her face, and she pulled it back behind an ear. A second later, her usual challenging style came back.

She raised an eyebrow. "Won't your parents connect the dots? They know plenty already."

"I don't think so. They'll probably think it's someone in my friend group. As for you and I, I won't tell them right away that I'm seeing you. To them it'll be like for most other people: we've been spending a lot of time together, one thing led to another... and now we're dating. They won't start doubting me just because I went to them for advice. They trust me."

Her lips tensed for a second, before she took the last bit of food on her plate. "So is that our story? Late nights working on this project led to more?"

"Yeah, let's keep it simple." I finished my food as well. I washed it down with more wine. "We'll wait for your dad and uncle's answer. If they say no, we amicably break it up a week after. If they say yes... we keep this thing going for a couple of weeks after we have the contracts between our companies signed. Whenever it feels like it wouldn't cause trouble."

Having finished her food, she placed her fork and knife in the right position on her plate. "That's simple enough. You can pick me up for dates—" she made air quotes for the last bit— "and we can go work instead, each of us doing whatever we need to do."

I nodded, relief soothing the tension in my shoulders. Being on the same page bode well for the plan. "We'll have to spend more time together than if we'd only been preparing the short-list proposal and the contracts, but I can't get too distracted. My family's company is preparing for transition, and I have a lot on my plate. I can't get sidetracked."

"I understand. We don't need to make a big show of it. I don't need big romance at this time in my life, either." She leaned back as servers took our plates away and offered us dessert. We both declined.

Soon after, I paid for our meal and we walked back to my car. Josué drove us back to the Martínez headquarters, with both of us in the back seat mostly in silence. When we got to her family's offices, I signaled to Josué he could stay in the car and I helped Lina out.

We stood next to the idling car, the doors closed as we exchanged personal phone numbers.

I buttoned up my blazer, a reflex from wearing suits every day. "You know, it's funny how you said earlier that you don't need a big romance. Yet here we are, two near workaholics, about to fake one for a few weeks."

I was rusty in the act-like-a-boyfriend department, but I would have wanted the extra seconds with Lina if I were developing feelings for her. I didn't have a crush on her, even, and I wanted those extra seconds.

"I'm sure a telenovela has used that trope before," she said. Humor hid in her words.

The offices for her family's company were glass, and a few people were visible working inside. Lina had her back to them, her eyes on me. The distance between us wasn't much, but I got closer anyway.

I leaned in. "I'm sorry if this is awkward. PDAs okay?"

Her nod rubbed gently against my clean shaven face.

I wrapped an arm around her waist and pressed my cheek against hers. "Anyone looking doesn't have to know touching you like this is highly unusual."

"I'll survive it if you do."

75

I chuckled, unsure of what else to do. Holding her didn't feel as unfamiliar as I expected, and that was the most confusing part.

"See you soon. We'll text." I kissed her cheek. "How about this? This is how we do it in Chile. A single kiss like this."

My intention had been to let her go, but she held me in place with a surprise hug. Her arms wrapped around me tight, keeping me close for several heartbeats.

"Thank you, Gabe."

She squeezed me in her arms; with both of mine around her now, I did the same.

Chapter 8

Monday

> **Gabriel**: Hey. Any news from Edgardo or Miguel?

Lina: Hey. No, not yet. They saida week, so they still have a few days

> **Gabriel**: Ok, let me know. I'm already working on the due diligence and documentation, so we can merge everything into the contract prep and send it to legal. Also, we should go out on a date before then

Lina: Good idea. My family has been asking about you

> **Gabriel**: Tomorrow night? I can pick you up after my game. It will be late if that's okay with you

Lina: What about Wednesday?

Gabriel: I can't. Meeting

Lina: Okay then, tomorrow night. What time?

Gabriel: 9. From work?

Lina: From home

Gabriel: Sure. But be warned, I have to work. We'll have to come back to my office... but I'll feed you. I'll get us food. You can tell your parents it was a short dinner date

Lina: That's fine. I also have lots of prep to do.

Gabriel: It'll be like college. Studying with my girlfriend ;)

Lina: I also remember studying with my girlfriend

Gabriel: We can compare notes

Lina: About our girlfriends???

Gabriel: About our WORK

Lina: sure, sure. But comparing notes on our girlfriends is still on the table. I remember my college ex fondly, she had gorgeous chestnut hair

Gabriel: I'm good not talking about my exes though, thanks. Do you date men, too? Otherwise, fake dating you just turned a hell of a lot less realistic

Lina: I date men, too. I'm Bi (My family doesn't know. Don't mention ex girlfriends). We're good

Gabriel: I said I wasn't planning to ;) See you tomorrow, Catalina

Wednesday

Lina: I think we should repeat last night

Gabriel: so you had fun

Lina: So much fun! HR reviews really get me going

Gabriel: lol you're a smartass. I didn't know that a month ago

Lina: Aren't you learning so much? But I'm serious. My mom badgered me at breakfast to know about my date and called me over lunch to tell me I should make you dinner and bring you some

Gabriel: I'll always say yes to food

Lina: Friday?

Gabriel: I'll be at the office again. I'm still working on restructuring a few things to make room for this project, in case a certain deal with someone I know falls into place

Lina: Sounds "fun", I'll be there

Thursday

Gabriel: Huh... I got your dad's email. Why do I feel bribed?

Lina: You're so positive. You're not being bribed, they're holding the answer hostage

Gabriel: But I'm getting home cooking

Lina: At my parents

Gabriel: yeah

Lina: Do you understand they're inviting you as my boyfriend

Gabriel: yeah. And also we'll hear their decision. And I'm getting home food

Lina: Don't you get home food, well, at home?

Gabriel: Sometimes, but most nights I fend for myself at my condo. And cook only once in a while, time allowing. If it weren't for your parents' offer for Saturday, chances are I would have ordered in.

Lina: Sigh. In any case, prepare for it. You'll be interrogated. I can help you practice. I'll shoot inappropriate questions at you tomorrow over dinner at your office

Gabriel: I'm fine, thanks. I haven't had a girlfriend in a while but I remember. Latine families are pretty standard that way

Lina: If you say so...

Gabriel: Flowers for your mom okay?

Lina: No need to overdo it

Gabriel: Flowers it is

Lina: We'll break up eventually so no need to charm the suegra

Gabriel: But they don't know that, and I want to leave a good impression

Lina: Then they'll never understand why we broke up. Don't be too perfect

Gabriel: Huh. How close to perfect am I? In your opinion

Lina: ha ha. You know what I mean. They won't speak to me for weeks when we break up, if they like you too much

Gabriel: So I need to tone down the perfect, or...?

Lina: You know what? Doesn't matter. The way things look right now they won't speak to me either way, when we end it. I could use the break to be honest

Gabriel: so I'll just be my usual level of perfect

Lina: [roll eye gif]

Gabriel: see you on Saturday.

Chapter 9

Lina

SATURDAYS TYPICALLY INVOLVED A few hours of work; my to-do list as a Chief of Staff was never fully done, and the extra hours helped. On that day I'd decided to work from my office, and I barely arrived home on time for dinner. I'd just made it to my room when my mom knocked on my open door.

"Are you going to change? Gabriel will arrive soon. Exciting! You should get pretty."

I arched an eyebrow and left my purse on top of my dresser. "Get pretty? I know I haven't had a boyfriend in a while, but it's not like I need to impress him. He knows how I look."

"Tah." The familiar irritated sound she made with her tongue told me enough, but she continued anyway. "Show some effort. It's a new relationship; show him you care."

I pressed my lips together and crossed my arms. "That may be one of the most old-fashioned things you've said to date, mami. Young people don't want to seem too eager."

She shrugged. "Maybe here they do, but not back home. Women take pride in how they look, and we flaunt it for our man."

My mom dressed well and wore make-up every day, even on Sundays. She definitely walked the talk. It didn't mean I would follow in her steps.

"Mami." I bit the inside of my lip. "Gabe is my boyfriend, not my man."

"What's the difference?" She smiled and winked at me. With two firm hands, she guided me into my walk-in closet. "Now go. Get pretty."

She left me there alone; I heard my door close. I shook my head, but gazed through my collection of pretty dresses. It would be half an hour or so until Gabe arrived, so I had time to freshen up my look if I wanted to. The flutter of nerves in my stomach told me I wanted to; feeling attractive would give me a boost of confidence that would help relax me.

I put extra care into my eyeliner and winged it more than I did for my working look; I curled my long hair and even put on some perfume. The dress I chose to change into hugged my body, and its neckline drew the eye to my breasts, one of my favorite features of myself. In case there were any doubts as to where I wanted his eyes— rather, any date's eyes, real or fake— the geometric pattern printed on my clothes provided further guidance.

By the time Gabe was scheduled to arrive, I was ready to impress my fake boyfriend.

I came into the large living room just as Gabe offered a bouquet of white wildflowers to my mom, interspersed with baby eucalyptus leaves.

He gazed at me from the foyer, with another bunch of flowers still in his hand. With assured steps, I approached him and smiled.

"Are those for me?" I asked.

He didn't check my neckline; he looked me in the eyes. "Yes. I'm showing off."

The glint I could see there felt better than catching him admiring my chest. His hand closed around my waist, and that felt even better.

Gabe brought me close to him; my heart jumped to my throat and, when he kissed my cheek, my eyes fluttered close.

He held the flowers between us, our closeness threatening to squash them. I wrapped my hand around the stems and missed; I held his hand around them instead. The kiss lasted for a moment too long, or time had slowed down— one or the other or both. He finally pulled back and let me hold the flowers by myself.

A self-conscious edge hung in the air as we stared at each other, so I cast my eyes to the flowers in my hand instead. Orange and pink petals greeted me— dahlias, if my limited knowledge was correct. "Thanks. They're lovely."

They looked like they smelled divine and, for the show of it, I dug my nose between them.

"Come, come," my mom said. "We'll put the flowers in water and then we can sit and chat while we wait for Edgardo to come home. He's bringing Miguel tonight, too."

Gabe picked up a bottle of wine from the console table in the foyer, which I hadn't seen before. "I also brought this. I hope you like it."

He offered the drink to me with a smile.

I grinned back and shook my head. Checking that my mom wasn't looking at us, I tsked. "You're really laying it on thick, aren't you?"

"Of course. Both to make it believable and to leave a good impression."

The door unlocked behind Gabe, and my dad and Tío Miguel appeared through it.

"Lina! Hola, hija." Dad left his keys on the console table and walked to us. He pushed a hand forward and offered it to Gabe, who shook it. "Un gusto verte, Gabriel."

"Igual, gracias." Gabe shook Tío Miguel's hand and greeted him, too.

"I'm glad you came." Tío Miguel's smile was the same one he gave everyone, and it belied his high self-esteem. "We have lots to talk about... though you're likely here for my niece, too, huh?"

I didn't know if the man had ever had a single self-critical thought in his life, and it showed in his casual and confident style.

"I'm mostly here because of her." Gabe glanced around my home's living room, and settled on me with a slight arch to his eyebrow.

I understood what he implied and shook my head at his ridiculousness.

———

Gabe

I sat next to Lina at the table, her family surrounding us. It had been a few years since I last had a first dinner with my girlfriend's family but, from the looks of it, things hadn't changed much in the Latine family dating scene.

They still asked a thousand questions of the new boyfriend, just like Lina and I had expected.

I just hadn't been prepared for the direct pressure of their interrogation.

"Well, it's clear you're a hard worker," Edgardo said. We'd been talking about some of my tasks and ongoing projects at the Sotomayor Group.

"I work hard, yes. Our company is important to my family and me— I'm sure you understand," I replied. "My parents made great sacrifices in coming here, so I want to make them proud."

"What a wonderful son," Iris, Lina's mom, added. "I'm sure they're very proud."

"I hope so." I took a sip of water. I didn't even taste the wine I'd brought; I'd given Josué the night off and I'd driven, and wanted to stay sharp for this dinner. "The next couple of years are critical. We have big plans in the making. Once those are done, then I'll feel settled."

"That's how it is," Miguel said. "Hard work will get you there."

"But you also have to think of fun and building your own family," Iris's eyes twinkled as she looked from me to Lina. "Work isn't everything, and you're at the age where you should think about that. At your age I already had Lina!"

Ironic, that I wasn't here for fun. Being Lina's pretend boyfriend was all about trying to be a good person and helping her, and reaching my own company goals. But her family didn't know that, so of course their minds went to us getting married. Only logical place to go, really.

I held back from rolling my eyes.

"Mom, please." Lina shook her head. "Bringing up making a family and kids the first time Gabe's here? We've been dating for just over two weeks."

"If marriage isn't on the table, then why are you dating?" She shrugged. "Like I said, the clock's ticking."

"People don't only date for marriage," Lina continued. "It could be for companionship, or... or..."

I placed my cutlery on the plate to signal I was done eating. "Or because you like each other, with no plans for rings in the future."

"But if you're going to live together and make a family, why not get married?" Edgardo said.

"We're far from ready for that," Lina argued.

Miguel shook his head. "Young people don't understand commitment."

God, her family was pushy.

"I think both Lina and I are pretty committed to our jobs." I placed my hand on Lina's in a sign of support; we could be a team in this.

"There's only so long you can wait as a woman!" Iris started, but Miguel interrupted.

"He's a man, he has more time." He pointed a severe finger my way, and softened it with a smile. "But that doesn't mean you can play with my niece's feelings!"

"I am not playing with her feelings." I rubbed her hand with my thumb. "We both know what we're in this for."

"We wanted to see if dating could lead to good things." Lina trapped my thumb between hers and the side of her hand, and squeezed it. It might have been a strange gesture, looking at it from outside, but in the moment its reassurance feathered away the tension in my chest. "The three of you are not making it easy."

"Yes, well, good." Edgardo waved both hands in the air in a dismissive manner. "Let the kids be. No need to force them into an engagement yet."

Lina and I exchanged a look; his *yet* hadn't gone unnoticed to either of us.

They'd forced us into a fake relationship. I was willing to shift my work priorities for a shot at a project that could win me the CEO position and bring new business to the company. I was willing to come to a couple pushy dinners with Lina's family, and date her, and let people think we were together for romantic reasons... but I drew the line at marriage.

"Yes, yes. We're just teasing," Miguel said. "Besides, it's either they get married and this turns into an anecdote for the wedding, or they break up— and then who knows we'll have another chance to make fun of our Lina again!"

He laughed, certain his joke was funny and everyone would appreciate it.

I didn't join him. His jokes so far had all missed the mark.

I arched an eyebrow. "But why make fun of her in the first place?"

"You're both so serious." Miguel shook his head, but the smile remained. "Maybe it's a sign you were made for each other. Lina's just like that."

"But you have fun, right?" Iris asked in my direction, after taking a sip of wine. "What do you do to disconnect from work? I swear, it took me years to get Edgardo to slow down."

"Work hard," Edgardo said, "but not so hard that you don't have room to take a breath. The heart can't take it."

"I try to keep my heart active," I replied. "I play fútbol twice a week. Sometimes on the weekend, for tournaments."

"Enrique does too!" Miguel jumped in. "What league are you in? The Latino one?"

"We're all in the same league." I left Lina's hand to drink more water, though I wished it was wine. "I see him around, especially during tournaments— we play on different teams. I also see Lucía sometimes."

"Yes, yes." Miguel drank from his glass. "Her boyfriend is on one of those teams."

"Have you been there to cheer Gabe on yet, hija?" Iris asked. "It's amazing how the two of you have orbited each other for all these years, families in the same circles, yet you're only dating now."

"It's all thanks to this project Lina came up with," I said. "Spending time together, driven by the same goal..."

"It's changing things," Lina added.

We exchanged another look. This time, the mix of humor and defeat in her eyes reached over the walls I had inadvertently built around me and her family. It made me want to wrap her in a blanket and let her cozy up in a safer place, where we could sit by the fire and focus on our goals in peace.

"Let's talk business for a bit." Edgardo's words interrupted my reverie and brought me back to the present. "You did that presentation for us last week. I brought Miguel so we can talk about it together."

"I'll go ask for dessert and coffee while you all talk about work." Iris went into a door I assumed was the kitchen.

"Should we help take everything to the kitchen?" I asked, but Edgardo motioned with a hand for me to stay sitting.

"Tah, no." Iris showed up again, another woman by her side, the latter wearing what seemed like a uniform. "Just be a guest, tonight. We have people to help us."

Iris and her companion moved around us, picking up dishes and glasses from the table and taking them to the kitchen.

Miguel turned serious, losing his teasing smirk for once. "Edgardo and I talked for a long time about this idea of yours. It's not a simple project."

"It isn't." I frowned. I considered taking Lina's hand in mine again, but regardless of my impulse, I couldn't justify it this time. My original message of teamwork had been passed on, or not. I focused on the conversation instead, and gazed between the two older men. "But we strongly believe that a strategic partnership would strengthen both our businesses."

"And it's not only doable," Lina added. "It's smart. This could benefit both our companies, and help Martínez and Associates grow."

"The numbers suggest that, yes," Edgardo flattened a hand against the table linen. "But it could stretch us out. I don't know if Miguel or I can tackle something like this, so we had to think hard about it."

"I can do it," Lina tried. "I can run the project."

"Maybe it'll be the thing that brings Enrique back," Miguel said.

"I can do it." This time, Lina's voice echoed tight in the space.

"We believe it can be done, yes." Edgardo nodded. "We're saying yes, Lina."

My eyes whipped to Lina, my heart beating faster at Edgardo's agreement. I wanted to check with her, celebrate with her, somehow. But she stared at her dad, eyes still and attentive.

"You are?" Lina's tone changed one-hundred eighty degrees. It had softened, and hesitation threaded through it for the first time.

"Yes." Edgardo's eyes shifted between Lina and I. "We'll supervise you, hija, but yes."

"Yes!" Lina hugged me in a blur of movement. Her perfume hit me, almost making me dizzy with the surprise of it. The smell was citrusy and not at all sweet, but it seemed like dessert, or a prize for surviving the worst of dinner. She grabbed me by the shoulders. "We're doing this!"

I couldn't help it, I surrounded her with my arms and brought her close; I squeezed her and kissed her cheek.

She blinked twice. I smiled.

"Let's celebrate with coffee, what do you say?" Iris said, and the moment broke.

Gabe

I had been good most of the evening, and managed to keep my eyes away from Lina's neckline. Discipline was a common aspect of my life, but it had been hard to resist when all I wanted to do was feast on the sight.

Right before leaving, my strength broke. With my stomach full and chest light after getting her family's approval for our project; and with us facing each other by the door, it was a little too easy to let my sight drop. And the sight was indeed glorious.

But I caught myself and looked away within a second. Chances were Lina didn't catch me, as she'd been gazing toward the dining room; her mom had appeared from the kitchen and walked in our direction.

"I'm going with Gabe to his car— to say goodbye," she said.

I offered my hand to Iris again, and we shook hands once she reached us. "Bye again." I'd said my goodbyes earlier, but it felt right to do so again. "Thanks for everything."

"Come back soon!" Iris let us out the door, and Lina and I walked down the porch and into the front yard.

My car sat on the masonry driveway, and we approached the driver's side. Her house was big for the city, with a great yard boasting large, old trees on the edge of the property, and a well-maintained lawn and flower pots. The building itself had the look of an old but fully renovated home, clean brick walls and white trim interspersed with big windows.

Lina sighed. "That was an intense evening."

I leaned sideways on the driver's door, my back to the house. Lina rested her hip on my car, facing me. She crossed her arms and it was very difficult not to glance at her neckline again, to see what her gesture did to her breasts. I almost did it, in fact, but stopped myself when I caught the tiniest sign of a squint on her part. She'd catch me for sure, this time.

I gazed at her eyes, instead. "Does your family have any shame about pushing you to get married?"

She raised an eyebrow. "You were being pushed into it right alongside me."

"Yeah, but I'm replaceable. Something tells me they would have done this with any boyfriend of yours."

"Didn't you expect it?"

The night was cool. Automatic sprinklers turned on, the spray covering the width of the lawn. The smell of wet dirt drifted in the air.

"No." I filled my lungs with the smell of petrichor. "I expected to be drilled about work and be fed until I was nauseous."

"Those things did happen."

I raised an eyebrow of my own. She was evading my question.

Her face relaxed and she looked toward her house. "Fine, yes. They're pushy. Especially since I turned thirty."

I shook my head. "There's time. I don't plan to get married for several years. Why should you?"

"Don't make me repeat their reasons; you heard them. They're sexist and see the world as a binary, with clear expectations for each. They only care about how they see me." She gazed at her house again. "I'm a woman."

She hooked a finger in my shirt's button placket and pulled me toward her, and I became extra aware of the fact. I nearly stumbled into her, leaning close to her by instinct. She stretched her neck high and talked into my ear. "I think my mom's watching from the window."

My brain, slightly fuzzy from the smell of her and the warmth of her skin so close to me, chose that moment to wonder at how it would feel, if she'd followed her statement with her teeth on my earlobe. It did so for some weird reason, at such an inopportune moment. Distracting me.

Who was I kidding; I knew why the image and the question had appeared in my brain. Because Lina was my type, and spending time so close to her, little pats and whispered words, heightened my attraction to her.

It wasn't until that moment that I realized exactly how dangerous that was. I should have created distance, let the heat in my lower belly die down, since I wasn't planning to follow through with any of it. But I'd promised I'd do this, show off like we were truly seeing each other in a new light. I couldn't pull away and be true to my word.

A different plan was in order. Still so close to her, I ran my hand up from her wrist, up her arm, and stopped it at her shoulder.

I wanted to make sure she heard every word. I brought my lips to her ear and lowered the timbre of my voice. "That's kinda creepy of her."

Lina laughed and pushed me away with a firm hand on my chest. "Stop. It's not like she's watching us make out."

"She never should watch you making out with someone."

She grinned, light from the tall decorative lights of the garden sparkling in her eyes. "It's fine. At this rate, she never will."

I pursed my lips as I considered her. "Please tell me that's because of the creepy factor, and not because you don't think someone will want to kiss you like that."

It wouldn't be me, but attracted as I was to her, I could see how sad it would be for no one to get to spend hours kissing Lina. If she wanted that for her life at all.

If she wanted that, she'd find someone. Probably earlier than I would ever be ready to think about that for myself. I couldn't see how she'd have any trouble finding someone whenever she wanted.

Humor didn't leave her face, but she raised an eyebrow at my statement.

She lifted a hand and called me down as if to tell me a secret. "It's only because of how busy I am. Letting myself relax enough to make out like that won't happen any time soon."

That I got. I looked into her eyes. "In that, we share the same fate."

"Yet here we are," she said.

"Fake dating you is full of ironies."

She stared at me for an extra second, before checking how close we still stood, then turning her eyes back to her house.

"Besides, if I fall for a woman or enby person, I don't think I'd get to flirt openly like this. Not with the way my family is."

I could still smell her perfume, clear above the petrichor, and my head still swam with images of kissing Lina for hours. Yet I heard the disappointment in her voice.

"That's sad." I lifted a hand to caress her face. "You should be able to flirt with anyone you like. You're good at it."

That changed her vibe. "You think I'm good at it? I'm not a flirt, typically. But I do like to go for what I want, so..."

"You could have anyone eating from the palm of your hand, if you wanted." I accompanied that with a serious nod of my head.

She laughed. "Too busy for that."

"And that's just sad, too."

I kissed her cheek and got in my car. I lowered my window.

"We have the green light now," I said. "Next step, writing the proposal and signing the contracts."

As I drove home, I spent a significant amount of time thinking of all the good reasons why I was doing this, and why I had decided to postpone dating for a few years in the first place.

I needed to sear the reasons into my brain. Nothing else would have the power to stop me from doing more than getting playful with Lina, for the sake of convincing everyone we were dating.

Chapter 10

Gabe: Tomorrow morning for the meeting with your lawyers— is anyone from your family going? On my side it'll be me and one of our lawyers

Lina: Tío Miguel is coming

Gabe: Okay. I won't be all business then. Just mostly business.

Lina: Responsible, professional... but a little distracted by me? I can work with that

Gabe: Yes, exactly. If you want to flirt a bit that would help

Lina: Right. I should probably flirt with you some, at least when we have other people around

Gabe: exactly. See you tomorrow, then. Looking forward to it

———

Lina

Morning came on a cold day. I hadn't checked the weather, assuming a warmer Fall day, and now paid for it. Our lawyers' office lived high in a skyscraper, and I stood at the building's feet waiting for Tío Miguel. A car stopped by the sidewalk in front of me, and Gabe appeared from the back seat. He found me by the main doors, wearing the wrong jacket and freezing my butt off.

"Hey." He kissed my cheek; the gesture appeared warm and friendly, and I smiled. The car that had brought him to the meeting went away. "What are you doing out here?"

He wore a wonderful wool coat, in a tight black and white pattern, contrasting beautifully with his navy suit. His wavy hair was slightly tussled; maybe he'd run his fingers through it in the car, or maybe he just wore it that way. A glimmer of mischief shone in his eyes, and I welcomed the flicker of warmth it brought to my insides.

"I'm waiting for Tío Miguel. He insisted I should be here, so he could find me easily." I rolled my eyes and sank my hands in my pockets. "I think he didn't want to go up there by himself, not that he would ever admit it. That, or he doesn't want *me* going up there by myself, who knows why. What about your lawyer?"

"He's already up there. He's waiting for us."

"So Tío Miguel is the only one missing." I sighed.

Gabe gazed around as if looking for someone, but then zeroed in on me. "Okay. Tell me the truth. How okay are you with me saying a few mean things about your uncle?"

I grinned. "I can likely tolerate some mildly mean things."

"It's just that... I don't know how you do it. The man is pretty bad."

This time, I laughed. "Is that all you can do? I can say worse things."

"But you can because he's your uncle. If I say it, then that's worse."

"True. I don't know how I would react if you said the same things I think about him." My hands were still very cold, and I took them out of my pockets to rub them together. I shifted from foot to foot. "But if you want to complain about him taking too long and making me wait in the cold, then I'm all for it."

Instead of getting a chuckle and a few choice words from him like I expected, he frowned and wrapped my hands in his. Warmth seeped into me through his skin, the sensation building through cells and bones until I got a mild shiver.

I closed my eyes and released a strained sigh. "Oh, that's good."

Gabe rubbed my hands, helping my blood circulate better. When I opened my eyes, he watched me closely, a small smirk on his lips.

"Does it feel good?" he asked. I nodded. "I'm going to kiss your hands now, and I think you will really like it."

"You are? And I will?" My eyes closed in a tiny squint, enthralled by the way he opened my palms in front of his face, but also distracted by my natural suspiciousness.

He kissed the center of my palms, his eyes on mine. "Miguel is walking our way. It might serve us well to make a little bit of a show."

If only my body could process his words correctly. Rather than acknowledging this was for show, when he kissed the fleshy hill of my thumb, and then the inside of my wrists— one at a time— my heart betrayed me with palpitations. At least I had warmed up, now. Wrong jacket, who? I could have made it work with a light sweater.

"Better now?" Gabe asked, a twinkle in his eye.

"That's a Latino man, right there. Romancing his lady." Tío Miguel's voice reached me from somewhere in my vicinity but outside of my view, and barely in my awareness. I still hadn't recovered from Gabe's kisses. "I still bring flowers to my wife every month."

I came back to myself with a small jerk of my head.

"Please don't bring me more flowers, Gabe." I took my hands from my fake-boyfriend and grabbed one of the coffees in the tray Tío Miguel carried. I didn't know why he'd stopped for coffee when we could have gotten some at the lawyers' office, but it explained his delay. I gave a cup to Gabe, then took one for myself. "The ones you brought to dinner the other night were nice, but I'm good for now."

"You don't like flowers?" Gabe took a sip of his coffee.

102

"I have mixed feelings. They die too soon, and it makes me sad."

Gabe frowned, but didn't say anything. Tío Miguel was the one to share his thoughts instead.

Mi tío threw the recyclable tray into the trash and concentrated on his cup. "Why so picky, Lina? Your boyfriend was nice to give you flowers."

"And you think I'm ready to marry him now," I let out. I steeled myself to hide my cringe; that comment had the potential to get even more nastiness from my uncle. I usually was better off shutting my mouth, but sometimes I just couldn't help myself.

Tío Miguel was about to say something but Gabe interrupted him.

"I won't give you flowers then, Lina. When I give you something, I want it to be because you like it."

If there had ever been anything to make me consider marriage— in a joking way— it was that statement and the way he'd kissed my wrists.

"It doesn't even have to be jewelry," I managed to joke.

"I'm sure I'll find something." Gabe offered me his hand, and we walked toward the building with his warming mine. "I have a bit of time."

———

Gabe

Miguel, Lina, and I stood at the building's foyer after the meeting. Gustavo, the Sotomayor lawyer my sister had sent to the meeting, had just left to return to the office. If I had been a little less selfish, I would have gone back to the office with him, both of us using the same corporate driver. Instead, I'd chosen the freedom of making the journey alone, and Josué waited for me nearby. In case it made sense to go with Lina somewhere instead.

"The next stage," Lina said, "is to prepare the information our teams will need to write up the division of labor part of the contract."

"Yes, I'll get started on that." I took a sip of my coffee, now mostly cold. It gave me something to do with my hands.

"¿Ya vienes a la oficina?" Miguel asked Lina.

"Ya casi. I need to talk to Gabe first."

"I get it. Saying goodbye to your novio, huh? I'll see you at the office." He shook my hand but spoke to his niece. "Don't take too long, work won't wait."

He left us and we waited until he was out of the building to turn to each other. She drank the last of her coffee, the bottom of the to-go cup up in the air, then threw it in the garbage.

She sighed. "Do you think he knows how much he contradicts himself?"

"I don't think so, no." I put my hands in my pockets. "So, what did you want to talk about? I doubt it was a ploy to kiss me goodbye."

She smirked. "It wasn't a ploy to kiss you, but it is relationship business. My mom reminded me that mi primo Luis is getting married next Saturday. She made a comment about how good it was that I wouldn't have to go alone now."

She lifted an eyebrow in question.

"Oh." I ran a hand through my hair. "Of course tu novio would go with you."

We chatted near the elevators, and a car full of people reached the lobby and emptied into the foyer. Folk in office attire surrounded us. The lunch rush had begun.

"To be honest, the wedding had escaped my mind." Lina ignored everyone around us, her eyes locked on me. I liked the attention a little too much. "I wouldn't have remembered if my mom hadn't mentioned it. I can say you had something else already."

It should have been easy to take her offer and skip the wedding; work had begun to pile high on my to-do list. I worried the inside of my bottom lip; why didn't the agreement fall ready from my mouth?

"It's okay, Gabe. I know I'm already asking a lot. And you're busy."

I studied her as she offered me another out. Maybe the no didn't want to come out for the same reason I had brought flowers and wine to dinner the other night. Because if I was pretending to be her boyfriend, I would pretend properly.

I had integrity, but it seemed I also had pride.

"I bet they tease you for attending these things alone." I finished my own coffee and threw the cup away.

"Don't worry about me," she said. "I'll be fine. I'm used to it. I just ignore them."

"Let's shut their mouths instead. What do you say?"

"That they will shift and ask us about getting married instead."

I chuckled. "At least you'll get my help to manage the pressure of *that*, this time. I am not marrying you at the end of this, Lina."

She looked up to the ceiling and scoffed. "I think I'll live. I'm not waiting for a ring from you."

"But maybe I'll get you a commemorative brooch."

She laughed. I grinned, despite the anvil chaining itself to my ankle, warning me that I would pay for this small show of ego.

"I'll text you the details." She kissed my cheek. "Thank you, Gabe."

I nodded and she walked away, never looking back.

A full minute later, I shook myself out of watching her go, and made my way to the office. I'd have to carefully carry that heavy weight chained to me now, and use it as a reminder that this was as far as I could go.

Chapter 11

Lina

EVEN THOUGH IT HAD been my mom who suggested I go cheer for my boyfriend at his soccer match, it was Lucía who roped me into attending one of his games. It meant I would have to work through lunch the next day to keep up with work but, as soon as Luce had realized both our boyfriends would be playing against each other, she called it a cousin bonding evening and begged me to come.

Guided by Lucía, I discovered that the league played at a semi-permanent structure that, from afar, resembled a large padded hangar. Soon, I discovered that it held eight small fields, all fenced and surrounded by bleachers. Players filled the synthetic surface, and observers formed small groups scattered around the space. After identifying the field where Gabe and my cousin's boyfriend played, we sat in the bleachers, Lucía's arm in mine.

"The game must be halfway done." Her neck stretched as she searched the teams. I followed her gaze, my eyes inspecting the crowd. "That's Rodrigo there, and... yes, that's your boyfriend, currently trying to steal the ball from him."

Gabriel pushed a foot between Rodrigo's legs, kicked the ball back and, skipping around him, caught the ball and ran with it toward the net. The fierce determination on his face looked good on him.

"I don't understand soccer, but maybe I like watching it in this format." I tracked Gabe as someone from the other team charged at him. They crashed against each other, and the other guy won the ball.

Gabe turned and ran behind him.

Lucía jumped up and put both hands around her mouth. "C'mon, Rod! Show them how it's done!" She sat back down and gave me a smile. "Technically this isn't even soccer. It's six versus six on synthetic flooring, which is non-regulatory— it should be on turf— but the league doesn't care because it's much easier to maintain. And it's not like it affects the show for us, right?"

I laughed. Gabe stood in the middle of the field, eyes on the ball, chest working hard and hands on his hips. He must have seen something in the game, because he took off on another sprint. His legs had a nice, full shape to them; his shorts tightened as he ran and offered that piece of information.

"No, it does not," I replied.

Gabe ran into two other players who were fighting for the ball and did his best to gain control of it.

Lucía stood and screamed again. I hadn't even noticed one of them was Rodrigo. "Don't let him take it! Push him!"

Other people around us stood as well, all yelling things toward the field.

"C'mon, prima!" Lucía pulled my arm to make me stand as well. "Cheer for your boyfriend! It's half the fun."

I stood, but said nothing. I limited myself to clapping.

"Oh, please." She elbowed me. "Look around you. We all do it. It's part of being in the league."

Lucía swung a hand in a big circle toward the opposite bleachers. In all of them, folk chatted with each other and cheered for their people on the field.

She clapped and pointed at the game with her chin. "Not that they would ever admit it, but they have this silent competition going, for who has the loudest supporter cheering them on." She gave me a cheeky side eye. "It gets you a lot of girlfriend points, if you scream. Both here... and after, if you know what I mean."

A chuckle escaped me. I wouldn't be screaming anything after the game, but I could play nice and pretend for the evening. For his reputation among the other players.

Before I thought much about it, I put my hands around my mouth and yelled the first thing that came to mind.

"Break a leg, Gabe!"

Lucía cackled next to me and pushed me with a hand on my shoulder. "Don't be ridiculous! That's for theater, and a real threat here!"

But Gabe had heard me shout and found me in the crowd, a frown clearing into a big smile. I grinned back at him and waved. A feeling a lot like appreciation sprouted in my gut, his smile sparkling in my chest like light through a prism.

"At least you got some points, huh?" Lucía wiggled her eyebrows. "Come now. I'll introduce you to the other WAGs."

"WAGs?" I asked as I followed her down the bleachers.

"Wives and girlfriends. As one of the league founders' girlfriends, you're one of us now."

She led me to a group of femme folk standing next to the waist-high fence delineating the playing fields. They all chatted with each other while stealing glances at the game, and made room for Lucía and I when we approached. For several seconds, they seemed to put all of their attention on us.

"Hi everyone. This is my cousin Catalina, but we call her Lina. She's Gabriel Sotomayor's girlfriend and it's her first time attending a game. Lina, these lovely people are Jenny, Marta, Essie, and Paola." She named each of them in order around us.

"I heard you yell at him a few minutes ago." Paola smiled. "That was an awesome cheer!"

I laughed. "It's my first time doing anything like it. I have no idea what I'm supposed to say!"

"You'll get the hang of it," Jenny added. "I personally just whistle. Mario, my husband— he knows when it's me."

"That's sweet." I grinned. "Thanks for the WAG intel."

They chuckled; three of them seemed quite friendly, except for Essie, who gazed at me with a bit more serious look.

"So do you all come here to support your partners often?" I asked as I glanced at Essie. A tingle of interest prickled in my solar plexus; she was attractive in that way that gave you a bit of a punch, rather than placid admiration.

Essie smirked. "I do. That's my husband, Óscar." She pointed at a guy on the opposing team to Gabe's. "Do you think we'll see you around, too?"

"My thing with Gabe is too new to know for sure." I grinned. "But I'll try."

"I don't know if you knew, but Gabe is my ex." The look on Essie's face held loads of irony and even some playfulness. "He's married to his job, so the league might be the best place to actually see him. If you want to accept advice from someone who used to have skin in the game, that is."

I raised an eyebrow. The tingles disappeared, eclipsed out of my consciousness by the scheming at play. Her tone was relatively neutral with a hint of pleasantry, but I didn't buy it.

"Oh, c'mon, Essie. Don't be like that," Paola said.

Lucía and I exchanged a look.

Essie lifted two hands in defense. "No harm meant, I'm sorry if I made it awkward. You would have learned about it at some point. Everyone knows! Don't worry— I am happily married now with someone who actually wanted to settle down. But maybe Gabe's changed, or maybe you're not looking for something serious. I shouldn't have assumed."

Even though flames licked the insides of my belly, I kept my face impassive. She may have wanted to create trouble, or maybe she was incredibly bad at reading social cues, but I wouldn't fall into the trap.

I shrugged. "It's fine. I'm married to my job, too, but we're having a wonderful time and seeing if it works."

"I'm sorry, I do apologize," Essie said. "I think I'm just shocked. He's known for staying single, you know?"

"Well, he's not single right now." I put my arm around Lucía's, and Marta seemed about to speak, but the referee whistled the end of the game.

"Oh— well, I hope to see you again." Marta smiled at me. "It's nice to see new faces."

Paola and Jenny grinned as well, before the four of them left. Essie's smile hadn't been as wide, but she hadn't seemed fully antagonistic, either.

"Wow, ¿qué se cree?" Lucía said to my side. "The gall. I mean, it's true you would have heard about it soon enough— I planned to ask you if you knew after, but I hadn't realized she was in the group."

"Maybe she's still upset about it"

"It's possible. Just don't let her attitude ruin it for you, okay? Even Essie's nice most of the time. She'll get used to the idea at some point. For now, let's go find our guys. I have an idea..."

———

Lina

Lucía went off in search of Rodrigo; I kept my distance from Essie but maintained a general sense of her location, tracking that she was nearby.

I wandered among Gabe's team members, clustered as they collected their things and mingled with partners and friends. I caught Gabe with his back to me, but before I reached him, he turned and saw me approaching.

He smiled. "There you are."

I stepped in close. I put my hands on his shoulders and, raising to the balls of my feet, kissed his cheek.

"Hi..." A hint of a question hid in his tone. "That kiss was... good. But don't hug me; I'm sweaty."

I raised an eyebrow and got a little bit closer. His shirt stuck to his skin, and I grabbed a handful of it and pulled him to me. A mix of pleasant product perfumes and clean sweat reached me.

I lifted my cheek to him. "Say hi properly to your girlfriend. I don't care if you're sweaty."

His eyebrows quirked, but he kissed me on the cheek. He hovered around my ear and said, "Is your cousin around?"

I responded to his ear, too. "She's around somewhere... but your ex is nearby. I'll explain later, but pretend we're in love, okay?"

He chuckled and nodded. He took a step away and crouched down to a bag I hadn't noticed.

"Let me change shirts, first." He stood with a dry shirt in his hand, which he handed to me. In the next move, he'd taken his wet shirt off.

I tried not to ogle, but I wasn't sure if I'd been successful. The sudden appearance of black tattoos around his shoulder and down his arm drew my eyes as if magnetized. My breathing caught, because if I as much as inhaled the wrong way, the ink might run away and disappear— the design was so *alive* on his skin, with a mix of geometric and organic lines, depicting a landscape mixing mountains and sea. His shoulders and arms and pecs all had definition to them, not too bulky, more like the kind you might guess came from a mix of lucky genes and general everyday movement, rather than weight lifting. No six pack but I did not miss it, when the general appeal of his torso was so yummy.

He threw his used shirt on top of his bag and reached for a towel from inside of it. He gave me his back as he dried the sweat off his hair and neck.

Once I started, I couldn't stop checking him out; truly seeing Gabe for the first time. His back muscles rippled as he moved, visible through the thin layer of plush flesh covering them. When I caught sight of the most biteable muffin top resting above the elastic of his shorts, I was forced to accept that I not only had a general appreciation for Gabe, but I felt more. In a different way than the tingling awareness I'd felt for Essie.

He threw the towel next to his used clothing and faced me again. He reached for his dry shirt, still in my hand, and pulled; I didn't let go, and ended up taking a step forward to him.

He smirked and lifted an eyebrow. "You seem quite enthralled."

The humor in his eyes made it clear, he thought I was acting. I released the shirt and he put it on. I hadn't moved, and he put his hands on my hips to bring me even closer. His arms went around me in a long hug, and I hugged him right back.

I reeled from the recent revelations, from discovering what had lived under the tailored shirts and suits, and the comfort spreading through me as his arms enveloped me.

"Lina! There you are."

Gabe released me from the hug and I turned to my cousin. It wasn't until I noticed her smile and the way her eyes jumped from Gabe to me and back, that I realized I hadn't hugged Gabe for the sake of anyone else.

Gabe put an arm around my shoulders.

"We found our boyfriends," Lucía said. "Should we go for dinner?"

"Uhm..." Gabe studied me, as I did him. Before he answered, I knew what he was going to say. "I don't know. I have lots of work."

"C'mon," Lucía insisted. She directed her words to Gabe. "Don't tell me you're as bad as my darling prima?"

"We're not bad." I put my arm around Gabe's waist. "We're committed. And he's even worse."

"Please." Luce took hold of Rodrigo's hand. "I get that you're both super busy all the time and incredibly goal-minded, but having a proper meal is healthy. You *have* to eat. You can go back to your work after."

"Just dinner, just an hour." Rodrigo said. "Think of it as intra-league solidarity."

Indecision tore my mind into two. I needed to work, but I'd go for dinner as a group; I was already out and having fun. A little bit more wouldn't hurt, and it would help sell the story with my cousin. But Gabe had said he didn't want this deal to take too much time away from his priorities.

"I barely know you, Gabe. If you're going to date my prima, maybe we can change that. And, Lina?" she arched an eyebrow at me. "Remember what I said about the silent competition among the guys?"

"What competition?" Rodrigo asked, and I laughed.

"I want to know this, too," Gabe added.

Essie passed us by. Our eyes caught for a minute.

I squeezed Gabe to me with an arm around his waist. "Let's go, Gabe. On a double date for an hour."

"We'll tell you about the competition if you go." Luce gave him a teasing smile.

"Okay, okay. Let's go," he said.

We walked next to each other like accomplices, and I enjoyed every second of it.

Chapter 12

Gabe

LUCÍA HAD DRIVEN LINA to the game, but I gave her a ride to the restaurant. I liked to drive myself to training; it seemed too pretentious on my part to have Josué take me there, when everyone else drove their very normal cars everywhere else themselves. Most of the guys had no idea I owned the playing fields and rented them out to the league for nothing; most of them thought I worked in corporate and was simply well-off. I was happy to keep it that way. Having a driver might make some of them search for me online and no, thanks. I didn't want the dynamics to change if they learned how much money sat in my bank accounts and investment portfolios.

We were halfway to the pub when I remembered to ask Lina about Essie.

"So what happened? You said something about my ex earlier?" I stopped the car at a light.

The restaurant wasn't that far away and it wouldn't take us too long to get there, which was a good thing. My to-do list haunted me, my work computer silently blaring an alarm at me from its case in the back seat. An image of the Board materialized in my mind, the dread of it fueling my fear that I might fail my parents and have the CEO role denied to me. The pressure of it all settled heavy in my stomach, but I did my best to ignore it for the next hour or two.

"Oh, yeah." Lina searched in her purse and came out with lip gloss of some sort. She pulled the visor down and painted her lips red. "I met her at the game. She dropped a few hints about her feelings about you."

I wished I could admire the effect of it on her lips, but I couldn't see it clearly in the dark car. The mild frustration of it surprised me; I had always thought Lina was attractive, but hadn't quite had a hook around the navel before, pulling at me to appreciate her beauty.

I frowned, both at hearing about Essie and the tug in my gut. "Wait. She what?"

"Yeah. Remember when I yelled at you to break a leg?"

That distracted me from the way my belly reacted to her and I laughed. The light turned and I drove the car forward."Yes. That was wrong— but funny."

And kinda sweet, too.

"Let's say I'd rather you focus on the spirit of my actions, rather than the details."

A grin stayed in place. "Let's do that. So what did she do?"

"Between my cheer and Lucía introducing me to a few people as your girlfriend, she seemed to take it upon herself to warn me against you."

I glanced at her for as long as I could afford to without risking an accident. "Are you serious?"

"Why would I lie to you?"

A car in front of us moved a bit aggressively, so I couldn't keep my attention on Lina like I wanted. I pressed my lips together; I really wished I could watch her. "It's not that I think you're lying— it's that I didn't realize she was still angry."

Lina didn't respond right away, and I didn't see more than a slight frown when I stole another glance at her.

"She indirectly made digs at you for working too much," she finally said. "Implied you wouldn't want to settle."

A scoff escaped me. "That's the core of her issues with me... though I doubt that was the whole story, from her side."

"I may have stopped her from saying more. Maybe that's on me." Her voice seemed pensive.

I grinned. "It's not like I would prefer you to hear her side, but... she has her own, and it won't be the same as mine."

Two beats later, she sighed. "I think I'd rather hear yours."

The pitch in her voice hadn't changed, but the words reached me like a whispered spell. I didn't know why, but the fact that she was content to hear my side and that was enough— for now— infused my chest with warmth. Which wasn't the ideal. Too tempting.

I took a fortifying breath. Not so much for the story I was about to share, but because I suspected it'd make us closer. That was vulnerable and scary in its own way. But Lina had showed up for me, and an explanation was the least I could offer in return.

"We dated for a while," I said. "For almost two years. She wanted us to get engaged; I didn't. But I wasn't clear enough with her. I wasn't opposed to staying together, but also... I wasn't planning to marry her."

We neared the restaurant. I turned on the blinker to get into the parking lot and slowed down.

"I see." The two words she uttered in the dark weren't as heavy as I thought they might have been.

I found a spot and parked the car. "We had a big fight when I finally told her I wasn't ready to propose. I told her it was because of the Sotomayor Group. Which was true. It wasn't the whole reason, but it was the most important one. She didn't take it well."

I switched the engine off. I could finally put all my attention on her; she gazed at me with a thoughtful wrinkle between her eyebrows.

Her eyes focused on me, clear. "I think she assumed the same fate for us, and thought I'd end up like her— disappointed."

"Still kinda shitty she took the liberty." I gave her half a smile, a corner of my mouth curled upward. "Imagine if I had been wanting to make it last with you. She could have gotten in the way of that, pulling away the veil of a new romance and warning you that I'm not good boyfriend material."

She shook her head. "With that kind of romantic statement, no wonder she wanted to marry you so badly."

I laughed, and we went into the restaurant.

———

Lina

Gabe sat next to me in a booth, Lucía and Rodrigo in front of us. Our food had arrived a few minutes ago; the smell of it reached me and I sighed. I hadn't been the one running for two hours, but I was hungry.

Gabe took a big bite of his burger and swallowed. "Mmh, that's good."

I smiled and ate some of the fries at the side of my beef dip sandwich. It hadn't escaped my notice that I had never seen Gabe be this casual, with sports shorts and a shirt, rather than in a suit, and eating a burger instead of the fancy dishes we'd had to date. The comfort of it opened a little door in my awareness, into a place where I could relax and bring down some of my walls. One or two at a time, but at least one for now.

Lucía must have seen something in the way I gazed at Gabe, because she gave us a teasing look I ignored.

"Aren't you happy you're not working right now?" my cousin said. "Much more fun to be out for food, telling us about how this happened." She moved a hand between Gabe and me.

My fake-boyfriend shook his head. "I thought we came for food and to hear about this competition among league players."

"I want to know about this competition, too," Rodrigo said. Lucía ran her fingers through her boyfriend's hair, pushing the longish tendrils behind an ear. "I've never heard of it."

My chest fluttered with a rare wave of longing. I rarely paid attention to the part of me who wished to know what love felt like, to care about someone enough to see them as your future. I spent too much time hoping my dad would start believing in me and let me run the business when he retired, to think much about real love.

I gulped and looked away. The weight of an arm around my shoulders took me out of my mood before I could fully delve into it. I gazed at Gabe, and when he winked at me, it was gratitude that fueled my smile.

It had been only a few seconds since Rodrigo's question, and I'd almost forgotten, but Lucía answered him.

"I have this theory I shared with my prima," she said. "That the guys in the league have this secret competition for who gets the most cheers from people."

Rodrigo arched an eyebrow and glimpsed at Gabe, who chuckled.

"There's always someone who brings that up during a game." Gabe left my shoulders to drink some of his beer. "Maybe there's something to this idea."

"You mean, like when I was trying to get that ball from you and I told you to break a leg?" Rodrigo smirked.

All of us laughed.

"Yes." Gabe grinned. "And, just as I got control of it, I told you at least my girlfriend was the loudest."

We laughed again, and Gabe and I exchanged a look. There was something in his eyes that brought butterflies to my stomach.

"Now it's your turn." Lucía took a sip of her drink. "I thought you guys have known each other for ages. I wondered if there was something there."

I startled. "You did? I didn't think you were aware we knew each other."

"Oh yeah. You always talked about the Sotomayors more after you came back from the gala."

Gabe chuckled. "That's probably because I always sought her out at Construction Cares. Every year, I counted on seeing Lina there. And I made sure to find her. Maybe she complained when she returned?"

I took a big swig of my beer. "I honestly don't remember what I would have said after returning, but I doubt I was complaining."

"What I don't get is what changed?" Lucía took a triangle of her pizza and held it in the air. "You've known each other for, what, ten years?"

I nodded. "Give or take."

"It's not like I was keeping tabs," my cousin said. "But I didn't think you guys hung out."

"We didn't." My fake boyfriend grabbed a fry from his plate and took a bite of it. "But the dress she wore at the Gala this year left an impression on me."

I chuckled. "Oh, please. I wear more or less the same type of outfit every year."

"And I noticed, every time." He grinned, a twinkle in his eye. "I almost invited you out a hundred times."

I turned to him, chin over my shoulder as I gave him a skeptical look. "You didn't."

"How would you know?" he asked. "I was careful not to show much. I didn't know what you'd answer, and I wasn't sure it was a good idea in the first place."

"Why? Don't disappoint me so soon, Gabe." Lucía smirked. "Don't tell me you can't be with a hard-working woman."

Gabe shook his head. "The opposite. I like that she's so driven. I didn't ask her out because I'm driven, too, and I thought I'd fall too hard. And I'd miss my deadlines."

His words were full of cheek, and he followed them with a big bite of his burger, like he hadn't just shared anything significant. Both Lucía and Rodrigo laughed; I chuckled, but his words still resounded in me.

Maybe the words were fake, but the fantasy mesmerized me.

"Well, you got over that, then." Rodrigo left his sandwich on his plate and shook a hand between Gabe and I. "Considering."

"I didn't." Gabe smiled. "She invited me out. And I couldn't say no."

I snorted, but he was right, in a way. Still, I couldn't correct him too hard, or I might end up revealing too much.

"I didn't invite you out," I said. "I proposed a business arrangement with the stadium bid. We ended up spending more time together, and here we are."

"Bet it doesn't hurt he's handsome," Lucía said, admiring my fake boyfriend. "He has a young Pedro Pascal thing going."

I studied him closely. His shiny, dense black hair had a slight wave to it; his dark brown eyes shone. He seemed to enjoy the comment, and it brought a playful energy that suited him well.

Would he be playful in bed, too?

Ugh, I shouldn't be going there. He might catch sight of that thought somehow, if I wasn't careful and it shimmered through my skin.

"Do you think I'm handsome?" Gabe asked, grin stretching wide.

His flirting pulled my attraction right back into the lead box where I liked to keep it. I wasn't a liar, current situationship aside, and pride swelled in my chest. Vulnerability and I had a shaky relationship, and I avoided it at all costs. Admitting to my feelings for Gabe would be shaking hands with the idea of exposing my heart, and I wouldn't do that.

I pursed my lips. "I think I can acknowledge he's handsome."

"Wow," Luce exclaimed. "Was that so hard?"

Gabe shook his head and Rodrigo laughed.

"I can admit he's handsome," Rodrigo added. "He even has a fan club we always tease him about. But his girlfriend won't admit she likes him."

I chuckled to hide my embarrassment. Protecting my feelings was a knee-jerk reaction, born from enduring constant bruising to my heart. But maybe I didn't need to go there so quickly, all the time.

I wasn't ready to put my true feelings on full display, but I could share a bit more. "I didn't say I didn't like him. He's a great guy and I like him a lot. What's this about a club? I want to hear about it."

"You don't want to hear about the club," Gabe tried. "Keep poking at my ego instead, why don't you?"

"No, no. I also want to hear about this club." Lucía turned to her boyfriend. "Do you have a fan club? You should. As long as I get to be the president, of course."

"I don't have a fan club, but thanks for the sentiment." Rodrigo gave her a kiss on the cheek. "It's a silly thing, but so fun to bug him about. Prime ammo for when you're trying to distract him or trash talk him."

"Go ahead, don't keep us waiting." Lucía rolled her fingers in the air as if to speed him up. "I have food I want to finish and, if my best prima is going to date him, I want to know how to tease Gabe at the family events."

Gabe groaned and faced his plate, focusing on his half-eaten sandwich. I took a bite of mine, but directed my attention to Rodrigo.

"It started a couple of years ago, when he was newly single. News spread that he wasn't seeing— what is her name again? Your ex? She's married to Óscar now."

"Essie." I washed down my food with beer.

"Essie! That's her. Well, they'd been together for ages, since before the start of the League. Gabe was one of the founders, right? Helped us find a place to play in. I wasn't around back then, but apparently he and Essie were the It couple. Until they broke up, Essie badmouthed him, and a group of defenders joined forces to cheer for him. One day, they arrived with signs, and we've never let him forget it."

Lucía laughed. "Were they hoping Gabe would choose one of them as the new girlfriend? Those of us cheering for our guys know when someone comes to the games hoping to meet someone, but I didn't know they would band together."

"They did that one time," Rodrigo said after drinking some of his beer. "But this guy here hasn't had anyone cheering for him from the bleachers since then. Until today, of course."

Rodrigo pointed at me with a lift of his head and went back to his food.

"The players are as good at gossip as others think femme folk are," Gabe said. "How can that still be a story people tell, two years down the line?"

"I'm more impressed by how much you must like my darling prima," Lucía countered, "to have broken up this two-year period."

Gabe pushed his now-empty plate aside. "Like I said... I'd always suspected I'd want this to happen if I spent more time around her. I was not wrong."

"Did you know, Lina? That this would happen?" Lucía smiled. "He's here giving you all the compliments, maybe you can share some."

Gabe said he wasn't a good liar, but wow, did he know how to deliver as a fake boyfriend. His comments were believable; I would have never guessed he was making it up.

"I didn't," I confessed, my heart speeding up, because I was about to say something closer to the truth than to a lie. "I always thought of him as attractive, but getting to really know him? That's what did me in."

Gabe leaned down toward me; I didn't quite realize what he was doing and turned to him— the kiss that would have landed on my cheek pressed against the corner of my mouth.

I blinked at him in surprise, my lips tingling like they were getting ready for a real kiss. He released a gust of air that tickled my face, and smiled right after.

Based on what he did when faking it, Gabe would be a great real boyfriend. The kind of boyfriend I might have wanted for myself, if I had been trying to find one.

Chapter 13

Lina: my uncle is driving me wild. I can't believe I'm saying this, but I think I'm going to go home. I'm still going to work, but I'm going to do so while well-fed, on my sofa, and in my PJs.

Gabe: sorry to hear your uncle is annoying you. Want to come over and work from here? I haven't seen you in a few days. They're going to start thinking we broke up

Lina: good idea. My dad was asking about you. I'll be at your office in 20. We can work on the shortlist document

Gabe: I'm at home, actually. Do you mind? I also felt like working in my pajamas. If you want to wear yours, I won't mind

Lina: casual date? My mom would tsk at me

Gabe: Meh, just tell her we're getting closer and she'll be happy again

Lina: lol, true. Have you eaten? I can pick something up

Gabe: I was going to order, but if you bring something that would be awesome. I'll send you my address and a code. You can use the code to park underground, and then to activate the elevator to my place. See you soon

---

Gabe

Even though I usually slept in my underwear and a shirt, while lounging at home I liked to wear joggers. The navy cotton covering my legs contrasted well with my gray shirt, and I decided it was a modest-enough look in which to see my fake girlfriend.

A mirror decorated part of the hallway wall, and I quickly ran my fingers through my hair to put it all in order. Once satisfied, I emptied the dishwasher and organized the small mess in my living room. It was good host behavior; nothing to do with the titillating notion of having Lina over. I did it to make my mom proud, really. Even if she wouldn't be there to see it.

When I thought Lina was about to arrive, I unlocked my door and set it ajar. There were only three doors on our floor: the elevator doors, a door to Jake's apartment, and one to mine. Having it unlocked meant that, when she arrived, she'd know exactly where to go.

Holding a pillow in my hand, I fluffed it and dropped it onto the couch just as my door opened. My heart leaped, before Jake appeared on the doorway, the finger he'd used to push the door out of the way still straight in the air.

"Oh. Hi." I picked the other pillow on my sofa and fluffed it up. "Thought you'd be Lina."

Jake arched an eyebrow. Neither of us were the kind to bring women around that much— if ever.

"Lina, huh?" He smirked. "Something going on?"

"Something's going on." I dropped the pillow on the sofa again, and checked my watch. Lina would be here any second now. She had never been late to a date; I didn't think she'd be late that night.

"Something work-related, or something... else?"

"Something... of both."

He took a few steps into my place, and put his hands in his pockets. "That's cool. And a bit surprising, to be honest."

I gazed around the room for any last-second things that need-ed to be put away. Mess wasn't my MO generally, but I needed to put the nervous energy running through my limbs somewhere.

I straightened and stole a glance at my friend. "I know."

"Hello?"

Lina appeared by the doorway, and Jake and I turned to her.

"Hey!" I strode to her and kissed her on the cheek. "Glad you made it."

"Hi, Gabe." She entered my home after I invited her in with a sweep of my arm.

I closed the door behind us, while Jake shook her hand.

"Lina." He gave her a friendly nod. "We've met before, at the gala a couple of years ago."

She smiled, and the sight stole a grin out of me. Lina tended toward being closed off, and the friendly gesture was rare. I wasn't surprised, Jake was the friendliest giant ever.

"Did Gabe invite you to work with us?" She asked. Her grin stayed, and it imbued warm fuzzies into my stomach. "I brought food. Plenty for three. My mom made frijoles charros today and sent enough for an army."

"That sounds delicious, but I need to go home," my best friend said. "I'm in the middle of a project I'm late for."

As friendly as Jake was, I expected him not to tell Lina what the project was about. I knew, as his best friend, just like I knew not to say anything. Jake was pretty private about his music.

"Can we still give you some?" Lina asked. "It really is a lot of food."

Jake looked at me, like asking for permission.

"Of course," I said. "Come with us. Take her food, then run away."

"It'll be my pleasure." He gave me a cheeky smirk.

Jake and Lina followed me to the kitchen. My friend sat at the island, elbows on the white stone covering it. Lina brought her cooler bag and put it on the quartz surface, her eyes all over my place.

"Your home is beautiful, Gabe. That view is amazing. Must be one of the best in the city."

Both Jake and I looked out the window. The city lights sparkled in the darkening landscape. After living here for a few years I had stopped appreciating the sight; with new eyes, I checked my place too, imagining what it might look like to Lina: the two-tone counters in gray and white, with bronze hardware, in an open space with a 6-place dining table and living room. Violeta had helped me decorate the space, making sure it wasn't devoid of personality, and pops of color contrasted with the mid-century lines of the furniture.

"Thanks. My sister helped me set it up." I stepped closer to Lina. "What do you need?"

She pulled out a big plastic container full of food from the bag. "Can I get a pot? My mom made me promise to reheat this the right way. No microwaves allowed."

I took a pot out of the drawer behind me and put it on the gas stove by the wall.

"Can I also get a ladle?"

My brain malfunctioned— or gifted me with an opportunity my awareness didn't compute— but I stretched around her to reach for the utensil drawer. My torso brushed against her back and she buckled... a soft wave curving her vertebrae at the touch.

I released a breath in surprise at the stolen moment. Tiny hairs on her neck fluttered, and I thought I heard an almost silent gasp escape her.

"Right, well." Jake cleared his throat. "I won't tell your mom if you don't, but I'll just warm up mine in my microwave at home. I really am in a rush. And maybe I'm not the only one..."

I made myself smile at Jake, like the whole situation had been on purpose. Like my fingers didn't shake as I took the ladle and gave it to Lina, who took it and added frijoles charros to the bowl I gave her next.

"Thank you." Jake took the bowl and got up. "I really appreciate it."

He waved at us and left. I turned to Lina and opened my mouth to say something, but she beat me to it.

"I think he bought it. Well played, Gabriel."

A gentle scoff escaped me, but I didn't correct her.

<hr />

Gabe

A few days later, I checked my watch and frowned. Where had the day gone? I had to leave soon for soccer, and I wasn't done with work yet.

My large computer screen shone brightly with mockery, its desktop interface broken up into several working windows.

They all waited for me to continue tackling my to-do list, infinite as it was.

"Fuck," I muttered, and rubbed my hands on my face.

How had my dad done it? With two kids at home he did spend time with, and a partner who also had needs. I know he'd relied on my mom a lot; he always admitted he wouldn't be here in his business if it weren't for her. But I had only me to take care of, and I wasn't sure I could do it all.

"You look like you need help." Jake entered my office with a travel mug, which I suspected was full of coffee. He handed it to me. "So I brought you some."

I lifted the seal and took a sip. It went down like velvet and support. "Thanks. Thank you."

Jake nodded and sat across the desk from me. "Don't you have to leave for soccer soon?"

I sighed. "I might have to skip. I'm running late on things."

"That's not like you." He frowned. "I hate to ask this question but... is this new situation with Lina distracting you? Don't get me wrong, I'm glad if it's distracting you. It's just not like you."

I crossed my arms, the travel mug still in my hand, and leaned back on my chair. I'd gotten rid of my jacket a few hours ago, and my shirt wrinkled under my hand. "You're right. It's distracting me and it's not like me. I mean, that's the whole point why I haven't dated since Essie. But it's not only Lina, it's also getting the contract and the shortlist application ready— everything is making my time run away from me. Suddenly it's normal work, plus this whole other project which is huge... and Lina."

"I think we like Lina, don't we?" Jake ran his fingers through his well maintained red-blond beard.

I raised an eyebrow. "Do we? We? What do you mean?"

"Different likes, but we both do. I like her because it's fun to have someone to bug you about, and because it's healthy to relax a little sometimes. She surprised you and it's nice to see it. And you like her because..."

Someone walked past my office, and I almost switched the glass from transparent to opaque. Any witnesses would only see us chatting, so I didn't, but I did push the button that would close my door.

"It's healthy to relax a little sometimes?" I repeated. "Are you serious?"

My friend's eyes stayed on me, unaffected. "And you like her because..."

"Is this an intervention? Don't push too hard, or I'll remind you why it would be healthy for you, too."

As close as we were, we rarely talked about dating. That way he wouldn't push me to derail my plans and start dating, and I wouldn't end up pushing him to admit he had feelings for my sister. Not that I knew for sure; the one time I'd asked him about it he'd told me he didn't want to talk about it, and I'd respected it. In exchange, he didn't push me too hard on my general lack of dating. The fact that he wanted to have this conversation at all bumped against our unspoken agreement.

He lifted two hands in a conceding gesture. "Let's not go there. Let's keep this about you. I'm much more comfortable with that."

I chuckled, but tension remained in my stomach. "Of course you are."

"And it sucks for you, but your mom taught us both well. If you need an intervention, I'm making this into an intervention."

Jake had a bit of a rough childhood, and I knew he saw my parents as his parental figures. When he said my mom taught us well, he meant it. We both had the privilege of having my parents guiding us through a lot.

"I don't need one." The words pushed through my tight jaw.

"Are we sure about that, though?"

I could avoid the conversation. Tell him I was going to be late for soccer practice and that I needed to go, or that I didn't want to hear it and he would respect my words, too. It didn't feel good to reject his attempt so I didn't, but I still wasn't ready to hear what he had to say.

I tapped my fingers on the desk and made myself ready.

"Okay. Fine." I loosened my jaw. "Let it out. I'll take it under advisement."

"You better. I'm the only one of your friends seeing you stressed like this, and I've known you the longest. It's my job."

"Fine, fine." I sighed. "Say your piece."

"You're working too hard, Gabe. And I know why you do it, and I want the same thing. But your parents wouldn't want you breaking up with Lina only so you can work."

"I know that. That's why the plan was to not meet anyone, so I wouldn't end up in this position."

"Haven't you known Lina for years? Technically you haven't met anyone new, and yet..."

"And yet." I pressed my lips together, frustration sweeping over me. "It's just the wrong time. If this had happened three years from now we'd be having a different conversation but, now? I'm trying to charm the Board with a business deal that is taking a lot of extra hours to achieve, eating away at the little time I had for myself. And there's soccer, which is supposed to help me stay healthy."

"And there's Lina," Jake said with emphasis, his eyes hard on me.

"And there's Lina."

"You must like her, why else would you have started it out with her?"

"Why else, indeed." I scoffed and looked up at the ceiling. "I just couldn't help myself, I think."

Because she needed help, and even then I liked her. I just like her more now. And wasn't that the problem? Lina was part of my life at the moment, and I liked it enough that, if I could add extra hours to the day just to see her, I would.

"So we're left with you either taking a step back from Lina, or you stop working so hard. Otherwise, you're going to burn out and not be good for anyone. Not even charming the Board."

I sipped coffee and rubbed my eyebrows. "Yeah. It just sucks."

"I can help more with the project side of things. Let me help." He rubbed his hands on his thighs, like he was ready to jump into it.

I smiled. "Thanks, Jake. I could really use your help. Or else, I don't know how I can do everything. I'll send you an email tomorrow with the details."

"So you're not going to break up with Lina? Good."

We stared at each other for a second. Jake was probably one of the people who knew me best, and he knew what he was doing. His gaze was direct and challenging; it made me want to relent and argue, all at the same time.

"I'll have to," I said, "but not yet."

He frowned. "If you know you want to break up with her, then do it. Don't string her along."

"I don't— I won't. Lina and I are on the same page. She knows my life isn't right for this relationship for the next couple of years and to be honest, neither is hers. We're just keeping each other company for a bit, but... there's the wedding we're going to next Saturday. And then the results for the stadium shortlist. I can't break up with her now. And I don't want to. It'd be like breaking up with her before the holidays."

"Talk it out with her, then. And if you're going to stay with her a bit longer... then at least enjoy it, okay? And don't skip soccer. Give me some work to do now—"

"Don't you have to finish that personal project of yours?"

"I can handle it. At least I'm actually single, unlike you."

"You're such an overprotective best friend."

"Just paying it forward, for all the years we've been in this together."

"I hate it when you go all softie on me. Because I love it too much to fight you."

"Go and enjoy life, Gabe. If you're going to date Lina for the next few weeks, at least do it properly."

Chapter 14

Gabe

JAKE'S WORDS STILL RESOUNDED in my mind when Saturday arrived, and Josué took me to Lina's to pick her up for her cousin's wedding. After asking Lina for details, I'd learned the venue was at the gardens of an old estate home, and that she would wear a two-piece yellow dress. I chose my suit accordingly, with dark gray pants, a tan belt, and a sand-colored jacket. If our outfits matched, we'd probably look more in sync. There was something about the idea that appealed to me.

I asked my driver to park by the main door and wait for me. Like that first night, the doorbell didn't give any indication it had rung, and I stood out there with nerves pinching my stomach. Like I was a teen again, picking up my date for prom.

Edgardo opened the door. "Gabriel, hola. Come on in, the ladies are taking a while." He gave a long suffering sigh and let me in.

"That's okay." I ignored his comment otherwise.

"Make yourself comfortable." He waved a hand toward the living room. "I'm going to go check on my wife, see how long she might be."

I nodded and he left; I sat on an armchair and took my phone out.

> **Gabe**: I'm in the living room, idk if you heard the doorbell

> **Lina**: What a gentlemanly way to tell me to hurry the eff up

I chuckled but typed an answer.

> **Gabe**: I never said anything about hurrying up. Take your time

> **Lina**: Not sure I believe it. Come to my room (up the stairs, through the hallway, 3rd door to the right) so I can see your face and see if I believe you

I raised my eyebrows. We were over thirty years old, but the part of me who felt like a teenager needed an urgent reminder to behave. Going to my girlfriend's bedroom at her parents' house for the first time didn't mean anything fun would happen.

I scoffed at myself, put my phone in my pocket, and went up the stairs. Once I found her door, I hesitated only for an instant, and knocked on it with two quick taps of my knuckles.

Fake girlfriend, I told my inner teen. *You're not supposed to want to do anything, anyway.*

When Lina opened her door and I got a glimpse at her, I could almost see my inner teen give me a sassy smirk.

The daffodil yellow of her cropped top and full skirt contrasted beautifully with the golden sand of her skin. The textured fabric called for my hands, my palms tingling with the instinct to run my fingers all over her. Test the way her dress might create fiction against my nerve endings, and feel the softness of her skin.

"Wow—"

The words got stuck in my throat, and my eyes still roamed her body when she spoke.

"I'm glad you like the dress. Thank you." Her smile was soft when I looked back at her. "I still need to finish doing my hair."

"Sounds good."

She squinted at me, the small smile still in place. "Okay, you don't look like you're annoyed or impatient. You can come in."

She stepped away and sat at her vanity. I leaned against the doorjamb, hands in my pockets, feet crossed at the ankles, and the door wide open. Just in case her parents walked by her room. And just in case my inner teen had any other thoughts on how I felt about Lina.

Her room seemed comfortable. The simple gray upholstered headboard went well with the lilac wall behind it and the white comforter on her bed. Small decor in a variety of bright colors sprung up on the surfaces of her furniture, including a reading lounge chair next to a small table. A wonderful bronze lamp stood proud next to it, and I could imagine Lina reading a book, cozy under the thick-knit purple blanket all too well.

She looked at me in her mirror's reflection. "You haven't asked anything about me living with my parents."

"Do you want me to?"

"No, but I expected it. Even if you're Latino."

I shrugged. "Maybe I haven't asked because I'm Latino."

She separated a strand of her hair and twisted it with her flat iron, creating long curls around her pretty face. A big section of her hair remained clipped high on her head.

"Did your parents make too much of a fuss when you moved out?" she asked.

"No. They're awesome. They made it clear they'd support us in anything we wanted. And it's not like I'm truly independent. I have what I have because of them, and I live in a family property. I didn't pay for it." I shrugged. "I don't think that's really different."

She chuckled. "I get that. I stayed here because my parents have a hard time letting me go— while I'm single, anyway. And I like the amount of money I'm saving. It could come handy one day, if I wanted to create my own side business. Or I'll just have one hell of a retirement fund."

"So if I'm hearing this right, you plan to move out married and with a whole lot of savings."

She unclasped the big section of her hair, and separated it into sections again. She continued curling it, each pass of the flat iron hypnotizing.

"I'm not waiting to be married to leave. I've fought some fights with my parents already; one day I'm going to be ready to fight for my right to move in with someone if I want to, and I will fight then. I just don't know if I want to go there simply to live alone."

I nodded, my eyes still fascinated by her movements.

"So are you going to stand there the whole time?" she asked. "I promise it's okay if you come into my room."

I raised an eyebrow and sat at the feet of her reading chair; my knees nearly touched the seat of her vanity. She worked on the section of hair closest to me, and I studied the way she twisted the flat iron and slid it down her long locks.

"It's relaxing to see you do your hair," I said after a while.

She sighed. "You're a good guy, Gabe."

In the mirror, her eyes locked with mine.

"What makes you say that?" I tapped a finger on my knee. "Because I said I like watching you do your hair?"

She left the iron on a silicon mat on the wooden surface in front of her. She shifted to face me more fully. "And for everything else."

I smiled. If our relationship had been real, I would have followed the drive to caress her face, maybe even kiss her. But her parents showed up at her door and interrupted the moment.

"We're leaving," Iris said. "Don't be late, kids. Hurry, or you won't make it in time for the ceremony."

"We'll leave in ten minutes." Lina went back to her hair.

"See you there," I added, and they left us alone.

Privacy with her like this shouldn't have made me gulp. We'd been alone in my home and it had been okay. It didn't have to be different now.

Only it was me now in her space, and it felt different, somehow.

I needed to distract myself. "Any family members I should be aware of?"

She shook her head. "I don't think so. Lucía won't be there, as this is the other side of the family. This will just be a standard one-day wedding thing."

I nodded. "So most of your family lives around here?"

She nodded as well. "Yeah. Both sides. Most of them came here over the years. Even my grandma, against her will. How much family do you have here?"

"Only my parents and sister. I have a hundred cousins in Chile, but we haven't visited much. Maybe that's why I'm so close to my parents, my sister, and my friends. We only have each other."

"I'm excited to get to know your family a little better." She put her flat iron back on the silicon mat and checked her reflection. "Shoot, I forgot the jewelry. I should have done my necklace before my hair."

She found a couple of shiny pieces in a drawer, untangled them, and put them on her vanity.

"I'll help." I stood and offered her my hand; she put her necklace in my palm. This would serve as another distraction.

I moved to her back and she carefully lifted her long hair. Leaning forward, I maneuvered the necklace in the space between her arched arms, lock at the back. I got it on my second try.

"Thanks." She let her hair fall, and tousled the curls for a more casual look. Within the next instant, she grabbed a bracelet and dangled it between two fingers. "Can you help me with this one, too, please?"

The natural thing was to kneel next to her, so I did. But in this position it was harder to ignore her perfume, or my proximity to her and what my body wanted to do about it, while alone in her room.

I frowned. My fingers moved over the soft skin of her wrist; her veins were no more than a shadow in her delightful light brown skin. What would her pulse be, if I checked? Was she affected by this at all?

It took me three attempts to handle the lock, this time. Once finally secured, I held her wrist in my hand and kept it there.

I lifted my eyes to gaze into her eyes. "Will you have to explain to a lot of people why you have a boyfriend now and, one day in the future, explain what happened that made us break up?"

"Maybe." She didn't pull her wrist away. "But I can get away with superficial half-truths."

"Anything in particular you want me to say? Or do?"

"Will you dance with me? People can't talk to us as much if we're dancing."

I smiled. "I'll dance with you."

She responded with a soft curl of her lips. "You'll make someone very lucky one day."

My chest turned concave with a mix of longing for such a future, for the vision of what it could be, if Lina was right. And for Lina herself. Maybe she could see that in me, and care.

But I wasn't someone who could offer all of that to her or anyone, anytime soon. I wasn't good enough to do it all, and I wouldn't do it halfway. Things had to get done right, or I wouldn't do them at all.

"I'm not that good." I held her eyes. "I could be better."

"You're already amazing. You will be great for someone one day, too "

"I hope so. One day." I broke and caressed her face. "Ready to go?"

———

Lina

Call me cynical, but the ceremony was meh. Gabe was far more interesting to me, in his semi-formal trousers and jacket combo, than a priest talking about sacraments. My cousin did look happy, though, marrying his fiancée. The venue was beautiful; the bride and groom had taken their vows against a lake backdrop, a flower arch around them, and a big tree above them.

During cocktail hour, Gabe and I fielded questions like pros, keeping to the same conversation we'd used with Lucía and Rodrigo. Same with dinner and the cousins at the table. It had gone so well, I'd started to believe the lies myself.

People milled around now, having finished their meals. They visited and chatted with each other and, from the look of the folk working the event, the dancing was about to start. The lighting changed under the white reception tent, and soft music played through the speakers.

Gabe and I still sat at our table, and he leaned forward and placed his elbows on it. "These arrangements are very pretty."

The centerpieces were a mix of white, pink, and lavender hues, contrasted by pale greenery. They weren't very tall but they were lush, and Gabe touched a delicate petal with the tip of his finger.

I mirrored him and leaned forward on the table as well. "It is very pretty. Do you have an appreciation for delicate things? Or aesthetically pleasing things?"

"The latter, I think." He gazed at me. "I also like strength. Like in a properly built structure, for example. I think that if I hadn't gone into the family business, I might have been a construction engineer of some kind."

I chuckled. "Mr. Engineer, are you telling me that math and building codes give you a boner?"

He laughed. "Don't go there, Catalina. Not when I'm about to dance with you." He cut me a look that held every letter in the unspoken words: *and this is fake.*

The music got a bit louder, and the MC announced the first dance. People surrounded the dancing area, but Gabe and I stayed put.

"Understood," I said.

He nodded and looked forward again. He took a flower out of the vase and studied it. I didn't know much about flowers, but this one looked like a type of rose. Its petals were light pink and slightly opened, and they rippled as Gabe twirled the stem between two fingers.

"You don't like these, then," he asked. "Flowers."

"They are pretty, they just make me sad."

The music changed, indicating that the general dancing portion of the evening had begun.

"I like them." He looked at himself. "I don't know if I can find a pin somewhere to put this on my lapel."

"Or we could do this, maybe?"

I took the flower from his fingers, our skin touching for a second. The tingle that sprung from the point of contact did something to my chest, and because of it, instead of ignoring it, I followed the impulse to put the flower in my hair. I tested the terrain of my curls with my fingers, found a spot that felt good, and tried to pin it in place.

"Here, let me." Gabe took over; his fingers moved gently on my hair.

Again, just like when he'd helped me with my jewelry, we were close. In my room, I'd hoped for him to kiss the inside of my wrist again, even if it didn't make sense, and I knew that I shouldn't want it. Here, so close that if I turned my head just a bit, I could align my lips with his, my thoughts led me on a slightly different path.

His lips looked soft, with tiny tension waves surging from concentration. The way I wanted to lick my lips and kiss him showed me just how dangerous this closeness was.

"Done." He took some distance and contemplated me. "I hope I didn't pull your hair too much. It looks really nice. You look really nice."

I smiled. "You look really nice, too."

"Thanks." He stood and offered me a hand. "Now, shall we dance?"

He took his jacket off and left it hanging on the back of his chair. He led me to the dance floor and, within ten minutes, I'd made up my mind: Gabriel Sotomayor was a great dancer.

He pulled me to him, hand to my waist, and guided me in a fast turn.

I laughed. "Gabriel. I didn't know you could move like this."

"The galas never give me a chance to show off." He leaned closer to me. "When they ask you why we broke up, you cannot tell them it was because I made a fool of myself dancing."

"Nothing foolish about you dancing."

Except me, maybe, who really enjoyed seeing him move to the music, and allowed myself to be mesmerized by it.

He released me from the turn, and we went back to dancing at a bit of a distance. His feet and hips continued to move to the rhythm of the music, while he unbuttoned his shirt sleeves and rolled them up his forearms. How was that so sexy? Simply witnessing the gesture had tingles showing up in all sorts of places.

When he was done, he grabbed my hand and continued dancing *with* me, a big smile on his face.

I stepped in closer to him, to talk to him discreetly over the music, of course. I didn't get much out of it, if we ignored the way his proximity lit me up. With the heat of our bodies moving, the smell of his cologne became clearer, and I took it in.

"You look like you enjoy dancing," I said.

"Why does it sound like an accusation? I do like dancing."

"Because it almost feels like you tricked me into being amazed, somehow."

"Oh, c'mon, Lina." He put a hand on my back, and we moved to the music, our bodies close enough to rub each other. "Let me have this. One thing I can amaze you with."

"Fine. But only one thing."

He laughed. "Fine. But maybe we shouldn't look like we're having such a great time together. Or it'll make it harder for us— you, really— when we break up."

"Excuse me. Harder for me, only?"

"Yeah. It's your family that is constantly bugging you about being with someone. My family doesn't care." He looked around the room. "And my family hasn't seen us together this way."

"I could tell my family you were actually just a random plus one."

He drew me even closer. "A random plus one who's dancing sexily with you?"

"I'm irresistible. That's why you came here even if you knew this was leading nowhere."

He smirked. "I see. That's the story you'll tell after the break up."

"Yep. Your reputation can take it, right?"

"Can it take that I wanted you so badly I took any crumbs you gave me, and accepted it quietly when you broke up with me?"

Instead of replying I smiled at him and lifted an eyebrow.

"Querida mía," he said. "That would be completely on brand for me."

I laughed in delight and let him spin me; my skirt swirled around me. When I came back to him, he held me tight again.

"When you laugh like that..." he sighed. "I can't fall for you, Lina."

I didn't respond right away. Perhaps because of the dancing, or maybe it had been his words— definitely the words— but tingling took root in my ribcage and cascaded down into my belly. My insides turned to jelly as we gazed at each other, eyes holding the connection as intensely as his hand on my back.

"We won't fall for each other," I finally said. As close to an admission as I could manage.

The white fabric of the tent changed colors, the light projectors creating bright shapes against it. The music continued its beat and, if it weren't for the fast rhythm of our movements, I could have pretended we were slow dancing.

He broke the connection of our eyes to glance around the room. "It's easy to get confused, with so much making it real. I'm sure there's a part deep in our brains that can't tell the difference."

"I think we'll be okay. We're both strong-willed. It would take more than a couple of months to get over being stubborn, when we already made a decision. When we already have an agreement."

"You're probably right."

His words were barely audible beneath the music.

We danced away the rest of the party, until we could leave without much notice or suspicion. He dropped me off at home, saying goodnight with a simple kiss on my cheek.

In my room, I took two tissues, a book, and a few heavy objects. I pressed the flower he'd put in my hair between one of my favorite book's pages, because even if I didn't plan to fall in love with Gabriel Sotomayor, something told me I would want to remember this night.

Chapter 15

Lina

THE WEDDING QUICKLY BECAME a small parenthesis in my life. Although I knew it had happened, and I had a drying flower as evidence, it seemed like an event from another life. Gabe and I returned to the pattern we'd established at the start, pretending to date but working together instead. A good month into this arrangement between us.

While my parents imagined we'd gone out somewhere, we diligently tackled our tasks in his office. We focused on the contract between our companies; we were on a deadline, as this draft would be presented as a part of our shortlist application. We drank coffee on the sofa facing his desk, papers in different piles around us, as we reviewed the paperwork we'd submit to the stadium project leads. We both worked on our own laptops, but we worked on the same document.

"Do you see anything you want to change? Last call." I studied him. He had a thoughtful and focused wrinkle between his eyebrows, his gaze running through the screen.

One of his feet rested on the coffee table, his bent leg helping to position the laptop at the right angle. His other leg shook. We'd both loosened up our working attires; he'd gotten rid of his jacket and tie, his top button open, and I'd taken off my heels and belt.

His shoulders looked wide in the shirt he wore, his hair messy from running his fingers through it. My fingers tingled with the desire to do the same; I could almost imagine what its texture would be like against my skin.

"I think it's done." He sighed and rubbed his lips together. I bit mine. He looked so hot, focused like this. He lifted his eyes, and that same focus directed at *me* brought a wave of awareness into my lower belly. "Do you like it?"

"Uh?"

"Do you think it's ready?"

I had decided that it was done a few minutes ago, allowing me the dangerous reverie, but I drew myself back into work.

"Yes. It's ready. We don't have time to let it rest for a few days before reading it again, but that's why we're asking your dad to read it."

"Okay, I'm printing it. My dad still prefers paper." He clicked a few times on the screen, and soon the quiet sound of a printer reached me from nearby.

Gabe stretched, arms long and thick above his head. He released the movement with a groan.

"I guess we're done with work for the night?" I asked, the vision of his chest widening in front of me still a mirage in my mind.

"That's probably the case. I might check my emails or something after I take the documents to my dad's office. You want to come with me? I think my mom is going to be there tonight."

I raised my eyebrows. "Why is your mom here? Have you told them anything about us?"

"They have an event I think. She comes to pick him up sometimes. And no, I haven't told them." He lifted a shoulder. "It'll come up. Soon, I think. Until then, I thought that it'd be best to keep it vague... it would prevent them from connecting the dots with the advice I asked of them. It'll look way more natural to them this way, right? Easy to see, that we spent all this time together and it led to more."

He smiled as he said that, an arched eyebrow betraying the irony of it all. I didn't share with him that the irony had started to evaporate for me, because all this time together coiled in my heart with building tension. Changing things slowly. Scarily. And I couldn't do much about it, except try to ignore it and hope for the best.

I sighed. "I'll go with you, then. I'd love to meet your mom."

"She's wonderful. She and my dad are." He smiled. "It's why I do everything."

"What do you mean?"

"I work this much and I have my whole damn future planned because I love them so much. They sacrificed a lot when they moved here. I was tiny— I don't remember, but when I understood..." He released a wistful breath. "You probably have seen something similar with your family. My parents worked so hard. I'm not about to let their efforts crumble down, just because it means I have to press pause on the rest of my life for a little bit longer. They trusted me to keep the Sotomayor Group going, to make it grow. I'm going to make it my number one focus, until I've achieved the next stage."

A surge of mixed feelings overtook my chest, a tear in the space between my lungs. His words made it clear, what was between us would stay a farce with an end in sight for him. They also highlighted our differences: his focus was on his family. I couldn't say that I worked for the same reasons. I admired Gabe for his choices; maybe having a family like the Sotomayors, so caring and supportive, made it easier to have an uncomplicated goal like the one he'd just shared.

I must have been showing some of my emotions on my face, because he frowned.

"Something wrong? Or you don't feel the same?"

"No, I just... I can't say I'm working this hard for the same reasons."

The printer had stopped working, but Gabe made no attempt to retrieve the papers.

"Why are you doing it?" he asked.

"Because I want to." I shrugged. "I want to be in this business, and trying to make a company that's already there grow makes more sense than starting over. Because as long as my dad gives me his stake and Enrique keeps wanting to stay away from the company, I *can* make it happen. I just need to survive the time before."

Gabe dropped his head to the side as he considered me. "I see why you need to be so determined and persistent."

My body stilled at his words, a semi-frozen state, because of course he'd sensed the strength of my will. I breathed through the comment, trying to process that his words were delivered with kindness rather than the condescension I was used to. I could take the words in; I didn't need to shield myself from them.

His eyes still searched my face. "Imagine what you could do, if your family supported you."

His voice delivered a lance to my heart, the spear flying past a crack in my walls. "Imagine."

He leaned toward me and put a hand on my shoulder. "I can't make what you want happen, but I can be there for you."

No wonder I was losing all sense of irony. My heart knocked at the closed door inside of me, wanting it to open wide and ask for more. For the first time in a long time, the idea didn't seem completely out of the question. Except that Gabe had just shown me that, if he were to ever accept my heart, it would be after he'd achieved his company's goals.

"Thank you, Gabe. For caring enough to be here."

He smiled. "Ready to take the papers to my dad?"

I nodded and put my things away while Gabe collected the documents and put them in a folder for Don Raúl. We left everything in his office, except for my heels which I put on, and we made the short trek to his dad's space. I followed him into it.

"Hola, hola," he said to the room. He put a hand on my lower back and pushed me forward, showing me to Vi, sitting across from Don Raúl and next to an elegant woman. The latter looked at me with kind eyes, a few lines on her face marking the million smiles I could guess she offered the world. "Lina, that's my mom there, Sonia. You know my dad and Vi."

"Hola a todos." I waved at them.

"Oh, Lina! This is a surprise." Vi got up from her place and gave me a quick hug. "I've heard that you've been spending a lot of time around here; I wondered when I might see you again."

"Yes, Gabe and I have been busy with the project. You'll probably see the results of what we've done so far, soon."

Gabe's mom stood as well, and she gave me a kiss on the cheek. "Nice to finally meet you." Her accent was soft and comforting. "Raúl has been telling me about this project."

She glanced between Gabe and I, a twinkle in her eyes. Don Raúl put a hand on my shoulder in hello, and then hugged his wife sideways.

"I brought the proposal, Dad." Gabe put it on his desk. "If you can share any notes you have by tomorrow night, that'd be awesome. The deadline is in five days, and we still need to send it to legal."

Don Raúl nodded. "Sure. Do you two want to come to the event with us? It's a gallery opening for a foundation I'm involved with."

"Yes, yes! Please come with us," Doña Sonia said. "That way I can get to know you better."

"Oh, no, I can't. I should head home," I said. "But I appreciate it. Maybe another time, Señora."

"Okay, but you have to have coffee with us soon," she said, "and you can't call me *señora* anymore. In our country you could call me tía, but if that's weird to you, just call me Sonia, okay?"

"Mom," Gabe laughed. "We're way too old to ask Lina to call you tía."

"I wanted to try," she smiled. "I only got Gabe's closest friends to call me tía."

Gabe leaned toward me, a smile on his face as he gave me what seemed like important background information. "My parents adopt every close friend I make. They're all in the family chat."

I chuckled.

"And I guess Lina doesn't count as a close friend, does she?" The twinkle in Sonia's eyes intensified.

"I don't think I'm a close friend, no," I said.

"It's okay. We won't ask you what kind of friend you are, not yet. But call me Raúl from now on, all right?"

Vi laughed. "I can ask what kind of friend you are. I don't have the same scruples."

"Enough," Gabe said. "Lina must be exhausted. We've worked hard today."

"Bye everyone. Lovely to meet you, Sonia."

I said goodbye and went back with Gabe to his office. His family's smiling faces were the last I saw.

————

Gabe

I returned to the Sotomayor headquarters from Martínez and Associates and ran into an empty elevator car. I'd spent a bit too long with Lina, and now I was late for a meeting with my dad and Jake.

It was an ongoing struggle. I was perpetually behind on everything, since agreeing to help Lina. I was sleeping poorly, stressed over the added pressure it had on my responsibilities. Even without faking this relationship with Lina, adding the project for the stadium already stretched my busy schedule. Somehow, I didn't want to stop.

I opened the door to the boardroom and voices went quiet for a second.

"There he is," Jake said.

"I made you coffee, but it might be a bit cold now." Dad pushed a mug to me.

"Yeah, sorry." I sat down at the table and the memory of the past hour sparked a smile. "Lina and I submitted the shortlist proposal."

She'd seemed so giddy, a grin I couldn't stop staring at making my heart flutter. Maybe that helped with the stress, that I enjoyed her so much. And that I knew there was a deadline.

"And now, we wait!" Dad clapped his hands once and rubbed them together. "We should plan a family weekend after the results are in. Maybe right after? At the lake house, of course. And you should invite Lina."

I hid a startle. I shouldn't be surprised; of course they suspected something was going on. It was the whole point of the plan. Maybe my jumpiness had to do with my guilty conscience... or to the fact that I'd started to accept that something *was* going on.

It was the logical conclusion, since I'd been having a harder and harder time not kissing Lina on the lips.

And, since the plan was to stay the course and not run away in response to my realization— I had to stick around, for everyone to believe the ruse— I had to at least ask her about going to the lake for the weekend with us.

I gulped. "I'll let her know, though she might be busy."

"So something is *really* going on!" My dad exclaimed.

"Yeah." I glanced at my dad, and I couldn't quite lie. "I'm feeling things."

"Then do your best to invite her over to the lake," he said, eyes soft on me. "Let's meet a different side of Lina, outside of work."

That was precisely the issue. Getting to know a different side of my fake girlfriend was waking up all sorts of confusing things in me.

At some level, I'd always known that would happen, if I spent time with Catalina Martínez. Thank God that everything was temporary.

Chapter 16

Gabe: Hey. Haven't heard from you in a couple of days. How are things?

Lina: Missing me, fake boyfriend of mine?

Gabe: Obviously.

Lina: I'm okay, just busy catching up with work

Gabe: Sadly, I know what you mean. Sometimes I wonder what I would do if I didn't spend 90% of my time working

Lina: Right? What is a life? Friends? I don't know her. Hence why I've neglected my fake boyfriend

Gabe: I've been catching up on work too, you're good. But let me take you out for a bit? I can pick you up from wherever

Lina: Sure. Pick me up from home in half an hour?

Gabe: Done

———

Gabe

I'd given the night off to Josué, and I drove to Lina's home alone. I rang the doorbell at her parents' house with nerves swelling in my stomach. Her mom opened the door.

"Hello, Gabe! Haven't seen you around much. Come in, come in."

"Hi, Iris. It's okay, I'll wait for Lina here. I want to take her for a drive."

Lina appeared next to her mom. "We're going out for a bit, mami. If he comes in we'll never leave."

She wore a low-cut sleeveless shirt, the coral tone of it accentuating the soft brown of her skin. The deep V-neck highlighted the fullness of her breasts and, when she leaned in to kiss my cheek, her perfume soaked my brain into dizziness.

It was Iris who sighed. "Ah, young love. I remember when Edgardo looked at me like that."

Lina surveyed me, as if seeing me anew. It became harder to breathe, a prickling sensation snatching my lungs. It insisted that I hide what I felt, but I didn't. It would help us if Iris could see it. Even if it made my hands tremble.

"Do you feel like ice cream?" I asked, the words stumbling out of my mouth.

Lina smiled. "Yes! Always."

I nodded and waved to Iris, who closed the door behind us.

We drove in silence for a few minutes. I couldn't say it was comfortable, because it wasn't— tension built in me. It pushed me to tie what I felt into a thousand knots, so I didn't do what I really wanted to do.

"You know, you're good at pretending to be an amazing boyfriend," Lina said out of the blue. "I think my mom is ready to start creating a wedding guest list."

That cooled down my feelings fast.

I scoffed. "Sorry, but I draw the line at a fake wedding."

I turned left, toward the location for a food truck I'd looked up earlier.

She laughed. "Don't you want to get married? Remember, I'm a woman and I'm counting down the days until you propose."

Her words dripped with sarcasm.

I smiled. "I want to get married. One day. For my parents, you know? They dream of that for Vi and me."

"I can't see that far. Until my work is settled and doesn't feel like a battle anymore, I can't imagine thinking of anything else. Otherwise I'd feel like I'm proving my family right and I'd hate that. Any serious relationship that could end in marriage before my dad retires would make them think I was ready to give up working."

"I can see that, but it's different for me. I can't date because if it turned serious, how could I choose? Ask my partner to let me work late every night until the transition to CEO was complete, be okay with being third on my list... I couldn't. That's why I didn't plan to date until the worst was behind me. That is, I didn't plan on dating, until you, Martínez and Associates, and your family's machismo got in the way."

Despite the web of confused feelings making a home among my organs, saying that out loud calmed me. We both had personal reasons not to let this fake relationship become real. And for me, one of those was that I wouldn't ask Lina to allow my half-assed attempt at passing our relationship for real to become our normal.

Several seconds went by before she answered. "I'm sorry this is disrupting your life so much."

I frowned. I wasn't sure how much I'd meant my words to sound like that. "It hasn't been that bad. It hasn't been great, either, but we've managed. Right?"

"Exactly what a fake girlfriend wants to hear," she joked. "It hasn't been great, but we've managed, yes."

Her words verged on self-deprecation, like my statement was an indictment on how much I took pleasure in my time with her.

I pursed my lips, hesitating as to how much I wanted to say. "When I say it's not that bad... I should rephrase. I've enjoyed the time I spent with you. It's just that things aren't what they could be... or should be, if this were real."

We reached the public area where the food truck would be that night. I parked near a walking path; trees lined the biking lanes where a few people strolled. Night approached, the sky in many colors, but dusk advanced enough that the park lights had switched on.

"What would be different, if this were real?" She turned to me, eyes bright.

"Maybe I'd ask my assistant to find out where they sell the best ice cream in North America, and then we'd take the plane there for a weekend so we could have it. Instead of me driving us to an artisan food truck."

"But I like this plan, too," she said. "I'm glad I've gotten to know you better."

We studied each other, sitting in my car, the park and its lights around us. If this were happening two years down the line, this was precisely where I'd kiss her.

I looked at her lips. They looked soft. Inviting. Two years down the line seemed like too far away.

"Ready for dessert?" she asked.

It took me a second to realize she meant ice cream.

———

Lina

"So why did you invite me out?" I asked. We'd just gotten our ice cream from a truck that boasted interesting flavors. I'd picked lavender and Gabe lemon; we'd taken our cones, heavy with cold deliciousness, and strolled away. "We typically go to your place and work, for our fake dates. We're having something close to a real date, instead."

The night was the perfect temperature; the park was mostly empty, the sky almost fully dark. A few people walked nearby, and in my head, I imagined we all enjoyed the calm evening.

"I wanted to talk to you." He closed his lips around the lemon-flavored dessert, the sight distracting me a little. "Didn't think texting was as good. Or a phone call."

I slowed down. Gabe seemed like the kind of man who would never break up over an email, and who would try to sweeten the moment with ice cream, to lessen the sting.

A flutter of nerves rolled through my guts, anchored in anticipatory grief. "Are we breaking up early?"

He frowned. "What? Why? No, we still have a few weeks left, right?"

"That's what I thought!" I licked the lavender treat, coating my tongue and my relief with its soothing taste.

"Okay, good. I mean, it's probably a good idea to continue with this for a little longer. A couple of weeks after we hear from the principal project lead, right? And after the contract is signed."

"Right. That's what we agreed to."

"Right." His tongue darted out again. "Good. Anyway, I didn't invite you out to break up with you, but..."

A cyclist rang behind us and Gabe stepped closer to me. Another ring reached us, and he put an arm around me to walk side-by-side for a few seconds, while a kid in a lot of purple and rainbow fringe passed us by. Once the riders were far enough ahead, he released me but walked closer to me than he had before.

He seemed to study the reduced space between us; while I felt a tingling awareness in my chest, he laughed.

"I invited you out to make it more serious between us, actually." He grinned. "To the outside witnesses, anyway."

Even if I knew it was all fake, the tingles electrifying my heart went from a hum to a strong current.

"Do you want to sit for a bit?" he asked, pointing to a bench nearby.

I nodded and we sat next to each other, an old, glorious tree hugging the space.

"So, how are we moving our relationship forward?" I cast a glance at him.

"My family has a lake house a couple of hours outside of the city. We go there as a family every once in a while, to take a break together." His lips kissed the ice cream again. Or so it seemed, to my infatuated eyes. "My dad wants to go there after we hear from the project lead about the shortlist, regardless of the results. And, well... he told me to invite you."

I frowned as I savored lavender once more. "What exactly does he think is going on between us?"

"I'm not sure." He stared at my lips on the ice cream, and the cold dessert suddenly felt tasteless. The gentle flavor disappeared, because my brain was more interested in learning what was going on through his mind. Wondering how his lips might feel on mine. Would I taste lemon on his tongue? It would mix perfectly with my lavender. "I didn't ask. But he assumes something is going on, and he'd like to get to know you better."

"Know me better, huh?"

His eyes lifted to mine. "Yeah. Because something is going on between us. I think he's surprised; he hasn't seen me with anyone since Essie."

I nodded. "Do you want him to see us together, though? Give him more reason to think we're a couple?"

"I don't know." He shrugged and took a big bite of his waffle cone. "He'd think it'd be weird if I don't at least invite you. But I could say you're busy."

Did I want to be busy? No, not at all. This was an amazing opportunity to see this family up close. Were they as amazing as I thought they were? Or would Sonia and Vi do the cooking and all the cleaning while the guys lounged around and took a nap?

"What's the place like? Are we thinking tight quarters, roughing it a bit?"

"Please." Gabe scoffed. "It's our second home. It's nice. It even has a helipad, though we rarely use it."

I laughed. "I truly didn't know what to expect. You all seem so unassuming."

"There are several rooms and a big shared living space with a view of the lake. We rarely run out of room but, because my parents will adopt every friend I have, we have sofa beds as well. My parents dream of a day when they can convert a room to bunk beds, if you can guess why that is."

I chuckled. "But no pressure from your parents, I'm sure."

"Exactly. They'd be just as happy if one of my friends had children and brought them over, as long as they get a bit of that sweet grandparent experience, apparently. Sadly, we're all forever single."

"Life just isn't what it was for the previous generations."

"Yeah. They don't bug us too much about it, luckily. In any case, there'll be plenty of space, if you want to go. We each can have our own room, spend some time with my family, then return to the city and keep to our plan."

What would it be like, to be with a mostly-new family like that, and pretend to be dating Gabe? My heart beat faster at the thought, because the images that came with the question tempted me more than they should.

"So you want to go?" Gabe's voice betrayed both nerves and excitement.

"Yeah. It'll be good. I haven't had a break since..." I frowned. "I don't know when was the last time I did something for me, and not for the company or my family."

"These weekends are my breaks and I enjoy them, but I get it if they're not your kind of thing. I don't want to get in the way of your goals."

"You're not. I probably could use a bit of a break... and a weekend away with your family might help with this curiosity I have. Are the Sotomayors as nice as they seem?"

"Oh, you know nothing, Lina. We need to be careful, or they'll try to adopt you, too."

"Didn't they learn their lesson with Essie?"

"They didn't try to adopt her."

He went back to his ice cream, silent after dropping that nugget of information. I nodded, and indulged in the make-believe that things could be different for us. That our fake relationship could turn real and not wreck our short-term plans, and that I'd find a warm family relationship in his world.

We spent the next several minutes in silence, until we finished our ice cream.

"How much will we have to pretend?" I asked. "Probably not much, right?"

His nod was slow as he looked at the ground. "If we're breaking up in a few weeks, we don't need them to think everything's going well. Right? And it'll get them thinking, when they realize we're not sharing a bed."

We walked back to his car, side-by-side again. At one point, his hand brushed mine. My fingers flexed, the instinct to take his hand strong, but unfulfilled.

Chapter 17

Jake: I think you should all come to the Sotomayor lake house in a couple of weeks

Gabe: Fuck's sake, Jake

Max: I'm in. Especially because Gabe's response suggests there's something going on

Jake: Gabe is taking his 'friend' and business associate to meet the family

Gabe: she already knows the family, what are you talking about?

Javier: not all of the family, evidently. I'm in

Jake: exactly. We're the extended family. And if these guys learned of this weekend and that I didn't tell them, I'd have to face the consequences. I'm not going to willingly have that happen

Max: I just can't believe you didn't invite us first, Gabe

Gabe: I don't want to overwhelm her

Javier: Somos un pan de dios. We would never overwhelm her

Max: hahaha god's bread, never got that one

Javier: My mom says that about good kids

Max: I know that, jackass. I'm pretty sure it's a Catholic thing

Gabe: Anyway, I don't want Lina to run away screaming at your guys' nonsense

Jake: what nonsense? You offend us

Gabe: I think you should all be too busy gallivanting through the world to come by

Jake: I will be there, your parents will insist

Max: and all I have to do is drop a couple of hints in the family chat that I want to go and they'll invite us

Gabe: I love you guys, but I don't like you at the moment

Javier: we'll be on our best behavior

Gabe: best behavior doesn't mean good behavior when you're all concerned

Javier: it's just because we're happy to see you finally breaking out of your dating celibacy

Gabe: I'm not breaking out of it. Just... temporarily pressing pause on it

Javier: that doesn't sound good

Max: no, it sounds amazing. I can't wait to see what's going on

Gabe: found a wife yet, Max?

Max: shut up

Jake: I'll send you all more details for the weekend at the lake asap

———

Gabe and Lina

Gabe: I have news. My friends may be coming to the lake house when we're there

Lina: Oooh. Looking forward to meeting them.

Gabe: Thing is, the house has several rooms, but not enough for everyone and for you and I to be able to insist on sleeping apart

Lina: I see

Gabe: I'm sorry. We can pretend to fight and I can sleep on the sofa

Lina: forget about it. It would make the weekend too awkward. Then I better not go

Gabe: no, of course you have to go. You said you could use a break. We'll figure it out. If just one of my friends can't make it, then we'll be fine.

Lina: what are the chances of that?

Gabe: decent. I think it'll be fine.

Lina: it will be fine. Don't worry about it :)

Chapter 18

Lina

THE SHORTLIST RESULTS WERE just a week away. Gabe and I spent our shared time working on our own stuff, and waiting. When my mom told me to go support my boyfriend's soccer game, it seemed like a nice change.

Rodrigo wasn't playing that night, so Lucía didn't join me. I walked into the field area alone, travel mugs in hand, one for Gabe and one for me, plus some food stuffed in my purse. If I didn't feel like my mother's daughter before, this would have done it. I'd brought a snack for my fake boyfriend.

Instead of going up to the bleachers with the other game watchers and WAGs, I leaned against the metal fencing around the soccer field, elbows on the rounded edge. Gabe ran past me without noticing, and I smiled. He looked cute when he focused. A frown stood out on his face, eyes shifting from the ball to the players, strategizing an attack. He sprinted, pushed the guy with the ball, and stole it from him. Two players came running to him and, after a quick glance across the field, he punted the ball to a team member far on the other side of the field.

"Show them how it's done, Gabe!" I yelled.

He turned to me with a bright smile and I waved. I hadn't told him I was showing up to the game.

The next time he ran past me, I whooped. He shook his head, but grinned again. When he approached me once more, I planned to yell something in Spanish, but he didn't give me a chance.

"We're having words at the end of the period!" he warned, and I laughed. At least half of that response tried to hide the sprinkle of awareness that his tone— half stern, half scolding— woke up in me.

When the referee blew the whistle at the end of the first forty-five minutes, Gabe ran to the edge of the field far from me; he grabbed a bag, a water bottle, and a towel he'd left there, then came to me.

"Hi." I nearly batted my eyelashes at him. Okay, well. I did. "I brought you coffee."

He put everything on the floor next to me, except for his water. He chuckled and stared at the travel mug I held to him, his fingers opening the latch on his bottle. Sweat shone on his skin, some of it condensing and streaking down his temple. A single drop fell from his chin.

He took a long swig of water. His shirt stuck to his chest, his lungs still in overdrive, expanding his already wide chest.

When I gazed back up at him, he stared right back.

He didn't say anything, but reached for the mug I held between us. He took a sip from it. "This is perfect, thank you."

I'd paid attention to how he liked coffee, so I was confident
he'd like it. Still, his words spread warmth through my chest. I
smiled, but it seemed the heat had made me lose my eloquence.
That, or how hot he looked, all sweaty.

"So. Words." I cleared my throat. "You said we needed to have
words."

"It's okay if you want to just... I don't know. Applaud. Say 'go
Gabe!'." He grinned and had more coffee. "I know you're helping
me in this competitive thing between all the guys here, but it'll
hurt too much when we break up if you're too good at it."

I seemed to need a deep breath after that. "What if I want to
bring a sign?"

He laughed and passed me his drinks, then used the towel to
dry the sweat off his face and neck. "Please don't," he groaned
into the towel.

"How about a compromise? I won't make a sign for everyone
to see, but I'll yell words for everyone to hear. Whatever words
I want."

The referee whistled again. Gabe leaned to me and kissed the
corner of my lips. I searched his face to know how on purpose
that had been, but I couldn't decipher it.

"They do say compromise is key in long-lasting love."

He winked and went back to the game, leaving me confused
and more than a bit turned on.

Gabe

The team we played that night was known for playing rough. I was mostly okay with that; I got to release a lot of tension pushing a guy extra hard. And I couldn't lie, I also liked the primal feeling of showing off for my girlfriend.

Fake girlfriend. I shouldn't forget that.

And I wasn't proud of it, but I figured, if I played soccer to get my heart pumping and do something other than work, then it was okay if showing off for Lina achieved the same results.

I may have been stretching my morals there, but I couldn't resist. It felt great to have her show up for me at the games. And as long as we both remembered how things would end, a little flirting couldn't hurt.

The captain on the other team ran to me at high speed. I glanced around me; I didn't have the ball, so I had to be in someone's way— and I saw him; another guy running right behind him with the ball.

I went in for it. I skipped around the captain and aimed for the other guy; he elbowed me and pushed me to the side. I took the hit, a burst of pain radiating from where he'd dug into my side, and I ran behind him. The rest of my team organized to defend from the attack, and I was the one protecting from behind. I tried to steal the ball, but he pushed me away.

"Don't let him do that! Referee!" Lina yelled from her spot at the edge of the field. "C'mon, Gabe! Give him hell!"

I chuckled and went back to it.

A scuffle exploded out of nowhere; three of their guys and two of ours pushed at each other. I broke them up, and we went back to playing.

The next time I gained control of the ball, I sprinted toward the opposing team's goalkeeper. I had two guys on my tail, and one approaching me from the left. My chances were high to score; I was in the perfect position to avoid an offside.

I was so focused on the guy to the left that I didn't see the one that shoulder-checked me from the right. I kept my balance and pushed sideways, the ball still between my feet.

It might have been an accident, or maybe not, but the elbow I got to my eyebrow hurt like hell regardless. When the next push dropped me to the floor and I burnt my knee against the polyurethane, I let inertia fall me to the ground.

The whistle went off. I took a few deep breaths and lifted my hand to my eyebrow. The dull pain at the spot exploded into shards when I touched; I winced, which caused another wave of pain to erupt. Blood stained my fingers.

Jaime, the guy acting as referee approached me. "You okay?"

Lina showed up right behind him. "Gabe! Are you okay? That asshole!" She pointed to the referee. "You're gonna give him a red card, right?"

I chuckled, but a few body parts hurt in the process. I winced again, and more pain erupted.

"You can't be here," Jaime told Lina.

"Chill, Jaime." I put up a hand, and Mario, a teammate, helped me stand. "She didn't know."

"He's hurt. Of course I wanted to check on him." Lina came close to me. She put a hand on my chest for balance and stood on her tippy-toes, inspecting my wound. "You need that taken care of."

"Gabe." Jaime warned me. "She needs to be out."

Lina turned to him. "You can talk to me. Gabe is my boyfriend, not my handler."

Jaime shook his head. "I asked you to leave. You didn't."

"Fine, fine, I'm going! But give that guy a red card."

"Don't tell me how to do my job." He pointed at me next. "There are three minutes left. Don't play them, go get that wound disinfected."

"But we'll play at a disadvantage—" I tried, while Lina hooked a hand around my elbow.

"It's fine, FIFA won't know. And I am giving that guy a red card, anyway. Not because your girlfriend said so."

Lina's smile blossomed triumphant anyway, and I let her guide me out of the field while the other guys went back to the game.

"Do you know where we might find a first aid kit?" she asked, trying to get me to sit on a bleacher.

"I don't know if we have any around." I didn't sit down. "But I have one in my car. Long story, but we have my mom to thank for it."

"Good. Let's go. You can tell me the story while I help you take care of that."

I tried to grab my bag, water bottle, and towel, but Lina didn't let me.

She gave me the mugs, and she carried everything else. "I'm a strong modern woman. Let me help."

I shook my head. "I'm not that badly injured."

She quirked an eyebrow my way as we got out of the field area. "The way that cut is bleeding, I'm reserving judgment."

An involuntary frown pulled at my cut, and I held back a wince. "Huh. I thought it was sweat."

"Honestly."

We found my car and I opened the back door; the first aid kit was in the underseat compartment. I gave the plastic box to my fake girlfriend, who'd been acting a lot like a real one.

"Okay. Sit there." She pushed down from my shoulder. I sat at the edge of the seat cushion, bringing my head to her shoulder level. Lina had me hold the first aid kit in my hands while she perused the contents. "Okay, gauze, good. Disinfectant tow-elettes... oh, wow, you have everything here. I'm impressed. Even a mouth to mouth device!"

I chuckled. "I don't think I'm going to need one of those."

No, if she wanted to put her mouth on mine, I wouldn't want it to be because of CPR.

"Har har." She put on the gloves, and my stomach dropped. I was disappointed she wouldn't be touching me skin to skin. It made sense, of course, but... disappointment was there, anyway, blooming in my stomach. "Let's do this, then."

She opened a disinfectant packet and unfolded the towelette. She dabbed at my eyebrow, slowly cleaning the wound and skin surrounding it. She focused on the task, her concentration visible in the slant of her eyebrows. Tension pursed her lips, and it brought a few images to mind I wasn't aware I had kept: when we worked together at home and she concentrated, the same gesture would shape her face.

"You doing okay?" She didn't look at me as she worked, but took a step closer between my legs. "I don't have great light here."

"Yeah, I'm good."

A little too good. The only thing that would make it better would be if I could throw the first aid kit away, put my hands on her hips, and pull her even closer. The desire to do just that built in my lower belly, collecting enough potential energy for a shockwave. Its power would hit my organs and liquefy them in the blink of an eye.

Mere minutes earlier I had been telling myself flirting wouldn't hurt, and it seemed to have brought my attraction to Lina to the forefront of my chest. She put the towelette in the red biohazard bag and opened another, continuing to clean my wound... and all I could think about was how much I wanted to make this real and thank Lina with a kiss. Maybe more.

I closed my eyes. It was a futile dream. This fake relationship worked only because it had an end. Because I didn't have to try too hard.

If I were courting my fake girlfriend, I'd work harder at it— I'd invite her out to real dates, and I would cook for her, and I would take every weekend off so that I could spend time with her. Half of my weeknights. When she came to my games, I'd greet her with a kiss. When I won a tournament, I'd kiss her like we were in the middle of a stadium and everyone was cheering for us.

I wasn't doing any of those things. Two-thirds of the time we spent together, we worked on our own stuff. How could she ever know I cared, if I didn't show her? And I couldn't, not without sacrificing the chance to become the Sotomayor Group CEO.

Not to say anything about how disinterested she seemed, when we were alone. I'd have to romance her, provide evidence of how good we could be together, if we made our relationship a reality. She was guarded for good reason, strong-willed, and though I liked that about her, it meant I'd have to take my time. Be patient. And yes, I'd be willing to wait. What I lacked was time.

First, make my parents proud. Show them I valued everything they've ever done. Then romance.

So no, I couldn't court Lina. She would never know I felt this way. Unless the universe conspired in my favor, and she was single in two or three years.

Her gloved hand continued to work, while the other held my jaw at the right angle.

"You have amazing eyebrows," Lina said.

I chuckled. Such a casual comment, when my heart had been tearing up in my chest.

"Thanks. I don't need stitches, do I?"

"I don't think so." She put the dirty towelette in the red bag, grabbed two small butterfly closures, and put them on my eyebrow. "But I'm not an expert."

She grinned with an arched eyebrow, and I smiled back.

She took the first aid kit from my hands and dropped to her knees with no warning. She left the plastic container on the floor, and used both hands to lift my shorts, one leg at a time.

"Did you hurt your knees, too?" she asked. "You fell pretty badly on them."

The answer died in my throat. I knew she was checking for injuries, of course I knew it, but my dick didn't care. Her head— and her mouth— were too close to it, and this position gave me enough material to imagine what it would be like, if she was on her knees in front of me for altogether different reasons.

"Uhm..." I gulped. "No. I think— I should be fine."

"Mhh." She opened another disinfectant packet. "Looks fine, just bruised and scratched, but I'll clean them just in case."

Her business-like demeanor was the only thing that saved me from tenting my shorts right where she could see.

I breathed in and out, thought about the Napoleonic Wars, and commanded my body to relax. This was not supposed to be an erotic situation; what had possessed my body? Lina was helping me clean up a wound, and I'd been pining, and all of a sudden, blood had vacated my brain and chest. It wasn't right.

"My mom!" I exclaimed and gulped. "My mom. She insists we all have emergency kits in our cars. First aid, blankets, hazard triangles, the whole thing. If not for us, it could help us help other people, she said. So we all have one."

Lina didn't respond right away. "That's sensible, and not at all a complicated story."

"Well, it's also because there are sections of road near the lake house without phone reception, and it was the emergency kit or a satellite phone just in case."

She laughed. "Now, that would be a rich person's kind of overkill."

"Or the kind of precaution that a socially-oriented person might think of. She's a social worker, you know?"

"I didn't know, but that helps me understand how she raised a guy like you, somehow. You're done, Gabriel. I think you might get a few bruises, by the way." She got up and passed me the kit; I locked the clasp while she put the used-up towelette and gloves in the biohazard bag. She made a knot at the top to close it and gave me a stern look. "Shower when you get home to make sure the whole system is clean before you change clothes." She waved a hand in circles in front of me, like my body was the system. "And make sure to add new gloves to the first aid bag."

"Yes, ma'am."

"Are you always this good?"

Her playful smile made me chuckle, because I hadn't been that good, the past few minutes, when I thought of her sucking my cock. And in bed, I wasn't all good, either.

"Can't say that I am," I admitted. "Not always."

She squinted at me, as if guessing what accounted for bad in my books. Worse of all, I couldn't even promise myself to behave, when potential energy continued to increase around my gut.

———

Lina

A few days after my greatest piece of acting to date— when Gabe had gotten hurt and I'd pretended to be mostly unaffected— I lounged on my fake boyfriend's sofa. We'd both spent our usual long hours at each of our offices, followed by a couple more hours working together at his place. Now that my laptop lay closed on the coffee table, I rested my head on the back of the couch and stared at the textured white ceiling.

I interlocked my fingers on my stomach; the soft clicking of Gabe's typing mesmerized my brain into a lull. Music played softly in the background, and my eyes unfocused. In my growing relaxation, it seemed easier to think of the other night when I'd helped him take care of his eyebrow cut.

The knee-jerk reaction I experienced seeing Gabe get hurt surprised me, just like the intense drive to take care of him. I'd let myself help him, but I didn't kiss his forehead like I'd wanted to, or run my fingers through his hair after I'd discarded the gloves. At best, I'd shown him friendship, which was something I could live with. More than that and it was too vulnerable. Too soft of a spot.

Aside from what it said about my growing... interest in Gabe, I didn't want to get used to taking care of him. That seemed like a direct gateway to becoming the kind of woman my family expected of me, and giving Gabe the wrong impression of who I was as a person. I pushed my comfort levels a lot already by asking him for this huge favor and being a fake girlfriend. The risk of confusing fiction with reality was too high, and I needed to keep my limits in sight.

Gabe's phone rang. "Mom? Hi, yeah. Mmh."

I closed my eyes as Gabe chatted with his mom. His voice wasn't particularly deep nor high, and it soothed me.

"Right." He chuckled, the sound throaty. "Oh, no. You could have come. Just text me ahead of time."

He let out another laugh, this once also low and breathy.

I shook my head and it lolled toward him; I opened my eyes for a second, catching the way he smiled and winked at me. I closed my eyes again and let out a small snort.

"She's good. Falling asleep on my couch."

"I'm not," I mumbled.

"Wait— what?"

While I had been close to dozing off as he talked to his mom, the way he exclaimed those words had me opening my eyes to track his face.

His eyebrow still sported purples and yellows from the injury, but he didn't wear butterfly stickies anymore.

"No, I didn't know." Gabe arched an eyebrow at me. "I guess Edgardo had Dad's number from before, right? Are you going to go to this barbeque?"

I closed my eyes again, this time for a different reason, and groaned. From the sound of it, my family had been up to some shenanigans.

"Mmh. Give me a sec. I'll ask her." He tapped on his phone. "It's on mute. Do you mind if my parents and Vi go to a barbeque your family invited them to? Apparently it's to celebrate that the two businesses are seeking opportunities together. My dad thinks that they'll have to invite your family for the day to the lake house, when we're there. You know, to be polite, in return for their invitation."

I sighed. "I told them about the weekend at your family's cabin. I think I gave them the inspiration."

"We have to say yes, don't we?"

I crossed my arms. "I think so."

Gabe unmuted his phone. "Okay. Yeah, let's do that. Yeah."

I closed my eyes again and took a deep breath. This changed our plans for the next few weeks, and we needed to be smart about it.

"Okay, Mom. Yes. Love you too. Good night."

How sweet, to hear his care for his mom. And how strange, to hear those words, and imagine what it would feel like, if they were for me.

Gabe turned off his phone, closed his laptop, and put both devices on the coffee table.

He sighed and lay back on the couch, his shoulder touching mine. Our faces oriented to each other; his eyes roamed my face, and the corner of his lips lifted in a soft curve.

"You looked like you could fall asleep there, for a second," he said.

"I wasn't going to." I bit the inside of my cheek. "But what would have happened if I had?"

"I would have agonized over it for a little bit. Should I wake you up? Bring a blanket and pillow?" He looked down to my lips, but lifted his eyes up to mine again. "Should I take you to my bed?"

"The more gallant option is the latter."

"Can't say I would have been thinking about gallantry." He wet his bottom lip. "I would have been thinking of something else. Including if you'd get in trouble for sleeping over."

My heart beat fast, taking the wheel of my emotions. I shouldn't think of his words as flirting, and I shouldn't respond to it. But I wasn't sure I was able to resist. "I'd be fine. My family is machista, but I fought those battles already. We just don't talk about it, because when they try, I bite their head off."

"So..." his eyes searched mine. "Do you want to sleep over here, sometime? It would add to the realism."

I gulped. "Maybe. We're going to have to amp up the pretense, anyway."

He turned sideways, so his body faced me more fully. "Because your family is coming to the lake house. And mine is going to your place for a barbeque."

I nodded. "We can't just play it cool with your family, when mine's going to be around."

A controlled breath expanded in his chest. His eyes never left mine. "Yeah. Your family half expects us to be deeply in love already. Who knows what kind of comments they would make about that. And who knows how my family and friends would respond to it, but I know they would get suspicious if I weren't always touching you, somehow."

"Oh. So you're handsy."

His nod was slow. "I think I'd be, if you and I were real."

Excitement feathered my skin, waking up dormant nerve endings. "I did promise I'd do anything to make this believable."

"I might have to kiss you." His eyes dropped to my lips. "For show."

I could see it all too clearly. The tempting image struck a chord deep inside, in the place where I hid the most tender parts of me.

I tensed and melted, all at the same time. "I think I'd be okay with that. Just don't abuse the privilege."

"Would I be abusing the privilege, if I kissed you now?" His voice rumbled, low and delicious. "To get used to it. So it's not surprising. So it looks natural."

It became harder to breathe. We stared at each other, the pull between us taut as we tested new territory. His face held a hint of humor, even patience, like this wasn't as serious for him, and kissing was a good and friendly addendum to our rules.

"Besos y abrazos no quitan pedazos," I said.

"Kisses and hugs don't tear you apart. What's that?"

"Something my mom used to say when I was a teenager. To discourage sex. Keeping it at kisses and hugs won't hurt me... because I wouldn't get pregnant from that alone."

He closed his eyes and groaned. "You're ruining the moment. I won't kiss you now that you mentioned unplanned pregnancies. It'll have to wait."

"You should kiss me soon, though. It won't hurt us to add that to the repertoire, right?"

"I'll kiss you soon." He opened his eyes and lifted an eyebrow at me. "I think I'll have to. Otherwise I'll lose my nerve, when my friends and family surround us."

"We'll have to rethink our break up strategy."

"We'll come up with something," he said and, sadly, I knew he was right.

Chapter 19

Gabe

NIGHT CAUGHT ME WORKING late again at the office. I'd taken off my tie, undone the top button, and crafted responses to the numerous emails piling up in my inbox. Once done with that, I had to review documents Jake had sent me earlier, to sign off on different branches' decisions for deals and projects. Only then would I be able to go home, before I did it all over again the next day. So on and so forth for the next couple of years, as planned.

It would be easier if I could concentrate only on work. My mind was adamant that thinking about Lina was much more interesting than writing emails. And, well, I couldn't blame my brain.

I regretted not kissing Lina two nights before. I'd been too busy to see her since then, and the moment when I'd asked her if I could kiss her replayed in my mind over and over again. In my imagination, I pressed my lips against hers in a different way each time. Knowing that I would get to make that a reality soon snatched my attention at the smallest opportunity, and my body buzzed with anticipation at the mere thought of it.

But that meant playing with fire. Many logical reasons existed to stop me, except that circumstances kept pushing us to move our relationship forward. And it tempted me, to let myself play it as if it were real, at least for a while. Until the inevitable break up.

Good thing that she was likely right: besos y abrazos no quitan pedazos. As long as Lina never learned that my feelings were a little more real than I was letting on, I could walk that line. It would be hard returning to my single life, but the more believable it was, the better for everyone.

I could live with that. I had to.

My phone dinged with the notification I had set for Lina. I clicked send on the email I had been working on and checked her text.

> **Lina**: the meeting tomorrow with the stadium bid project leads. Do you think it's a good thing that they want to ask us a few questions?

I stared at her text and rocked my chair from side to side. From so many people in my life, a text like that would have been a normal occurrence. From Lina it seemed like a huge deal, because it carried her doubt. Like she was nervous, and she was okay letting me see it.

The knots making it hard to breathe smoothed into silk at the possibility that Lina trusted me enough for it. Maybe it meant I'd managed to get through some of her walls, despite her guardedness. The idea blew oxygen into the building fire inside of me.

> **Gabe**: I think so. Why bother scheduling a meeting with a bidder they're not truly considering?

> **Lina**: I hope you're right. Less than a week now until we hear the results. Maybe we're neck-and-neck with other bidders.

> **Gabe**: could be. We're going to learn a lot from the meeting itself. Are you feeling prepared for it?

> **Lina**: of course. Especially since Tío Miguel and my dad will be there. I need to show them I'm on top of things.

> **Gabe**: We'll show them together. Are you at home yet?

> **Lina**: About to go home. You?

> **Gabe**: Not yet. I should be able to go home in an hour or so.

> **Lina**: Did you ever consider getting a sofa bed and toiletries in your personal washroom at the office?

Gabe: haha, no. But I'll admit I've caught up on sleep on the sofa before. Made the glass opaque, locked the door, and caught a few Zs a couple of times. More comfortable than I imagined, to be honest.

Lina: Are you running yourself to the ground, Gabe?

Gabe: Are you worried about me?

Lina: you've been a wonderful friend. A little bit of care is warranted.

Gabe: how little?

Lina: a little.

Gabe: okay, okay. I'll take that. And I'm not running myself to the ground. This will be only for a couple of years.

Lina: I keep telling myself the same. I hope we're both right. Good night, Gabe.

Gabe: Sleep well. See you tomorrow.

I know I shouldn't feel anticipation over seeing Lina, but if I couldn't blame my brain, I couldn't blame my heart and body, either.

———

Lina

After multiple visits to the top floor offices of the Sotomayor Group, I could simply say hi to Cynthia and walk past her reception desk toward the offices at the back of the place. I'd escaped my dad and uncle who would arrive together soon, with the excuse that I needed to pick up the Mexican cookies I brought to the meeting. The smell of cinnamon and sugar wafted from the box as I made my way to the boardroom, and I imagined I left a tempting trail of spiced sweetness behind me.

I didn't make it to the boardroom. To my surprise, my dad, Tío Miguel, Raúl, and Jake stood together chatting in the boardroom. They all turned to me as I approached them.

"Lina," Raúl said as he kissed my cheek. "What's this?"

He grabbed the box from me and Jake helped him open it.

"Hojarascas," I said. "My mom made a few different types for everyone to enjoy."

"Do I smell cinnamon?" Jake took one from the box and took a bite. "Oh god. This is delicious."

"Iris is a great cook. I'm very fortunate," my dad told the group.

"And if you're wondering," Tío Miguel added, "I'm sure Lina has learned a thing or two from her mother."

"Wait until Gabe is here to say stuff like that." My dad smiled. "It's for him that our Lina is showing off, right? Or are you trying to show off for the in-laws, too?"

"I brought this for everyone," I said.

Jake put the box on the table, and offered me coffee. He made me some at the small brewing station set up in the room while I caught up with Raúl.

"Where's Gabe?" I asked.

"He was wrapping up a call, the last time I checked. He will be here soon. Come, let's sit."

Everyone found a place around the table, but I hesitated. I checked my watch; Gabe had less than ten minutes to arrive.

"I'll go see if he's ready." I turned on my heels and stepped outside, opening the glass door to the boardroom, only to find Gabe taking strides in my direction. I kept the door open for him instead.

"Hey," he said. "I made it."

"Glad you're here." I offered him my cheek to kiss on the way to the meeting room, my hand still on the handle.

He didn't go in, and stopped in front of me instead. He took my chin between thumb and forefinger, turned my face toward him, and placed his lips on mine.

It was nothing more than the press of our mouths together, but my body reacted like I had never been kissed before. My knees weakened and everyone around us disappeared, my attention fully focused on the way his lips brought tingles to my skin, and his warm fingers held me in place. It lasted only a few seconds, but by the time it was done, it had pushed the button inside of me that wanted me to ask for more.

That simple kiss wasn't enough.

"C'mon, you two," Raúl said. "We need to get ready."

"Sweeter than the cookies, huh, Gabriel?" Tío Miguel added, his quip followed by his usual out-of-place, unconcerned laugh.

"What cookies?" Gabe asked, guiding me to two empty chairs next to each other. "Oh. I see."

"Hojarascas," Jake explained, taking another one from the box. His accent was better in Spanish than I'd expected. "Sit. I'll make you coffee."

Gabe nodded to his friend in thanks and he and I sat side-by-side, and I didn't say a word. I was still reeling from his kiss.

"Soon enough?" he muttered my way.

I didn't know how to answer the question, because there were reasons to say yes, and many more to say no.

"Don't distract me," I replied at the same volume. "This meeting is important."

He chuckled. "Thanks for that. It does wonders to my ego, to know I'm distracting you."

I shook my head and chuckled as well, just as Gabe opened a laptop and set up the call on the big screen. If my reaction made him feel good that was fine, I supposed, but I had to work hard at bringing down my internal response. Him kissing me that way in front of people was a big part of the point, but I wasn't supposed to react so strongly to it. I should have known;

if I'd lost all scruples I'd ever had at this pretense, and I had lost all sense of irony in faking a relationship with Gabe, then it was time to accept that my feelings were more involved than I was prepared to admit out loud.

Chapter 20

Gabe: what are you up to

Lina: reviewing an internal policy document :(boring

Gabe: that sucks

Lina: I bet you get to tell an employee to do that for you

Gabe: yes. And I like to threaten Jake with it when he pisses me off

Lina: I would tell Enrique to do it, but I'd rather not give him any reason to step into the business

Gabe: understandable

Lina: hey, I don't think I can go to the next couple of games. I need to catch up with work

Gabe: oh. Okay. I should probably skip a couple of games, too. I also need to catch up. But we just started the season tournament, I have to play it

Lina: I'll try to go in a couple of weeks, then

Gabe: maybe for the final, if we make it?

Lina: I'll make sure to go to that one. I could stop for lunch sometime this week?

Gabe: better not. I'm fully booked with meetings this week

Lina: Oh, okay. Well, text you soon, then

Gabe: talk soon

———

Lina: Two days until we get the shortlist results

Gabe: Nervous?

Lina: Maybe

Gabe: Should I go to your office and wait for the email together?

Lina: No. Can I go to yours? If we didn't get it, I don't want my

dad and uncle to see my first reaction

Gabe: of course, come and we'll have lunch. We'll check together

Lina: and what about dinner tonight?

Gabe: if you're okay with us having dinner at my office, too. I really need to try to catch up

Lina: I'll go to your office, no problem. It gives me something to say when they ask why we broke up. "He's an even worse workaholic than I am"

Gabe: yeah, I don't like that

Lina: worried about your reputation?

Gabe: maybe. See you tonight

———

Gabe

Dinner had gone off without a hitch, both of us settling into our usual routine. We talked once in a while, making random comments as we worked and ate, until we broke and admitted we needed the rest. Lina and I went to each of our homes separately and, this time, there was no kissing at all.

In a different life, we would have gone home together, worked together there, then gone to sleep together. Kissing would have happened several times throughout the evening.

Could that be normal life? Was that how my parents did it, at the height of building the Group, and trying to balance it out with being a couple and having kids?

The thought wouldn't have crossed my mind, if Lina and I hadn't ended up in this impossible situation, causing all lines to blur.

A sigh left me before I stuffed my mouth with food again. Today we ate together in my office once more; the shortlist results would be announced in less than an hour and, as planned, Lina had come to my office to have lunch and wait.

I'd been late for lunch, with a meeting that had gone past the scheduled time. Lina didn't seem angry about it. She'd taken it in stride, and now sat in front of me on my couch. We picked at our take out boxes and ate mostly in silence. I worked through a document another VP needed from me, and she worked on her emails.

Her hair was up in a loose ponytail today, the waterfall of it resting on her shoulder. Her fingers played with the ends of it as her eyes ran across her screen. My fingers would have loved to do the same, intermingling with the brown locks and her skin alike.

Frustration burnt a quiet path in my stomach. Why did we have to be in the middle of big career crossroads? This was the wrong time, and we had to have an expiration date. I had to stop myself from going any further, or the fake break up was going to hurt like hell.

Who was I kidding, I was in deep enough it was going to hurt like hell regardless.

At this rate, all I could do was ride this thing pulsing behind my breastbone and hide in work for a few weeks after the break up. I had enough piling up that it was the best option, anyway.

And all this time, Lina was probably thinking of our application, fully unaware of the quality of my feelings.

Time for something different.

"Only half an hour until the results are published. Getting nervous yet?" I asked.

She scrunched up her face. "Don't ask me if I'm nervous. It makes me think about it, and I don't want to think about it."

"I'm nervous," I admitted with a shrug. "I want to get it, too."

She cut me a glance. "You can be nervous. I can't."

"Of course you can be nervous. This is a big deal for us. If we get shortlisted, then we only have two competitors left. Makes the chances of us getting the stadium deal a lot more real."

She didn't say anything at first. She looked down and away; when her eyes returned to me, they were steady yet closed off. I wanted her to open up to me, tell me what she hid inside of her, but I didn't ask. It didn't seem fair, when getting closer didn't serve our goal, and we'd go our own ways soon enough.

"What would you do, if we don't get the contract?" Her voice was soft and hard at the same time. A challenge and her version of vulnerability, I guessed.

I bit the inside of my lips. I played around with my food, and responded after having a bite. "I would set it aside for a couple of weeks, but I'd go back to it. Do an analysis of the situation, see if there are comps in the market to set my eyes on. If we find a similar project somewhere in the Global North, it would be easier to correct and edit what we have, than starting completely from scratch next time we try."

She pressed her lips together, her eyes never wavering from me. Her takeout box rested on her lap, her hands still next to it. "You would want to try with us again?"

I frowned. "Wouldn't you want to try again? I believe we optioned it in the contract."

She mirrored me, no wrinkle between her eyebrows, but a cloud over her eyes. She bit her bottom lip. "I would. I don't know about my dad and uncle."

"I'll help you try to convince them."

"We might need to get married for that one; they won't trust me again if this one fails." She scoffed and smiled at me, the corner of her lips telling me she meant for me to take it as a joke... but I saw the sadness in her eyes, and I couldn't laugh at the situation.

I listened to the hallway and checked through the glass wall of my office, making sure we still had enough privacy; when I confirmed no one seemed to be coming our way, I clicked the button to make the glass opaque and put my feelings into words.

I spoke in a loud whisper. "I know you're joking, but fake marriages are a hard no for me, Lina. A couple of months doing this is different than letting my parents believe I found what they have. And you don't want to marry me, anyway." I put my mostly-eaten food and laptop on the coffee table, my computer screen going black— I had completely forgotten about it. "I haven't been that good of a boyfriend, even, for you to consider me as a real candidate. Even if it is to get your family to give you another chance."

She pursed her lips and squinted at me. "I don't like it when people tell me what I should want."

"This is not even real."

"But you don't get to decide what I want for myself."

I frowned. "Fair enough. I take the words back— but not what I meant. I hope you don't settle for someone whose idea of a good time is take out at the office. You deserve better than stealing time from the day job, or standing around at a soccer game."

Funny, that I would make a dig at myself like that, in the hope I'd convince both of us not to take this fantasy forward.

"I do. I will not settle." She stilled, and her eyes never wavered from me. "The day will come when I'll look for someone who wants to spend time with me and have work-life balance. But that day will come when I can have a work-life balance, too."

As much as I liked to be right, that one hurt. Maybe because somewhere inside of me, I had hoped that the little I gave her would be enough.

"I'm glad," I made myself say. I drew circles on my folded thigh with the tips of my fingers, the fabric smooth under my skin. "Do you have an idea when you might start thinking about that?"

She stared at me as if wanting to ask more, like maybe she understood the question breathing beneath my words.

She didn't ask, just like I didn't explain. Too risky for Lina, who liked to feel strong, and for me, who couldn't ask her to wait and feel righteous about it.

"I hate what I'm going to say..." she put her food on the coffee table, too, and ran her fingers through her hair. She sighed. "But I don't know. Depends on whether my dad retires as planned, and Enrique stays away."

I disliked the part of me who relished in the fact that her answers might not come for a couple of years from now, just because it gave me a chance at matching our timelines. It was a selfish part of me, because it meant keeping Lina on tenterhooks, depending on the men in her life to give her a chance.

How much more like the men in her family did that make me?

God, I needed to get my growing feelings in check.

I took a deep breath. "Even more important, then, to do what we can to get a contract in place, whether with this stadium or some other project. You hope it'll get your dad to leave you his share, don't you?"

She crossed her arms and stared at the floor. "Yeah. At this point, I don't see another way."

"Have you told them how you feel? They would be wrong to stop someone with your passion from running the business."

She gazed up at me from under the ridge of her eyebrows. "I have told them in every single way I know how, short of begging. I've shown them with my actions and used my words. They hide their heads in the sand, and tell me to wait and see."

Her voice was tired and ragged, and it reached deep inside of me.

"I'm sorry, Lina. Of course you have. I don't understand them, as men and as business owners, and it came out as if I doubted you. But I don't."

"I don't understand them either, but I don't have the luxury of waiting for an answer. They might never even accept the question. They're machistas— as simple as that. And it sucks for me."

I frowned and stared at my lap. "I don't know what to say. I don't know how to help you in this, that won't just be another man taking over."

"You're doing all I asked you to do. You're doing fine."

"I want to do more than fine. I want to be there for you."

She shrugged. "It's okay. You're not my real boyfriend."

And the fact hurt.

"Hey," she added. She reached forward with a hand across the sofa cushion. "Sorry. I got a bit defensive. But I appreciate it. You've been a great friend."

We gazed at each other for a minute. I took her hand; it was warm in mine.

I gave her a nod. "It's almost time. Let's clean this up, go get a coffee, and we'll get on that website."

"Refresh every five seconds, making myself sick every time."

I chuckled. "Let's not do that, okay?"

———

Lina

Gabe cleaned up our lunch and stepped out to make us coffee. While alone in his office, Violeta came and sat where Gabe had been.

"Hey! I heard you're getting the results for the shortlist now? I think my dad and Jake are joining us."

"Yes. The results should be shared publicly on that website—" I pointed to my screen— "and we should get an email with a copy of the official letter attached as well."

"Sounds good. I hope we get it. The contract between yours and our companies is almost ready; hopefully we're shortlisted so we can keep moving forward, full steam ahead."

"And if we don't get shortlisted?"

"Then we'll spend this weekend at the lake making each other feel better and try again."

I chuckled. "That's exactly what your brother said he would do."

"Yes. That's our style." She smiled. "Did my brother feed you well for lunch? So boring, having lunch at work. Good food is the least he could do."

He'd ordered Cuban for us, and it had been good, but I didn't think of it as a boring date. Maybe because it was fake, or maybe because Gabe and I were both workaholics, or maybe because I enjoyed his company no matter what...

I frowned. "It was good. You have a good brother, Vi."

She opened her eyes wide. "Oh, I know that! He's the best. I just also like you very much, and I hope you stick around for a bit. A work lunch is no way to romance your girlfriend, that's all."

I leaned on the back of the couch. "Where do you get your romantic ideals, Vi?"

"Romance novels, of course. And my parents. Doesn't matter, really. Romance should be the basic standard. How are you supposed to fall in love, otherwise?"

"What about having things in common, and spending time together, no matter if it's at the office?"

She grinned, the gesture so pretty on her, and so much like her brother's, her dad's. "Then maybe you'll stick around, if that's your idea of romance. That's what matters most. What your idea of romance is. I just hope it's the same as Gabe's."

I cocked my head. "You don't know me that well, Vi. What if I'm not good enough for your brother? I thought you'd be more protective of him."

"If he broke his singledom for you, you must be a pretty big deal. I asked him once, you know, when we'd both drunk a bit too much— I don't think he remembers this— but he told me he wouldn't get together with someone until he could make sure this place was strong—" she pointed around her and the building— "and he could build a relationship like my parents'. And he's a man of his word."

I gulped. A flutter of nerves moved under my skin. "That he is, I've come to learn."

She squinted at me. "So, unless a determined, value-driven, loyal man scares you... I hope you'll stay for a bit."

The change in tone lifted the veil over her statement. By instinct, I squared my shoulders as if expecting more word volleys from Vi. I even tightened my abs, like her comments would turn into punches. Somehow she'd managed to share a few warnings with me, hidden in between a kind tone and what seemed like encouraging messages.

Don't play with him. Be strong for him.

The realization made me chuckle. "Oh. Now I get it. This is how you're protective of him."

She continued to smile as she nodded. "That's right. I want him to be happy."

"I want that for him and I, too."

Gabe returned, and his eyes jumped from Vi to me.

He gave me one of the mugs he carried. "What did you do, Vi?"

"Only my duty as your sister. I gave her a bit of a talk." She lifted a shoulder.

Gabe frowned. He sat on the arm of the sofa next to me. "What did she tell you?"

"That she wants you to be happy," I replied, "and that she hopes that I stick around."

"Oh." His shoulders relaxed. He drank from his coffee. "That's not so bad."

Vi was the one to watch us closely, this time. "I also said that I hope there's enough romancing going on, so that you two fall deeply in love."

I laughed, this time, but Gabe groaned.

"Don't, Vi." Gabe asked me to squeeze closer to Vi, so he could sit on the couch next to me. "We're just seeing how this goes. Don't put pressure on it."

Vi shook her head at me, as if puzzled. "But pressure is what I do best!"

I laughed and woke up my computer. "She's committed to your happiness. I think it's cute."

I refreshed the page, but the results were not there yet.

"Dad should be here soon, right?" Vi asked. "He said this morning he wanted to be here for the results."

"Yeah. He texted me that he's in a meeting, but he should be able to make it.

"And Jake?" Vi added, her eyes on my computer. She refreshed the page this time. Two seconds later, she sighed. "Still not there."

"I don't know if Jake will come," Gabe said. Something about his tone made me look at Vi with curiosity.

Interesting. Vi didn't reply, nor looked in her brother's direction.

I sipped from my coffee and checked my watch. "Three minutes late."

My stomach turned into knots, and I bit my lips hard.

"I think we're gonna get it," Vi said. "We're so gonna get it."

Gabe rubbed my back. "It's okay. Even if we don't get it, we can try again."

"I'm refreshing again..." Vi said. "Nope. Not there yet."

I don't know what face I made, but Gabe put both our mugs on the coffee table and brought me to him.

"Come here," he said. "It's okay."

"I'm okay. I'm okay," I said, but all he did was hold me and rub my back.

No wonder I was having a hard time separating fantasy from reality, when he was so good at making me feel he was the kind of boyfriend I wanted.

"Where's Dad? I'll go get him. But first I'll refresh just in case... Ah! It's there—"

Time slowed down. Gabe hugged me tighter. We all leaned toward the screen, reading the three names listed there.

"WE GOT IT!" Vi jumped off the couch. Gabe and I did too.

I jumped into Gabe's arms, and he held me even tighter, before putting his hands on my shoulders.

"Lina! We got it!"

I gasped, no words out of my mouth.

Vi gave us a hug and marched out of the office. "I'm going to go tell Dad!"

"Lina—" Gabe wrapped my face in his hands. "Lina, we did it. We're shortlisted."

I put my hands over his. "We're almost in. We're so close!"

He dropped a hard kiss on my mouth, and breathed his words into me. "We did it."

And I didn't care about anything else, I kissed him like I wanted to kiss him. He tensed up against me, and I wrapped my arms around his neck and plastered myself to him, and hoped the warmth of my body would melt him and let him kiss me for real, this time.

And he did. His hands shifted, one down to my neck and the other to the back of my head, fingers tangled in my hair, and his tongue made its way into my mouth, and he tasted like espresso, and it was me who melted, to the point he had to help me stay up on my feet with his strong arms around me.

"Guys!" Vi yelled, and we nearly jumped apart. I would have taken a step back, but Gabe held me in place. "Oh, sorry—anyway, I told Dad! He's calling mom."

"I called Sonia," Raúl said, joining us in the office. "She's making pastel de choclo at the cabin in celebration."

Gabe let go of me in stages, like it was hard for him to do. Once free— bereft— of his arms, Vi hugged me again.

"You're gonna love pastel de choclo," Vi said.

My heart beat wild in my chest, my lips still tingling from kissing Gabe. I stole a glance at him, who looked at me sheepishly; I would have asked about his shy look, if my mind could make any sense of things, and I could find the words. Raúl approached us, anyway, and I had to put my focus on him.

"Congratulations, you two." He hugged Gabe, then he hugged me. "Well done. This is great."

"Thanks, Dad."

"Now the work really begins," I added. "We need to sign the contracts, study our competition, complete the final proposal, and hope for the best."

"Let us know how we can help," Vi said. "This is a family business, right? This is how we do it. All together."

I was so high from the kiss I didn't even have it in me to feel the punch of that, reminding me how different things were in my own family business.

"Want to call your dad?" Gabe asked me.

"No, I'll do it in person. I should go."

He nodded, his eyes still reserved. "I have soccer tonight. I'll see you on Friday. I'll pick you up at five, then I'll drive us to the lake house."

"Sounds good. See you in a few days, okay?"

Chapter 21

Gabe: I saw Enrique at the game (we won). He talked about sheep, for some reason? Said he wants to get into animal farming

Lina: yep. That's what he's into. Currently finishing up his degree. Also, thanks for winning.

Gabe: yeah, I won alone, sure. For you ;) but it just makes it all worse, that your uncle wants him to run the company. The guy is into sheep. What????

Lina: lol yep. I know. But I can't be too upset about that. It keeps him away, and he's all about sustainable farming. Just like I'm trying to push for accessibility in construction. We are related after all, and we have social causes we favor

Gabe: oooh, tell me more. That sounds great

Lina: Sustainable sheep farming? Ask Enrique ;)

Gabe: Sigh. Listen, girlfriend. You know what I was asking about. Accessibility in construction?

Lina: Listen, boyfriend. That's a trade secret. Sharing that with my competition is a bad idea.

Gabe: where do I start proving you wrong? I think I'll start by saying that accessibility isn't something you should gatekeep. It's something we should all be incorporating into business.

Lina: Yes. Good argument. But you have way more resources than I do to push it forward, earning a name in the market faster than I could. Not that I'm doing it for marketing purposes

Gabe: too bad for you that I'm a good son and I listened to my mother talk to me about accessibility a long time ago. You saw our notes on this when we were preparing the proposal (which we won *together*, remember? We're already teammates). We do accessibility consistently.

Lina: yeah, but it's not the specialization of the Sotomayor construction branch.

Gabe: ooooh. Now I know what you're planning. Good trade secret. Thanks for sharing.

Lina: only because I know you won't actually play dirty. We can share.

Gabe: We already are

Lina: Right. Well, my eyes are closing. Goodnight, Gabe. See you tomorrow at 5.

Gabe: bring a swimsuit

———

Gabe

DRIVING INTO THE MOUNTAINS brought a deep sense of peace to me. Lina turned out to be a great copilot; we chatted right through the section of the road without cell service, time moving fast as we filled the car with banter.

My soul calmed down completely once I saw my family's lake house lit up among the shadowed trees. It was the one place—and time— where I could let go of the sense of responsibility I held for the Sotomayor Group, and simply be me.

The appearance of the large cabin filled me with shimmering warmth each time. A mix of traditional with its big logs, and modern with its huge windows, it cast a warm glow in the midst of the dark forest. Through the wide and tall glass panels, I could see my family puttering around and waiting for us. The tingle in my chest morphed into a delightful mix of awe and affection.

"Wow, this place is gorgeous," Lina said. "I'm a little sad for past me, because I didn't know this existed when I gave you attitude at the convention."

I chuckled. "So you're saying you would have been friendlier, had you known it could have scored you an invite?"

"No, just that I'm happy that in our weird circumstances, I get to be here today."

I parked the car and gazed at her. "I'll invite you over sometime, when we're broken up. If people don't get too weird about it."

"Oh. I hadn't realized." She undid her belt buckle, her eyebrows heavy on her face. "People will expect us not to be friendly anymore, when we break up."

I grabbed the wheel tight in my hands. "I asked Vi. The contract will be ready this week. That gives us two to three weeks to figure out the break up, right?"

She sighed. "We'll have to stop spending so much time together."

All the inner glow in my chest grayed out, shadowed by a passing dark cloud overtaking my lungs.

"We can always text." I frowned. "Insist the break up was friendly. We can say we discovered we're better as friends than as a couple."

In my mind, I heard the echo of words my dad shared with me ages ago, when I'd had a crush on a friend, and he'd told me that a good partnership required friendship, too.

"I guess we can do that," Lina said. "It's been nice to have someone who understands, to talk to."

"Yeah. It has been. So let's go have a nice weekend to celebrate the success of everything we've managed to do the past few weeks."

We took our things out and I opened the door to the cabin with my heart in my throat.

———

Lina

Gabe opened the door to his family's home away from home, and coziness seemed to explode straight into my mind.

"My favorite brother is here!" Vi jumped up from her spot in the living room across the house, and came to us as I studied the view.

A huge stone fireplace stood proud at the center of the large side wall. That alone won me over. It drew the eye to the living space in the great room, helping distract from the stairs to my side, the closets tucked underneath it, and the door nearby. With the fire crackling and warming up the space, all I wanted to do was sit at the luxurious, huge sectional in front of it, get one of the several throws littered around the space, and cozy up with a good book and a nice drink.

The open, vaulted ceiling helped highlight the magnificent windows across from me. They hugged the sitting area, and offered a wonderful view of a large deck and a darkened land-scape. On the other side of the tall, two-story high windows, the dining space boasted what seemed like a 12-place table at first sight. Next to it, and closer to us still in the foyer, an elegant open kitchen with light stone countertops, bronze metal finishes, and sleek-white cabinetry filled the space.

"This place is amazing!" I told Gabe's parents, Raúl and Sonia, as they approached as well.

Vi gave her brother a kiss on the cheek, then she did the same with me.

"Wait until you see the deck in the daylight, and sit around eating delicious food and chatting. It's my favorite part," she said.

The furniture and finishes made it clear the place had been decorated both with money and love. Leather, wood, gold, and light colors in multiple details helped give the home dimension rather than make it feel stuffy with the huge logs.

"Where's Jake?" Gabe dropped our bags on the floor as he hugged his mom.

"He's on his way," Sonia said. She hugged me next. "He's bringing Max and Javier from the airport."

Gabe put a hand on my back. "So they're both coming?"

"Yes." Raúl's smile sat wide on his face. "It'll be good to have everyone here."

"Good thing we'll have enough beds... but barely! Soon we'll have to expand the house." Sonia's smile matched her hus-band's.

"And you love that, don't you?" Vi laughed. "If Jake and the guys will be here soon, should we start making something to eat?"

She and her parents went to the kitchen, while Gabe showed me the rest of the house. The principal bedroom was behind the door I'd noticed earlier off the living room, while the second floor boasted five rooms with queen beds plus a large bathroom. When we entered what would be our room, Gabe closed the door and crossed his arms.

He faced me. "I guess we're sleeping together after all, since everyone will be here. Are you cool with that?"

"Yeah. I'm comfortable with you— comfortable enough." Correcting my admission was a knee-jerk reaction that didn't sit well in my stomach. Gabe gazed at me, putting no pressure on it. Like he knew my walls came up by instinct and didn't get annoyed by them. "Are you okay with it?"

He nodded. "Friends can sleep together. I considered jumping in with Jake, but if you're okay sharing a bed with me, then that's better. Less suspicion from others."

"Yeah. We're supposed to be having a nice weekend away... maybe we can make it good. Enjoy our time together. We've earned it, right?"

He stared at me as a slow smile curled his lips. "Let's enjoy it, yes."

Before I could say anything else, the boom of laughter reached us from below, loud enough to get through the wooden floor.

"My friends are here," Gabe said. "Let's go meet them."

We returned to the living area, and I was met with a delightful scene: Sonia leaned on the kitchen island, wooden spoon in hand, a big smile on her face as she listened to someone I didn't know tell a story from his perch on a barstool. Vi took the spoon from her mom and mixed something in a large pot, the only thing cooking on a six-burner gas range. Raúl casually poured steaming water into it while Vi stirred. The two of them grinned as well, and all faces in the room tracked the guy in the middle of a monologue.

"So I drove like I was in a Formula 1 race to New York, because of course Javi was there, and begged to the universe that he'd see my email and wait for me. He did, we hopped on his plane, and Jake had a new phone for me as soon as we hit the tarmac."

"All because you wanted to bring us alfajores," Sonia said. "Thank you."

"Anything for you all," the man replied, a cheeky smile on his face.

"Six dozen, though." Raúl scoffed and shook his head. "We'll have enough for everyone for the whole weekend, I think."

"Including Lina's family tomorrow?" Gabe asked as we approached the crowd in the kitchen, and everyone turned to us.

"Well, hello there!" The storyteller got off his chair and hugged Gabe, then stared at me. "I'm Max. Very glad to meet you and see you're real."

I offered my hand and he took it, but used it to bring me closer and kiss my cheek.

"You didn't think I was real?" I asked when he released me.

"I wasn't sure. Jake refused to tell us more on the drive here."

"I told you she was real. What else did you need?" Jake came and kissed me on the cheek as well. Like they had all been trained by this Chilean family in their traditional manners. "You can see for yourself, now."

"I assure you, I'm very real."

"Good." Max nodded and put his hands in his slack pockets. He still wore a casual suit, like he hadn't had a chance to change after office hours. He had a similar build to Gabe, with lighter brown skin and darker hair, and incisive brown eyes. "Sometimes I wonder if we're cursed, all single for so long. That, or I'm right and romance is dead."

"Please." The only man I hadn't met yet joined us. His hair was straight black, his eyes blue like Jake's, and white skin. He also kissed me on the cheek. "Ignore him. He's the cynical one of us. I'm Javier, and I do not think we're all cursed."

"Hi, Javier. I'm glad to hear that. I'm sure there are very good reasons why you're all single."

"Just like there's a good reason why Gabe isn't anymore, right?" Max smirked. "I can't wait to hear the story."

"Anyway," Gabe said. "Now you met my friends. I'm sure you'll find them all a delight, because they will all behave so wonderfully and not bug you at all."

"Oh, I think I'm going to have fun, as long as they can take as good as they like to give." I gave them all my best smile, before Sonia and Raúl called us for dinner.

Chapter 22

Gabe

AFTER THE MEAL, WE all had a drink and played cards. Lina sat next to me the whole time, on an evening where things felt more real than they ever had.

My parents were the first to go to sleep, leaving my friends, Vi, Lina and I by ourselves. We all took our drinks and sat on the deck, sprawling over the outdoor furniture.

"I think it's so sweet that you call Sonia, tía," Lina said to my friends.

"I don't think she could be anything else to me." Jake sipped from his drink. "I've known her for so long."

"The only closer thing would be mom, and that'd be weird," Vi said. "You do have a mom."

"I do, though the Sotomayors feel more like family."

I put an arm around Lina on the couch we shared. "Jake and I have been friends since before we were ten. In many ways, Jake, Vi, and I grew up together. These guys, though," I pointed to Max and Javier with my glass, "they are a later addition."

"But we call her tía as well, just to make her happy." Javier smiled.

"The three of us were kind of adopted by the Sotomayors," Max added. "Jake has been around the longest, compared to Javi and I, who have been around for only ten years. But they've been there for us this whole time."

"*Only* ten years?" Lina asked. "That's a long time, no wonder you all seem like family."

"We're all family, no matter how we all got here," I said.

Lina turned to me, her eyes shiny as she gazed at me. "I can feel that. It's wonderful."

"I feel like getting in the hot tub." Vi gazed at all of us in turn. "Anyone else?"

"I'm thinking of going to sleep, actually," Jake said, and Javier nodded.

"What? Why?" Vi asked.

They continued chatting but Lina leaned close and it called for me.

"Where is the hot tub?" Lina asked. "I haven't seen it."

"If you want to get in, we can go change and I'll show you."

Before I knew I'd be sharing a bed with Lina, the expectation of getting to spend time with her in the hot tub had been the highlight of the weekend ahead for me. Now it made me nervous... because I would be sharing a bed with Lina, and enjoying her company while scantily clad could amp up the time in the privacy of our room, rather than simply serve as a lovely memory to keep.

But we changed clothes anyway, taking turns in the bathroom, and I guided Lina to the side deck, where the hot tub lived among the trees. No one else was around.

"Wow." Lina leaned on the deck fence and stared into the forest, then turned to watch me by the hot tub. She arched an eyebrow. "This can hardly be called a hot tub. It's a small swimming pool."

I smiled as I took the protective cover off. String lights hung in criss-crossing lines above us, casting a soft glow on the space. The treeline, shining bulbs, and house reflected on the still water, until I turned on the jets and everything turned turbulent. It would take a few minutes to fully reach the right temperature.

"It has a swimming pool function, actually, but I'm running it as a hot tub right now." I submerged a hand in the water. Still cool. "It's nice for the fall and winter weather. But it also had to be big, because we're all tall and big, and it's a bunch of us. In the summer, it's nicer to simply jump into the lake."

"I love how you put these hangers nearby, too." She walked to the side arch with hooks on it, where she hung our towels.

She also took her shirt off, revealing a bikini top with ruffle at the bottom line that barely covered her belly button, and which had a deep V that tantalized me with a view of her breasts. Especially as she bent down to get rid of her shorts as well.

I gulped. In desperate search of a distraction, I focused on my next task and loosely folded the tub cover. The sight of Lina undressing, showing me tempting new expanses of skin, burnt an image into my retinas that I couldn't unsee, and certainly wouldn't forget. Not that I wanted to. The curves and lines of her thick thighs, wide hips, and full ass proved to be just like I'd fantasized they would be. I needed to be in better control of what the view did to my insides, or to my cock. Turning away from her wouldn't be an option for long.

"How do I get in?" she asked.

Just like that, my time was over.

I took a deep breath, returned to the tub, and checked the water's temperature again. My parents had arrived early in the day to do maintenance and up the water levels, and now we got to enjoy it; the warm liquid promised relaxation. I put my hopes in it— that it would soften *everything*.

Maybe if I framed the moment as an opportunity to create a good memory for future Gabe, and let myself enjoy it rather than suffer for what wasn't mine to touch, I could make the most out of my circumstances.

I approached the arch and removed my shirt, which I hung from a hook. Facing the wall, I adjusted my half-hard cock, and hoped the loose fabric of my swimming trunks would hide it. Once done with that, I found the special inset staircase for the pool and dropped it to the floor.

"Ingenious." Lina leaned against the hot tub, the curve of her body delicious on her cocked hips.

I held out my hand to her, and she went up the stairs to the pool, each step bringing a satisfying wiggle to her thighs. I got an eyeful, and I loved every second of it. I would definitely remember that.

Lina sighed as she got in the water, and I followed right behind her.

"Oh, this is an amazing way to let go of a week of hard work," she said.

"I love it so much here. We can actually see the lake from here in the daylight. It's beautiful."

We sat side-by-side in two individual places, and I let the jets soften my muscles. My eyes closed.

She sighed. "I think there's a knot in my neck that is finally loosening up."

"Do you want warmer water? It makes you melt and it feels amazing."

"Mhh. Melting sounds divine, but I make no promises. I think you've noticed I can be... wound up."

"Is that what you call it?" I set the heater a couple degrees higher and sat back, squirming to find a comfortable position again. "Wound up?"

She crossed her arms. Her breasts pushed together, and a drop skated down her skin and in between them. I fisted my hand underwater, to stop myself from following its track with my finger.

"It's what others have called it. I think of it more like..."

"A shield?"

"Strength." Her head fell to the side, her eyes gleaming my way. "Though I can see how it might appear as a shield from outside."

"And I see how it requires strength to be in the position you're in."

"Yes. I need to be strong, to not let things deter me."

"Doesn't it get exhausting? Always making yourself tough, to withstand the hard stuff. We all need a place where we can let go. Have someone else make the decisions."

"And I'm going to guess you have that here. With your family."

I nodded. "Do you have such a place?"

She didn't answer right away. The space between us filled with the sound of bubbling water and the rumbling motor jetting it around.

I mirrored her, my head turned to the side. Her gaze jumped all over my face.

"I don't know," she said. "And I don't know how to make it happen."

My lips tilted in a small smile. "I think that telling me something like that counts. Letting me know the parts of you that need a little help."

"But what if you make fun of me for it?" Her voice was low, her confession seeming to constrict her throat. "Or dismiss it?" She gulped. "Make me feel like a fool?"

I lifted my hand. Wet and all, I caressed her face. "I don't ever want to do that." My thumb left a trail of water on her skin as it made an arch on her face, but she didn't seem to mind. Her eyes were fixed on mine. "I think of it more like a privilege, to be someone you would trust like that."

"I suppose that if I want to know what that feels like, I have to give you a chance to prove you mean it."

My breathing turned fast, my lungs feeding oxygen to the fire igniting in my blood. I could hear my pulse in my ears, the rush of it filling my mind and helping me forget why I shouldn't rub her bottom lip with my thumb. Pushing me to do it anyway.

My eyes were glued to her mouth, taking note of every detail as it became pliant under my touch. "I'd like to think I've shown you who I am."

Her nod was slow, contemplative. "You told me you're not always good."

"I didn't mean I'd play with your heart, Lina."

She wrapped her fingers around my wrist, and for an instant I worried she'd push my hand away. But she didn't.

Her warm skin stayed in place, a beacon of light glimmering from the point of contact. She closed her eyes and sighed.

She whispered, "I think I would have tried to open up, if we didn't have to break up."

Gallons of liquid lead filled my chest, moving slow like lava and with the same consistency, pressing down on my stomach. I wanted to grab each ounce of it and throw it away, far, where it wouldn't weigh down my heart with responsibility. It scared me to let myself imagine, hope for a way to make it work, because I knew my limits. I didn't know if I could do it all, and have it all. Give her everything.

I let my hand curl around her neck, my thumb now on her pulse. It was fast like mine. "If you're still single in a couple of years, can I try again? Do it properly."

"Are we being ridiculous?" she asked.

As much as I hoped she meant we were being ridiculous for waiting for two years, she could be trying to put me down gently. I would have asked, but Max's laughter reached us from around the corner of the house.

"I hope you guys are decent!" he exclaimed as he and Javier appeared.

"We brought you drinks. I hope the same you had earlier works."

I didn't let go of her nor turned away, until my friends were already up the stairs and settled in the water with us.

"Jake and Vi went to sleep." Max offered me one of the glasses he carried, and groaned as he relaxed into the water. "Separately, Gabe. Chill."

"I didn't say anything." I helped Lina reach for her glass, taking it from Javier and giving it to her.

"We don't talk about it," Javier added in her direction.

"I wondered." Lina sipped from her glass. "But what I'm hearing is that I shouldn't ask."

"Neither Gabe, Jake, or Vi talk about it," Max offered. "So we don't."

"This isn't about how I feel about it, which isn't bad, by the way," I said. "But why should my opinion matter? So I'm not going to talk about it until they do. Besides, it's more fun to tease Max about his situation."

"Oh?" Lina smiled. It helped the weight in my chest dissipate.

"I need to get married. Soon. For inheritance and business reasons. And to stick it to my dad."

Javier scoffed. "It's complicated. And absurd."

Lina laughed.

Max snorted. "Please, let me forget for the night. My lawyers are on it, and I'm hoping a bride falls from the sky for me. Otherwise, I don't want to think about it. Gabe can tell you another time, Lina."

We continued to chat, laugh, and de-stress. Even if it helped, one thing took hold of my mind. I wanted to clear up a few things with my fake girlfriend, and come up with a way to get it all, even if I couldn't have it all today.

———

Lina

I got into bed, ignoring the nerves fluttering in my stomach and pushing them way down. I pulled the covers higher, up to my shoulders. The sheets were white and soft, but the comforter stole the show. It looked like an oversized knitted blanket, made with the chunkiest light blue yarn I had ever seen. I tested its texture with my cold hands— it was nice and soft under my fingertips.

The house logs shaped the walls, but the ceiling had been covered by white shiplap; it helped make the room feel bigger and cozier, somehow. The window to my right was closed, curtains drawn, and the door to my left remained shut. Gabe was still in the bathroom down the hall; we had taken turns getting ready to sleep. I was pretty confident we'd managed to hide that we'd both changed in the bathroom, instead of in the bedroom like a couple who saw each other naked occasionally.

I took a deep breath. I wouldn't be opposed to seeing Gabe naked occasionally. But I couldn't think of that, when I was about to share a bed with my fake boyfriend and not get him naked. I had always run my life by making myself strong in the face of difficulty. I could make myself strong in the face of temptation.

And for once, I was with someone who got that about me. To the point I'd opened myself to him, through a stone door I hadn't opened before. Heavy, it had only moved enough for a crack through which to show him who I am, but maybe it had been enough. If he'd tried to kiss me again, this time with no witnesses, I would have let him.

Gabe came into the room, looking freshened up. He rounded the bed to what I deemed to be his side, and I followed him with my eyes. Only my lamp was on.

He got in the bed casually, like we did this often. Like he didn't mind at all that I'd taken claim of the left side of the bed. He simply adjusted his pillow and lay on his back, an arm above his head and the other on his stomach. One knee was up, the blankets scrunched up between us. He was on easy display to me, and his legs and wide torso reminded me why I was tempted in the first place. I stitched my strength around me with silver threads. I wasn't sure if I had the capacity to move the stone door again. It wasn't until that moment that I realized that, after so long finding comfort in my might, I'd forgotten how to be soft.

But Gabe was soft. Maybe he could teach me. If I managed to thaw enough to let him in.

"You know—" he scratched his stomach, the fabric of his shirt wrinkling with the motion. We both lay on our backs, but I turned my head to him. "I can't believe a little over two months ago I found you at Construction Cares for our yearly check-in. Now we're in bed together."

"Things like this happen. Two colleagues getting friendly and leading them to bed. We just decided to fake it."

He snorted. "Stranger still."

This weekend could help me decide if I dared show Gabe more of the vulnerable me. Saturday would show me what we could have.

I took a fortifying breath. "What's your family's morning routine like? Pajamas or not for breakfast, that kind of thing."

"PJs for breakfast. Whoever is up first starts getting things ready. It's usually brunch, but it'll be different tomorrow morning since your family is coming. So we'll get up, everyone but my parents will make a quick breakfast while they get ready for the day. That way, after we all clean up, they can start cooking. Then we all get ready."

"So everyone helps?" I asked. "Even your friends?"

He nodded. "House rules. My parents have never wanted to hire staff for this house; they think that doing these things ourselves will give us character. In the city it's different, but here? They only have someone to do maintenance if no one's visiting, but nothing else. They say that this way we'll never forget what it's like to look after ourselves and people we care about."

"Quite progressive. In so many ways, I'd never know you're rich." I turned to my side to get a better look at him. "Lake house aside, you don't seem to throw cash around."

He shrugged. "My parents weren't rich back in Chile. My mom is a social worker with very strong equity ideals, who's kept us all in line. I don't think the Sotomayor Group would be what it is, considering the amount of social-forward policies we have, if it weren't for the way Max and Javier invested in the business. They're our strongest shareholders, after the fours of us. It's given us a lot of leeway to do things differently."

"How did you meet them?"

He smiled and scratched his jaw, one hand still pillowing his head. "College. Max and I connected immediately; we both clocked each other's last names in two of our classes and found each other, and when we realized we're both Chilean, I immediately invited him for once— like the number eleven in Spanish, *once*, as in elevenses. A Chilean version of high tea, to give you an idea— anyway, I digress. Max met Jake through me, and I met Javier through Max. We've been pretty close since."

I smiled. I didn't have friendships like his, focused as I was in earning my dad's trust. Hearing him talk about his family and friends made me think that I might have been missing out.

In the silence that followed, he turned his head to admire me. Warmth spread through me at the openness lighting his eyes, his brown irises beautiful and comforting.

"Are you too good to be true, Gabriel?"

The grin that took over his face bloomed slow. The light in his eyes turned into a playful glint.

"I'm doing things right, if you're asking yourself that."

I smirked. "Show me more of that tomorrow when my parents, Tío Miguel, and my aunt are here, and I will sing your praises."

"How about we just have a nice day tomorrow? Let's enjoy ourselves. Then end the day with a walk by the lake."

"It's a plan. Good night, Gabe." Moving slowly, I turned off the lamp and lay on my back, sheets once more up to my neck.

"Good night, Lina."

But I heard him take a deep breath and remain immobile, just like I did. I don't know who fell asleep first, but I suspected that both of us were dealing with thoughts and longing well into the night.

Chapter 23

Lina

I WOKE UP A few times during the night, never for long. The first time I did, Gabe's arms were around me, the room had been dark, and I had been half-asleep. In that hazy state, it was easy to let myself melt into the embrace, and sleep with the warmth of him all around me. Next time I woke up, I was using his arm as a pillow, and one of mine was around his stomach.

I dreamt of us rolling in bed, enjoying lazy sex in that infuriating way where you were just about to orgasm but couldn't, not by the dream alone. Gabe teased me in my dream, but I never begged, because I couldn't, even if I wanted to.

When I awoke for the day, I did so fast. Gabe was spooning me again but, instead of it being a cozy cocoon, my body lit up with awareness. His erection poked against me, and my breath hitched when I realized I had known it somehow, and my brain had filled in the blanks.

I didn't dare move, because my heart pressed the brakes while the rest of my body pushed on the pedal, asking me to give in and tear the stitches I'd sewn the night before. This was a chance to soften to him, to connect with him, stone doors still in place. Tempting, to bridge the gap between my emotions and my mind, letting my body take over and patch the chasm between reason, fear, and everything else.

The change in his breathing was so subtle I wouldn't have noticed, if it weren't because I lay so still. I didn't know if he was awake or sleeping, but the way his lungs worked faster and rugged, I guessed he was dreaming of something very much like I had been.

Want. Feeling wanted in return. Despite our goals and responsibilities, my walls, and our deadline.

"I'm sorry," he grumbled behind me. "It's a morning thing."

Of course I knew that it happened a lot for penis-owning people. But pain shot through me regardless, like he'd rejected me. The reason why I protected myself in the first place. So I tried to repair the fabric of silver around me, and looked for words to minimize the moment.

"That's a lie," he added before I could joke it away. His voice rumbled behind me. "It's you. I'm attracted to you. But you don't have to— we don't—" he sighed. "I'm sorry."

He made to give me space, his arm leaving my tummy and waist, but I grabbed his hand and held him in place. My heart lodged in my throat, and the shaky organ attempted to jam the brakes into my chest, but my body fell into the inertia of the moment, pedal to the floor at full speed.

"I'm attracted to you, too," I admitted. "I'm glad I'm not alone in that."

Gabe released a gust of air that caressed my neck, my ear, sending a shiver down my spine. "I haven't been with anyone since Essie, and being so close to you, kissing you... I'm suddenly starving."

Blood drummed in my veins. My body took command, and I pushed my backside against his erection. When he groaned, my brain aligned with my body and overruled my heart.

I couldn't open the door to the soul of who I was, but I could open a window.

"It's natural we feel this way." I let my fingers travel up his arm and to his body behind me, and I put my hand on his hip. I dug my nails into him, thankful for the light padding around his form, letting me feel like I could grab him to stay right next to me. "We've focused too hard on work and neglected connection. And now it feels like it could be right there for the taking, and our bodies know it. Because this is what it could feel like, and this is what would happen, if this were real."

He didn't answer right away; his hand advanced up my tummy and under my shirt, discovering the hills of my body, and stopping right at the swell of my breasts.

"If this were real," he said, his voice low and deep like thunder, his thumb caressing the underside of my breast, "this is where you would get to know a whole different side of me. And I don't know we should do that, when we have only two weeks left, and then we have to pretend we never were that into each other in the first place."

My brain knew he was right, but some ancient part of it overruled that, too. "We said we'd have today."

"Lina..."

"What would you do, if this were real." I pushed on his erection again, and he responded like he couldn't help himself.

"I... I would pin you on the bed. On your stomach." He took a deep breath. I gulped. "And I would tease your back until you were squirming under me. Then I'd put a pillow under your hips and use my tongue on you, until your writhing was too much to take and I let myself sink in you."

"I think I'd like that—"

"And I would tie you to the bed, so I could take my time and play with you and exhaust you from orgasms alone. Have you give up the fight you put up for everyone and everything, because you want me to take over. With me, you give in. Fuck."

He grabbed my breast and squeezed, and I buckled, because the idea that he craved to dominate me electrified me all over. In bed, I could let him work me up until I surrendered to him.

"But we shouldn't— I can't." The arm under my neck curled, squeezing me in a not-so-loose hold around my throat. "I don't even have condoms here. Nor the privacy for it."

"Don't give up on me, Gabe. Please."

He groaned.

"Do you want this?" I asked, the warm skin of his forearm a shock to my neck.

"Lina. Yes."

"Then use your hands on me, and tell me what you'd like to do. Let me imagine."

"It's a bad idea." The hand on my torso retreated back to my tummy, and it went a little lower than before, but he stopped before he reached the elastic of my pants. "It's only going to be more confusing, and still unfulfilling."

At this point, I needed this. I looked for reasons to make this okay for both of us.

"What if it's a gift we're giving each other?" I asked. "For those nights when we're working alone at night. To remember what awaits us in the future, when we've achieved our goals. So I can remember what it's like to be wanted."

"You want to feel wanted?"

"I want it. So much."

"And you'd feel wanted if I used my fingers on you? If I told you how I want to be rough with you until you come so many times you lose count, and melt, and let me see you like that?"

"I'd feel wanted if you broke down every wall until I came apart in your arms."

"Fuck. Lina." He squeezed his arm around my neck further, and I stretched it back to feel him harder against my throat.

I pushed my ass against his cock, and he rubbed himself on me. I left his hips and grabbed his hand on the rounds of my belly, guiding it over my clothed sex.

I took a broken breath. "Tell me what you'd do if I let you take control of my vibrator."

He moaned. "Do you have one with a remote?"

I nodded. He rubbed me over my clothes, and I wish I could see him losing control. He squeezed my neck harder, as if to keep me in place as he had his way with me, unaware I was getting my way with him, too.

"What would you do?" I insisted. "If you want this, this morning... then I want it too."

"I want this so badly," he confessed, his teeth finding my ear. "You sure?"

"Gabe. I need it. Touch me and tell me."

A whine arose from deep in his throat, and his hand found its way under my clothes. Straight under my underwear, two fingers circling on my clit twice, before making their way to my entrance.

"God. You're so wet."

"Tell me. What you'd do."

"First, I'd give you a warning. You don't order me around. I'm in charge." The tips of his fingers slid around my clit, teasing me without fully touching the head of it— like a punishment.

My vocal cords shook as I gasped. "Yes, sir."

"Fuck. Yes. Just like that." He rubbed his nose on my earlobe. "I'd tie your hands behind your back, or on the headboard— depending on how wild you get."

"Would you tie me up more? Knots and ropes to set me up just like you wanted?"

"And belts and scarves and ribbons. We'd get creative."

I trembled, and his erection rubbed against me faster, and his fingers twirled around my clit, pulling on it and massaging it until my eyes rolled back.

"Then I'd open your legs— get that vibrator in you. I'd stand at the foot of the bed, and I'd play with you until you couldn't think straight anymore."

"Until I'm shaking and crying out?"

"Until you need my cock in you, in any way I wanted to fuck you. And I'd fuck your mouth, never letting go of that remote, so that sucking me felt like relief to you."

I wrapped one hand on his forearm around my neck, and snaked the other until I could put my hand on his erection over his clothes.

"You like that? That okay?" he asked, and I surrounded his length as best I could from the position he held me in.

"More," I said, and he fucked my hand while playing with my clit. "I'm close."

"It makes you horny to think I want to do these things to you?"

"Yes."

"Do you like knowing that I'd come all over your tits, and tell you to play with it on your nipples, while I set that vibrator to a hum, and sucked on your clit myself?"

"Fuck, Gabe—"

"Fuck, sir."

I came hard enough to see stars in our still dark room.

"Holy shit," he said behind me, his thrusts insistent in my hand. "You come so perfectly in my arms."

I still trembled as his fingers left my clit. His hand wrapped around mine on his cock, and he thrust into our joined hands a few times before he came with a strangled moan.

———

Gabe

I hadn't come in my pants since I was a teenager, but the moment I had just shared with Lina had painstakingly deconstructed each layer of maturity I'd ever thought I had in me. I was thirty-three years old, and I had devolved into a young buck with just a few whispered words.

"Jesus," I said. I released her neck and put a hand on her hip, catching my breath. I closed my eyes. "Was that okay?"

"Yes, sir."

I groaned. "Don't tease me. I'm serious."

"It was more than okay. It was great." She turned around and faced me. She put a hand on my face, and my heart finally began to slow down. "Thank you."

I frowned. "Don't thank me, either. I didn't do it for you— I wasn't being generous. I couldn't help myself."

"I wanted it, too. Don't forget." Her thumb caressed my cheek. "And I love that I get to have this little secret, for the years ahead."

A smile curled my lips. "That we had this stolen moment, when we faked a romance?"

"That I know what my good friend, good guy Gabriel Sotomayor is like in bed."

I scoffed. "You know nothing yet."

The words escaped my lips before I could examine them, and now my face warmed up in response.

Lina laughed. "I have an idea of what you're like. And I'll treasure it."

The frown hadn't left my face, and I gazed at Lina in the dim light of the early morning. "This part— my attraction. That isn't fake. It's important to me that you know that."

Her grin softened, her eyes still and bright on mine. "Thank you."

And, because I was more selfish than I wanted anyone to ever know, I gave her a kiss on the corner of her lips.

"Let's get up before I think too hard about how difficult it'll be to go back to being friends with you."

"We're becoming stronger friends, that's all— ones that had to get some things out of their systems. Friends who might one day look for something more... maybe even with each other."

I nodded, but the smirk on my face was how I let it be known that I doubted I had her out of my system yet.

Whispered words reached us from the hallway, steps in the direction of the stairs.

"We need to talk." I caressed her face in the same way she had mine. "On our walk tonight, okay?"

———

Lina

Gabe's and my family sat around on the deck, our stomachs full of pastel de choclo. The memory of its caramelized golden surface filled my memory with joy, as we all shared warm drinks after a late lunch. Gabe had his arm around me, and being close to him felt easier, better, after we'd let go of our rules earlier in the morning. We sat together, me almost on his lap in a wide chair. Our parents, my uncle, and my aunt sprawled over the outside furniture, while Lucía, Vi, and Gabe's friends played cards on a blanket nearby.

"That meal was truly delicious," my dad said. "I don't think I'd ever had that before."

"You have to send me the recipe," mom added. "I'd love to try it one day."

Sonia shook her head. "I'll make more one day and send it to your office. I hear you keep sending food to the Sotomayor VP floor."

My mom laughed. "Only where Gabe is. We're trying to take care of him."

"Thank you, but there's no need." Gabe chuckled. "I'm doing well."

"I was taught that the way to a man's heart is through his stomach." Mom waved a hand in the air to reject the notion. "I know nothing will compare to Sonia's food in your mind, but I'll try very hard to be a second favorite."

"We should be teaching our Lina how to do that, though," Edgardo added. "We want him to like her food as second best!"

He laughed, seemingly unaware of the brief look that Sonia and Raúl exchanged.

"I've never cooked for Gabe," I said.

"¡Hija! Pero, ¿cómo?" My mom tried, but Gabe spoke before she could add more.

"I am good. Thank you. I'm a decent cook and I can take care of myself."

"You have a management degree, I saw in the documentation. Right?" Tío Miguel asked Gabe. "My son is finishing a master's degree in it."

Tía Soledad, Tío Miguel's wife, sat nearby. Quiet as always, but seemingly interested in the conversation.

"Specializing in sustainable agriculture, I believe?" Gabe said, his hand squeezing around my shoulder.

"Well, yes, but management, still." Tío Miguel frowned. "The basic concepts are all the same, and Edgardo and I learned by doing. We didn't need the degree to get here."

"Degrees didn't use to be necessary. I only made it through undergrad back in Chile." Raúl shrugged. "But it's different for the new generation."

Laughter exploded from the folk playing cards, but the rest of us continued our conversation as if nothing had happened.

"It helps them network, for sure," my dad said. "Quite the friend group your son made for himself."

Gabe released a gust of air through his nose, a rough sound accompanying it from his throat. He frowned. I didn't think he liked the implication that his friendships were about networking with powerful, rich people.

"So lucky, to have a son who's followed your steps so closely, Raúl." Tío Miguel added.

"I'm very proud of both my children," Raúl replied. "Each of them brings something to the table."

"I should introduce you to Enrique, Gabriel," Tío Miguel said out of nowhere. "I'm sure you could encourage him to see the potential in joining the family business."

"I talked to Enrique this week." Gabe reached for his cup of cedrón infusion and took a sip. "He talked about sheep."

"Precisely why you could talk to him! Man-to-man."

Gabe shook his head. "Gender is not relevant at all."

"Ay, young people!" Tío Miguel said. "That's not what I meant."

"Besides, I like doing business with Lina," my fake boyfriend added. "We wouldn't have made the shortlist application deadline if she hadn't done such a wonderful prep job."

"I've known Lina for years," Raúl said, "and when she came to propose this deal to us it was incredible."

"If I inherit the company—" I kept my eyes on Raúl— "it would be a pleasure to continue doing business with the Sotomayor Group."

It was a risk to say that here, with my unpredictable uncle present and surrounded by people who didn't know me very well. But the words spilled out of me, unbound and full of hope.

Raúl smiled at me. "I think we could do amazing things together. More deals like this stadium business. Now let's just hope things will turn out the way we want, huh?"

"I thought you'd want to wait and see if we actually get the deal." My dad put his hand on my mom's leg. "What if Lina misjudged?"

"Lina didn't misjudge." Gabe's eyes were serious as he challenged my dad. My breathing quickened, and warmth flowered inside of me. Whatever happened between him and me, one thing was clear. Gabe was on my side. "She's done everything perfectly. If we don't get the stadium, it's because our competitors offered a better deal."

"And the contract is written to open the door to similar deals." Raúl's smile was conciliatory, and when he directed it at me again, it turned genuinely warm. "We already thought about it, and we want to keep working with Martínez and Associates. It's a pleasure to know Lina is our point of contact. She's wonderful. An asset to any business."

My heart beat at double its normal pace. I didn't know if the Sotomayor's support would have any impact on my family's vision of the future, but I wanted to wrap their words in a gold ribbon and tie them to every one of my doubts. I put my hand on Gabe's knee and squeezed; he dropped a kiss on my temple.

"Lina is wonderful, for sure." My mom nodded, her mouth tilted in an upward curl. "And it's always a treat to hear your daughter is held in such high esteem."

"Of course she is," my dad added. "We raised her well. People like the Sotomayors would recognize that, easily."

"Gabe complements her well, too, eh?" Tío Miguel's eyes sparkled. "We can see his influence in how this deal happened, too. He's great as a leader, for sure. You should be proud."

I schooled my face into neutrality, even if my chest ached with the stabbing pain of my uncle's casual insult.

Sonia grinned in my direction. "We are. As for Lina, well, Gabriel likes her. That's all I needed to know. Her business instincts are clearly sharp, as well."

"It's been a gift to get to know you all," I said, and the feelings behind my words were one hundred percent true.

Gabe

We said goodbye to Lina's family, and I took a deep breath of relief.

"We're going to stay outside a bit longer." My dad put an arm around my mom's shoulders. "Anyone want to get drinks with us?"

"I will," Max said.

"I'm getting in the hot tub." Jake gazed at Vi, then away. I smirked.

Javier smirked, too. "I'll go with you."

"I'll have a drink with you guys," Vi said. "Then I'll get in the tub. Later."

"Do you want to go for a walk?" I asked Lina, ignoring the weird tension that Vi and Jake had barely managed to hide. "Sunset's coming up soon. We can sit on the dock."

"Yes! Go romance your girlfriend," Vi said, and pushed us toward the stairs that led to the lake.

"Shall we?" I asked, and Lina nodded. I'd learned her face well enough in our time together to know that, even though she didn't broadcast it, she was sad.

We followed the trail that led to the water, sparsely paved with big, rustic rocks. It was a bit of a winding path, designed to turn the steep decline into a gentle descent. We strolled slowly through it, ancient trees lining the clearing.

Five minutes into our walk, I spoke over the sound of wind on leaves. "There were several things that could have put that look on your face, but which one is on your mind?"

It took her a beat to answer. "Can I hold your hand?"

I jumped at the opportunity, and took her hand in mine.

She sighed. "I don't know if it'll ever stop bothering me, how my family talks about me."

"I don't think you're supposed to get used to it. It shouldn't be like that in the first place."

"Theoretically, but it is like that. I have to live with it, somehow."

No wonder she'd felt like she needed to harden up, when her very family put her in this position so often. It was easy for me to stand where I was, and want her to soften for me. It wouldn't be me at risk. Things were different for her.

"Thanks for the way you stood up for me. I don't think they will change their minds, but that made me feel better."

I squeezed her hand in mine. "Of course."

The fragrance of trees gave way to the scent of water, and the general wet greenery and sand smell of its shore.

"It was great also hearing your mom and dad adding their two cents. Refreshing. I spend so much time with my family I forget there are other types of people. Supportive and encouraging people."

"Well, my mom has been amazing that way. She helped my dad learn, and the both of them helped us grow differently. Words like intersectionality and equality were common in my house. My fights with my sister as kids were all about fairness and justice— we were those kids, you know?" I chuckled. "When we grew up Mom told us about her own family, and how she went through things like you have."

"A bit of a miracle that she found your dad."

We stepped onto the dock. The wooden structure went several feet into the lake in a large T shape, unoccupied at the moment. The boat and other water implements were secure in the shed.

We stood at the end of the wooden structure, and I gazed across the lake to the shore and forest across the water. "I think he sees it as a miracle that he found her. He adores her."

"Takes a special kind of man to adore a woman who talks about equality at home, and demands it of her partner."

"And it takes a special kind of person to stand in her truth even when her family tries to cut her off, like with my mom. Someone who will not settle for a partner who won't celebrate that kind of authenticity in her." I pulled Lina's hand to draw her attention, and dipped my head in invitation to sit. Hopefully she read between the lines, and heard how I was talking about my parents, but could be talking about her, too.

We sat at the edge of the dock, legs hanging down and feet almost touching the water.

I reached for her hand again. "My mom and dad... They're everything to me."

She sighed. "You've said that before, but I think I can see it now, too."

"I guess it makes sense, that you see how we are together, then you have your own family reminding you things are different with yours, and it hurts." I pursed my lips, undecided on my next words. But if we were going to have this conversation, I needed to share how I felt. "It's like your parents are not on your side."

The faintest hint of lake fog floated over the water; the breeze that danced around us was warm for the fall.

Lina sniffled, but when I checked on her, her face was composed. "You know, when I asked you to join this project with me, with us— I knew why I was doing it. It would finally make them consider my proposal for the first time. I did that on purpose. I knew they would see you and your family as the key to making it possible. I thought I could take it, but it is hard. The way they see you as the leader."

Water sloshed against the dock posts in a soothing rhythm, a contrast to the anxious waves in my veins.

"I asked you to be my fake boyfriend to get here," she said. "And we did. I got what we wanted— we both did. Even if we don't get the stadium, the future has promise. But now, having you be part of this makes me invisible, and I still may not get the company."

"If we were together..." I bit the inside of my lips and didn't finish the sentence.

"If we don't break up... my family will think they were always right. They will see how I spend time I don't have with you, how I pamper you with food and coffee, and every look I give you will be adoring and full of hope to them. They'll think I'm patiently waiting for a ring, and that my focus finally shifted to the future they always assumed I would want. If it were only about ignoring them or correcting their beliefs, that would be one thing. But I worry any chances I had of inheriting the company would turn to smoke, because being with you would tell them that the risk of me changing my mind was higher than ever, and wasn't worth taking."

My heart sunk, a plop as it fell right into the lake.

"I remember a story my mom told me," I said. "How there used to be people who went to University in Chile with the sole purpose of meeting someone there and getting married. The degrees became part of their dating resume, rather than the reflection of what they wanted to do in their lives."

She nodded, eyes on the water below us. "I can't risk it, Gabe. I don't care if someone chooses to stay home and take care of their family, as long as it's fulfilling to them, but that's not me. I can't imagine getting stuck in my current position, even worse if I tried to start again somewhere else. Convincing my dad to give me his share of the business is the option I'm going for. If that doesn't work out... well. He will retire in a couple of years. I'll know then what my future will be."

A few pops of yellow tinged the trees around us and the lake. I sighed. "And that's why we need to break up."

"We've always planned for it."

"Yeah." I looked at our linked hands and brought them to my thigh. "We both have good reasons for breaking up."

And yet, after these weeks together, and after what we'd done that morning, this conversation didn't feel like planning for it, but like we were both trying to remember why.

Lina seemed more clear than I did, her voice heavy and echoing how I felt, but also determined. So I brought my reasons up again, a little bit for her, and a lot for me.

"Remember when I told you about my break up with Essie?"

"Yes. She wanted to get married, and it was one of the issues."

"Yeah, but it wasn't the main one. It's that she wanted us to be, well, us. She didn't like that I made work and my family the main thing, and I get that. No girlfriend would like that work was such a huge deal for me, and I don't want that for my partner and I, either... but I'm just not at a place where I can have that balance between life and work. Not yet."

"I get that. I wonder sometimes if I'd even be able to find a partner, busy as I am. I like all genders, and even then I feel like my dating pool is tiny. How many people would want to date someone who can only offer a few meager hours a week? That's just not right."

I nodded. "My parents had a rough few years there. Trying to raise us, trying to offer a home to Jake as well because he needed a safe place... my mom and dad both worked full time and ran a family home and a family business that needed to be pushed to grow..."

"Yeah, I'm sure they worked super hard. My family did, too. They immigrated here and hit the ground running."

"One night I came downstairs after my bed time. I wanted to sneak in and grab a toy. I don't think my parents heard me, but I froze when I realized my mom was crying." Even after all these years, my throat still closed up, and my hands went cold at the memory. "My dad hugged her and rocked her; they were on the sofa. He kept telling her they'd be okay, they'd make it. It would be just a few more years like that, building what they'd started, and then they'd get to slow down."

Lina leaned closer to me, her chin on the tip of my shoulder, paying close attention.

"When I say I hope for what my parents have, I understand it comes with sacrifices like they went through. Why would I—how *could* I achieve better? I don't fancy myself particularly special and, to be honest, I don't think I could do what they did. Do it all, and do it so well." I shook my head. "My dad wants to retire early. I want to see him enjoy our privilege, and see him and my mom enjoy it all. I want them to have freedom. To do that, I have to take over as the CEO, and do it well. Then I can have my freedom, too."

She sighed. Instead of looking at me, she rested her temple on my shoulder and looked at the water. "You're such a good son. A good person, really."

"My dad and I are planning a two-year transition. I'm doing everything I can to make it happen. I don't want to be so self-centered that I put my desires in front of this, for them. Or to ask a partner to be patient with me while I make this happen."

To ask that of Lina, as much as I wanted to.

Lina squeezed my hand. "I think that's up to your partner to decide, if that's something they can live with. But you'd have to ask first."

And it was at the tip of my tongue to ask, but that wasn't all I'd be asking of Lina. I'd also be asking her to live with a family that thought I was the reason for every success in our lives. She was a proud, driven woman, and I adored that about her... asking her to let me have the glory would make me self-serving in a whole different way.

"When I asked if I could try this again with you in two years, I meant it, Lina."

My voice had a shaky quality to it, and it sounded hoarse in my ears, but I made no effort to hide it.

"I don't know where either of us will be in two years but... if we're going to tell everyone that we think we're better off as friends, then it'll be easier to be in each other's lives. Beyond just working together. A future together could still be an option."

I pulled away from her; as she lifted her head, I grabbed her face with a hand around her cheek. Her eyes were wide open, her brown eyes dark in the vanishing light. For a moment, I simply gazed at her, at the way her unpainted eyelashes faded at the tips, at the baby hairs at the edge of her temples, and the way her lips parted. Then I kissed her, fully meaning to, and for us alone.

Her lips moved in a languid manner against mine, and her tongue echoed their unhurried rhythm. I held her head in my hands, both of them now gripping her face. My breathing was slow, never mind the rapid pace of my heart. There was nothing desperate in the way we kissed. It tasted like acceptance, imbued with resignation.

I rested my forehead on hers.

"We should see each other less, I think." Her hand fell on my chest. "So that the break up is a bit easier... a bit more subdued.

No one would expect us to spend time together if we're broken up. So we might want to... taper down."

I sighed. We were ridiculous, after all.

"We'll do that. We'll start spending less time together, be a little off during the barbeque next weekend."

"I still want to go to the final game, if you guys make it."

I turned away. Orange brushes had given way to purples in the sky above the trees.

"If we make it?" I scoffed. "We're ruling this tournament. We play Rodrigo's team on Thursday, and I think we can win. Then the final is on Sunday."

"And we break up a week after that."

"Okay, then. We have a plan."

We stayed like that, sitting in silence as the sun set, her head on my shoulder. We walked back when the light around us turned blue, and made it back to the cabin right as night fell in our little corner of the mountains.

We woke up tangled up again the next morning, but we didn't do anything about it this time.

Chapter 24

Lina

DAD AND TÍO MIGUEL had left a while ago and I was mostly alone in the office. I had flicked off the ceiling light more than an hour ago; the dim glow shining from my desk lamp fit my mood much better.

I sighed and rolled the wheel on my mouse for the hundredth time. I'd reached the bottom of the page several minutes ago, but my index finger moved by inertia. I rested my head on my free hand, my elbow on my desk, and closed my eyes.

It had been three-and-a-half days since we came back from the Sotomayor lake house and I had last seen or heard from Gabe. He'd dropped me at my home last Sunday, no kiss on the lips, nor the corner of my lips, not even my cheek— just a soft "bye, Lina." And I'd been thinking about him non-stop ever since.

Sure, I was almost caught up with work, but I missed him. Pride helped prevent me from texting him and asking how he was doing, or proposing I stop by his place, bribe him with food, and pretend there was nothing complicated about us spending more time together.

Two things stopped me. One, it's exactly what my mother and the rest of the family would want me to do; feed my boyfriend and hope he'd want me around more. Two, doing so meant I had lost track of my goals again, and if I didn't fight for them, no one else would.

I was alone in that. Gabe couldn't help me; in fact, having him around would get in my way. We'd even discussed it openly. We were in agreement.

I didn't know what kind of choices I'd make if I were selfless like Gabe, but I doubted he'd be making mine. Willing to do anything for what I wanted, even giving up the person I'd developed feelings for. He was doing exactly the same, but for much more noble reasons.

"Cousin!"

Lucía's scream made me jump, and I straightened in my chair before she could see me slumping on my desk, daydreaming of a man.

"Yeah?" I called, just as she came into my office.

She grinned at me. "Ready to go?"

I squinted at her and did the math. It was Thursday, Gabe had mentioned the game he was playing against Rodrigo, and according to my watch, it was past 6:30.

"No," I said. "I'm not going."

I scrolled the page back up, and refreshed my inbox. The same three emails I had been ignoring waited unopened. I only cared about one of them, the one carrying the final version of the contract that had started it all.

"What? Why?" Lucía rested a hip against the edge of my desk. "It's the semi-finals. You have to go."

I pursed my lips, torn. I wanted to go, but Gabe and I had decided something different.

I frowned. "We're not... I'm not..." I bit the inside of my lips. "I'm trying to give him space."

Lucía stared at me for a long breath; her expression didn't change as she stood, pulled out the chair in front of me, and sat on it.

"Everything okay?" she asked. "Are you two fighting?"

I shook my head. "No. But I don't know if we work as a couple. I think we're better off as friends."

Her eyebrows rode high on her forehead. "You could have fooled me. I thought you two were on the fast track to a serious, long-term relationship. You looked so cozy on Saturday. Don't think you can fix it?"

"What do you mean, fix it? Fix Gabe and I?"

She nodded. "Yeah. You know, fix the problems instead of just breaking it off. Gabe is the first guy you're into in years. Why not take it a little further, and see if this could actually work?"

I leaned back on my chair and crossed my arms. I knew I shouldn't go, even if I really wanted to. I should push away the longing, and get used to the idea that we were about to end. I should put the words together, and tell my cousin that she should go alone, and that I'd just go home...

"C'mon, prima." Lucía's brow remained furrowed. "At least come to the game with me and keep me company. See him run and get all sexy and sweaty and make up your mind then, okay?"

Selfish. Could I live knowing I was being selfish? Because I wanted more time with him before we ran out of time, and maybe it was a terrible idea... but ignoring it was worse.

I missed him. Whatever we'd started hadn't been satisfied, and Saturday hadn't been enough. The next ten days let us complete the circuit and do what our bodies needed. A poor analog for what I really wanted, but as good as we could get for now.

Lucía presented the perfect excuse to find Gabe, and gave me a chance to convince him we could have a few more days to remember.

Gabe

"You're a beast, Gabe!"

If I hadn't been in the middle of a simple jog, I might have tripped. As it was, my heart stopped working for a second, and I felt a little faint, upon hearing Lina's encouragement from the bleachers.

A hesitant smile appeared on my face and I gave her a quick wave, before returning to the game.

Lina had come to see me play ball, like she'd known I had wanted her to. I had almost texted her a hundred times during the week, and I spent every spare moment coming up with excuses to reach out, but I shut myself down each time. Having my soon-to-be-ex-fake-girlfriend here filled me with stormy feelings, and suddenly the ball and the game mattered a lot less.

Thoughts of what I might do when the game ended and could talk to Lina distracted me enough, that our captain punched me playfully on the shoulder, and called me out to get my head back in the game.

I did my best, but when the whistle blew at half time, I couldn't get to Lina fast enough.

"Hey." Sweat dripped down my temple, and I used the bottom of my shirt to dry it. It bought me a second to figure out what to say next, while I half-hoped she would take the lead.

She did, her eyes quickly lifting from my midriff to my eyes. "Lucía insisted I come cheer for my boyfriend."

My heart fell to my knees, at the thought Lucía had forced her to come somehow. "Oh. Well. Your cheering still needs work, but maybe that's good, considering."

"I wanted to see you, too," she added. I searched her eyes to see more of what she meant by that, but she glanced at Lucía. The latter stood with Rodrigo, their arms around each other some distance away. "How long is your break?"

"Fifteen minutes. You want to talk about something?" My lungs still hadn't fully returned to normal, and I took a deep breath.

"Yeah. But maybe we should wait until after the game?"

That didn't help my lungs recover. "Did something happen with your family? Are you okay?"

"Nothing happened with my family. Nothing new, anyway."

"With the contract? We're still waiting for the finalized signatures and then we start with the final proposal, right?"

"We're signing tomorrow and everything else is on time, too. No, I want to talk about what we agreed to during the weekend—"

"C'mon, Gabe! We need to discuss a plan of attack for the second half."

I lifted my hand in the general direction of Mario, our Captain, whose call interrupted Lina and I. I told him to wait with a gesture of my hand, without looking at him. "I have to go—" I told Lina— "but can you tell me quickly?"

"Gabe!" Mario insisted and I lifted my index, to ask for one more minute.

My eyes never left Lina. "Don't leave me hanging. I'll be too distracted."

"Why do you have to be so cute?" she asked. Instead of saying more, she went up to the balls of her feet, put one hand on my chest, the other around my neck, and kissed me.

When she released me, I made several attempts to say something, my mouth doing something weird that undoubtedly made me look like a fish.

She smiled. "Go. More later."

"More kisses?"

"Gabe!" Mario insisted. "I swear to God."

"Go," she said, made me turn around, and went as far as to slap my backside.

Nothing had changed since the weekend, except my willingness to be proven wrong. Would Lina show me I could have it all?

———

Lina

"Looks like my favorite prima may have decided to mend things with her boyfriend..." Lucía sat next to me, after sending her real boyfriend back to the game.

I faked a sigh. "He looked too hot running." I shrugged. "And I like him too much."

Liked him enough, in any case, to be weak for him for the next week and a half, if he was okay with that.

"I knew it!" she exclaimed. "You didn't look *better off as friends* on Saturday."

"Doesn't mean we're going to stay together." I bit my lip. "It just means that it works right now."

"If it's working, why would it stop working?"

"We're too driven. Work is more important than—" I was going to say each other, but that was wrong; it lodged in the pit of my stomach with a wave of nausea. I couldn't say it. Work wasn't more important than Gabe, it was just extremely important right now. I cleared my throat. "Look. You know how hard it is at the office, right?"

She crossed her legs and shook her foot. She raised an eyebrow and gave me a once over. "You mean, how our dads make it impossible for us, and my brother is just about to leave town altogether to get a break from Dad, and my cousin is steering the ship as best she can and with so much zeal that it can only be her running the show in the future, so I need to figure out a plan because I can't stay?"

I had been gathering words to start on my response, but the last part stole them all from me. I closed my mouth with a snap.

"Mmh, yes," Lucía said. "I can see you didn't expect that."

"No, I didn't. Luce— you want to leave?"

"I will at some point. My dream isn't to do admin work forever, you know? I don't want to fight you for the company, either. You deserve it."

My breathing became fast and shallow. The whistle blew in the game, the sound of the referee stopping it for some reason, but after a quick check to make sure Gabe hadn't gotten hurt, I continued studying my cousin.

I locked eyes with Lucía. "There are other roles. If my dad gives me his share, I can make it so you could take over your dad's position if you wanted. You'd have to go up in the ranks to gain experience, but I can help. I never meant to make it seem there was room for only one of us— We could be the Martínez girls, running the company."

She hooked an arm around mine and patted my forearm. "No. I don't want to stay. I don't see my future in the company. But give me a bit of time before you kick me out, okay?"

"I would never kick you out."

"Perfect, because I'm still figuring it out."

"Okay. Yeah. Wow." I took a deep breath. "I didn't expect that."

"Good." She smiled. "Feels good to know that you have everything in control, but I can still surprise you."

"I don't have everything in control," I confessed. I found Gabe in the game, and caught him running with the ball toward the goal posts. "I didn't plan to like Gabe so much, for instance."

"I think it's a good thing that you like your boyfriend."

I scoffed, because if that was true, it wasn't true of a fake relationship.

My eyes found Gabe again, and caught the moment he scored. I couldn't help it, I jumped to my feet and yelled, "You're a fucking rockstar, Gabe!"

He shook his head and laughed as his teammates slapped him on the back, and I sat down to a laughing Lucía.

"Fine, fine," my cousin said, mirth in her eyes and her smile. "I won't bug you about your choices. I know you're doing your best to set up your future, and if that means focusing on work, then so be it. It's not my business. But if I were you, I would want to know if I could make both things work. Because this?" She pointed between me and the field. "This is fun. And you look silly, and invested. You get to enjoy your life, too, you know?"

"I want to enjoy my life too."

I hadn't been planning to include a partner yet, but now that I'd had a bit of Gabe, I wanted more of *him*. I couldn't reconcile it all together; I knew I couldn't be with him until I had my work future secure, but maybe I could have him for ten days.

———

Gabe

We lost. My team got eliminated from the tournament.

Disappointment coasted through me, yet it didn't feel as sharp as it usually did. I couldn't look at the other team jumping up and down in celebration but, overall, I was fine. Because as much as I'd grumble about losing in the semi-finals later, the kiss Lina had given me had risen to the forefront of my mind above anything else, even defeat.

"Let's go out for drinks," Mario said to my side.

I nodded but didn't look at him; I looked for Lina instead. "Where are we meeting?"

"Flannery's. You better come." Mario put a hand on my shoulder. "I'll personally kick you off of the team if you leave with your girlfriend. This is a mandated team-building, crying about our defeat into a beer event."

I chuckled. "Fine. I promise."

"You get to see your girlfriend every other day. Your team only loses the tournament one night a year." He pointed an accusatory finger at me. "Because we're not losing the Spring tournament."

"Fine! Now let me go. I'll be there."

As soon as Mario released me, I turned around and searched for Lina again. She took fast strides toward me; disappointment faded, replaced by sparkling hope. A grin stretched on my face, and I took my shirt off to dry my face and neck with it, my eyes fixed on hers as much as I could. The way her eyes checked me out, the curl of her lips, the anticipation in her features...

When we met, I was ready. Her arms came around me, mine around her, and I pulled her up and off her feet, our mouths together like I'd won the World Cup.

My team disappeared, the other guys did too. The lights around the field shone on us alone, no one else around; their chatter and laughter was distant white noise.

I held Lina against me, her soft and full body resting against mine, and we kissed and kissed, our lips and tongues dancing with each other and for each other alone. My heart skipped every other beat, and I hugged her a little tighter.

"I've missed you," she said, and air left my lungs in a relieved gust.

"I've wanted to call you every day." I frowned. "That's a lie. I wanted to reach out every hour."

"I know we said we should create distance, but I don't think— I mean, why? It's like breaking up before we have to."

"Right." My hands settled on the rounds of her hips, and I frowned. Of course the plan still was to break up, but...

"We both have plans." She sighed. "I won't get in the way of your parents' freedom, and I can't risk not proving myself to my family. But they don't actually know what we do when alone. Since you agreed to do this with me, we've spent time together and they never knew we weren't a real couple. They won't know that what we do together now is different from the past few weeks. We can tell them our time together wasn't as good as it should be, but... but in reality, when we're together..."

Her eyes glimmered, open like they rarely were.

"I see. You're saying we can still tell them what we decided, that we're better off as friends. But until Sunday next..."

Lina nodded. "Yeah. Until then, these next ten days..."

"Why, Lina? It's going to make it harder to break up."

"You're in my system." Vulnerability danced in her eyes. "I didn't like these past three days."

"I didn't like them, either." A long strand of her hair fell next to her face, and I ran it between two fingers. On the second pass over the silky strands, I put it behind her ear, hoping for an unobstructed view.

Almost everyone had left the playing field, and we stood in each other's arms mostly alone on the synthetic surface. The lights were on, a game still ongoing on one other field. Everything remained background noise, focused as I was on Lina.

"We'll go back to our lives, after," she said. "We'll work together, by phone and email to make it a bit easier at first; we'll break up and focus on our goals like we both want to. But over the past few weeks you made your way into my... my... life. And maybe if we let ourselves do what we've been pretending to do, it'll be a little easier when we break up."

How could it be easier? I weighed the possibilities, and they all came with a cost. If we started giving each other space now, it would hurt— it already hurt. It meant swallowing my torn emotions, and crossing my fingers I'd get a chance to test what I felt in two years. If we didn't go our own ways now, and we used this time to do some of what we wanted... If we did, and I knew what it was like to be with Lina, it would hurt even more afterwards... If I was able to let her go.

I frowned. "That morning on Saturday, you said we feel this way because this is what it would be like if this were real. That we just need to... complete the task."

Her nod was slow. "Our bodies don't know we were faking. We kissed, we slept together, we hugged... It's like we promised it something and didn't deliver. And the attraction is real. Why do you have to look so hot taking your shirt off, drying the sweat on your forehead, and letting me see these biteable muffin tops?"

I scoffed, she grabbed said rolls at my waist.

"They're squeezable, too," she added.

Could this be attraction only? The way my heart beat, the way my organism craved a few amazing days with her, I didn't think it was as simple as that. Because if I could brave some honesty with myself, I'd have to admit I wouldn't be simply scratching an itch. I wouldn't be faking it, and the break up would feel even more real.

But for ten days it would be glorious.

The question was, could I give her what she wanted, and deal with what it did to me?

"You want to feel wanted," I repeated from Saturday. "And I want you."

"And for the next ten days, I'll show you that I want you, too."

"It's not only attraction for me, Lina." I gulped. The final whistle for the last game rang nearby, and I ignored it, too. "Are you okay with that?"

Lina's eyebrows wrinkled like the words I'd shared had pained her. I loosened my grip on her, but she tightened hers around my neck.

"It's not only attraction for me, either," she whispered. "But it's all we can give each other, when we only have a week."

"Prima!" Lucía approached us, and Lina didn't let go of me as she turned her face to her cousin. "Are you leaving with Gabe?"

"I have to go to the pub with my team," I said. "You can come if you want."

Lina shook her head. She spoke to me only, Lucía still several paces away. "No. I would want to go home with you, and I shouldn't. Not tonight."

"Lina..."

She kissed me. "What time does everyone leave your office tomorrow?"

"Five-thirty. But you know I often leave after six."

"I'll be there at six. Then we'll go to your place. But we won't work, once we get to your apartment. Tomorrow only."

Her words scorched a fiery trail on my skin, my lower belly heavy with the power of them, holding them captive. I nodded. She smiled, kissed me again, and left with Lucía.

And left me in a whirlwind.

Chapter 25

Gabe

I DIDN'T FEEL MUCH better the next day, counting down the minutes until six o'clock with a tornado twisting in my rib cage. I kept checking my watch, then my phone, then the computer's clock, like one of them would surprise me and reveal that it was indeed a lot later than it was.

In reality, I had barely made it to five. My watch had just informed me it was 5:14, when my door opened and I lifted my eyes to find my best friend.

"Hey," I said.

Jake stopped a few steps away from my desk. "Hey. Are you going to work at the office for much longer? Most people are getting ready to go."

"No. I'm waiting for Lina, then we'll go to my place."

"Things are going well, I take it?" He smiled.

"Well..." I scratched my jaw. "We're... fine."

My childhood friend squinted at me, just like when I invited him to sit with me at school all those years before. "Are you still thinking about breaking up?"

"C'mon, Jake." I shook my head. "I told you before. The plan has always been to break up, and Lina knows it."

He raised both eyebrows. "I don't get you two, then. I would have never guessed, last weekend, that you were on your way to the end."

I sighed and closed my eyes. "It's not that I *want* it to end. But I'm late on everything, half the things on my calendar are past due—"

Because I'd had to carve time out of my days to accommodate a fake relationship with Lina, and it'd wrecked my work schedule. And now I'd said yes to spending even more time together, this time not even working side-by-side while having a meal.

Not that I regretted the mess I was making of things for myself the next ten days, but I'd certainly pay for it.

Even though I couldn't have finished that sentence even if I'd wanted to, Jake took the option from me with a firm voice.

"Then figure it out, Gabe." Jake took another two steps my way, a fiery intensity in his eyes. It was the closest to anger I'd ever seen him. With his imposing size, it could have been a terrifying sight. "You found someone you like, and she likes you back. You get to be with her! What the hell are you doing, letting her go?"

Shock froze my brain in time. The space between us crackled with a sudden electrical charge, as we watched each other process what he'd just said. The only reason I wasn't scared was because I knew him. I trusted Jake. But his anger surprised me.

It took a few seconds, but Jake's shoulders slumped. As much as he spoke to me, I was pretty sure he spoke from his own experience, too. He rubbed his forehead, while I released a slow breath.

Jake stared at the ground, then up at me again. "Talk to me and I'll help. You know that. And talk to your parents. They'll help, too."

My nod came slow, his words still trickling down to my chest. I wasn't sure I dared imagine a future where I didn't have to let Lina go, but I recognized the truth in my friend's statement. I felt something for Lina. Something big; something important. How could I let her go?

Jake's message harpooned into my heart and latched.

"Love you, Jake. Thank you," I muttered.

His eyes were sad. "I want to see you happy."

"I want the same for you."

His lips tilted in a small smile. "I know."

———

Gabe

After Jake left, and with nothing left to do but wait and count down the seconds, I managed to work for a bit. But when I received a text from Lina, I dropped everything.

Lina: I'm ready to go. Can I go to your office a bit early?

Gabe: yes, I'm ready whenever.

Lina: Good, because I'm coming up to your floor now

I jumped out of my chair, strode toward the elevator, and found her just as she exited the car. She grinned at me, eyes sparkling. She opened her mouth to speak, but I grabbed her face in my hands, plastered my body to hers, and kissed her. I kissed her like my life depended on it, giving myself into it until I'd run out of breath.

"I've been waiting for you," I said. "I've been waiting for this."

"Me, too."

"Come to my office for a second. I have to turn everything off, get my things."

"Okay."

She held my hand as we retraced my steps back to my space. Most of the floor stood in the near-darkness of dimmed lights, spaces empty, waiting for the cleaning crew later in the evening. Once back in my office, I got behind my desk, ready to turn my computer off. I started with my open documents and spreadsheets, any and all details invisible. My preoccupation wasn't on the sensitive company information I usually dealt with, but on my next few hours with my... with Lina.

"Are we alone?" she asked.

"Seems like it. Most people should be gone by now."

I'd just cleared my screen's desktop of the windows I'd been working in, when Lina got between me and my desk.

I stared up at her.

"So, I was thinking," she said. "You spend a lot of time here, right?"

"Yes. I go to meetings sometimes, as you know, but this is my home base. Why?"

Lina's voice was barely above a whisper, but I heard her clearly. "Since we have only a little bit of time to make memories, I think I'd like to make one here. So you remember me when you're working late into the night."

Distracted by the look in her eyes, the comforting size of her in front of me, the tempting shape of her body, I managed to find the control for the glass walls and made it opaque. I also closed the door with the push of a button. It locked automatically, and its click broke the momentary silence around us.

Her thighs were right in front of my face, her skirt stretched over them. I put my hands on them, one over each, and rubbed them up and down. I lifted my gaze at her again. "I couldn't forget you."

"But I want you to think of this, too." She bent down, hands on my face, and kissed me.

My hands left her thighs, caressing up her body and following a path to her shoulders, then down her arms. I held onto them for balance; her tongue made a pass on my lips and it made me dizzy.

"I will think of it." I admired the lovely view of her breasts, better displayed from this angle, almost overflowing out of her low-cut shirt. My blood went from humming to a buzz, and I brought my eyes back up.

She gave me a knowing smile. "You can look all you like."

"If I look, I'll want to do more."

"Haven't you realized? I want you to do more."

I surveyed my office, buying myself time. Blood already rushed to my cock, the mere suggestion of taking Lina in my office sizzling in my veins. Clouding my mind. "You know the kinds of things I want to do to you. Waiting until we're at my place might be best."

To my surprise, she grabbed her phone and tapped it a few times. Then she left it on her side, screen down.

She pushed my chair back. "You know I'm the kind of girl to go for what I want, right?"

"Yes. It's one of the things I like best about you."

"I want to go for you. Now. Here." Her hand made a path down my face, my neck, and my chest. Two fingers found a way through my shirt's buttons; her nails scratched my skin through my undershirt. "We don't have to choose. I'll still go home with you. If you're okay with us doing something here, too."

I gulped. My heart beat fast. My hands grabbed her arms tight, to avoid starting to grab anything else. Everything else. "Are you sure?"

She licked her lips; her eyes closed for an instant, a hiccuped breath escaping her. She sat on my desk and put one foot on each side of my thighs on my chair; her knees remained together, the skirt just over them. My hands gave up the effort to play nice, and I grabbed her calves and squeezed. My eyes caught on a hundred tiny details: the shape of her in front of me, the way her chest expanded and contracted, the faint texture of her bra visible through the thin fabric of her top. Could I feel her nipples harden through it, if I palmed her breast? Could I pull the silk and lace combo down, freeing her breast to suck into my mouth?

"I want to remember this." Her chest expanded as she took a deep breath, which left her with a tremor. Her head fell back. A small moan escaped her. "Seeing you lose your mind for me."

My mind had lost the battle as soon as she'd put her heels on my chair. My slacks tented. My cock took over directing the show, with Lina as the star.

"Look at me." I covered her knees with my hands. Her eyes were hazy when she did as I said, her eyelids half-closed. She was turned on, and I hadn't touched much yet. "What did you do, Catalina?"

She smirked, but it went away when a wave of arousal moved through her. "I have a vibrator on my clit, and it's on. An app controls it from my phone."

I groaned. My eyebrows furrowed with tension, my body taut with the need to see for myself. "Say the word, and my tongue will help you along."

"Tongue. Fingers. Cock." She opened her legs. "Take me here, on your desk."

Any reticence I harbored evaporated in an instant. Without hesitation, I pushed her skirt back around her hips; I didn't want any obstructions but her panties in my way.

My hands ghosted over the inside of her thighs, my eyes on the prize. "That's the last you demand of me. If I'm to have you, to take you here like this is a banquet and you're the main meal, then I'm in control. Are you okay with that?"

She nodded.

"Say yes, but only if you mean it."

"Yes. Yes, Gabe."

I could smell her arousal, and I took a deep breath to fill my lungs with it. "I'll stop if you tell me to stop. I'll retreat if you push me or fight me. But, Lina?"

Her eyes remained steady on mine as she leaned back on my desk, the weight of her torso on her straight arms.

I kissed the inside of her thigh, then nibbled on the other. She moaned.

My eyes locked with hers again. "I want you soft." A bite, closer to her panties. "I want you willing." A kiss. "I want your body pliant." I ran a finger down the fabric of her underwear in a gentle tease. She bit her lip. "I want you desperate for me."

"Yes, Gabriel."

I nodded, my cock straining against my trousers and my whole body falling into line. I wanted her. Not only her body and this moment— but this could be a test. If I were brave, maybe even a start.

Using only the tip of my right index finger, I pushed on her panties, aiming for her vibrator and her clit. Her labia parted for me to find a small, thin bullet vibe lodged between her lips. I pushed, she whined. Her panties added pressure on her flesh, the fabric stretched.

I clasped my fingers around the crotch and tugged. She shifted her hips on my desk, freeing her underwear to slide down her legs. "Good girl. I'm going to devour you."

Her undergarment complied to my pull, and I made sure to keep her stilettos on as I got rid of the piece of fabric. I put it in my pocket.

I guided her feet to my shoulders. The heels dug in on me. I smiled.

"You look hungry." She bit her lip. "I love it."

I'd loosened my tie earlier, and it didn't resist me as I deftly undid the knot. My eyes locked with hers, the fire there grabbing me by the guts. My cock, so hard it hurt, begged for attention, but I continued to ignore it. All I wanted was the fast rise and fall of her chest, the heat in the way she looked at me, and to play with her body until I couldn't hold back anymore.

The knot on my tie now undone, I held the strip of silk and pulled slowly. A smirk curled my lips as she tracked my movements and moaned. It took several seconds for the tie to part from my collar and, once free, I was quick to wrap it around my hands and pull on it twice, testing its strength

"Is that vibrator teasing you, Lina? How close are you to coming?"

"It's on low." She gulped. "I'm steady, but not close yet."

"Good." Still moving slowly, I wrapped her knees with my tie. I stared at her as I made a knot to secure her legs together. It would help keep the vibrator in place. "There's much I need to do before I let you off this desk."

I hooked my thumbs on the back of her knees and pushed her thighs against her torso. She fell back, her hands pushing the keyboard and mouse away, and two pens scattering to the floor. At first she caught herself on her elbows, but gave up and rested on her back instead. Her fingers held on to the edge of the desk.

"Yes, like that." My voice had turned rough in my throat. "Keep your knees up."

My hands caressed down the back of her thick thighs, grabbing at the fleshiest part. My eyes sought her pussy, now revealed to me. I braced her legs with my left forearm, while my right hand explored her full labia and glistening flesh.

I groaned, and slid my finger down the seam of her lips. "Are you ready for me?"

The bullet vibe blocked her entrance, and I pushed it up her slit. I wanted it still on her clit while I played with her. I inserted a finger, she moaned. It came out wet, and I bit my bottom lip. I inserted two, then three.

I lost my mind, and I hadn't even used my tongue on her yet. "Fuck, Gabe."

The way her juices spread all over my skin as I pumped her with my hand had me in a chokehold. I pushed my fingers knuckle deep, with half the force I'd like to use if I were using my cock, and she still writhed. I closed my eyes and focused on the sounds of her, of my fingers in her, then bit the tender flesh and focused on the taste. A moan built in my throat, and it soon filled my head. Nibbling on her lips, my fingers playing with her, her whimpers and twitches telling me I was getting exactly what I wanted from her... I was in my happy place, and I let myself forget about the rest of the world for a few minutes. Her pussy was my new home.

"Gabe. Jesus— Gabe. I have condoms— I need you—"

Her words brought me back from my haze; I caught myself rocking on my chair, desperately seeking stimulation on my cock, and only finding a poor mock of it against my own clothes.

"Fuck." I took my fingers from her and rested my forehead against the forearm bracing her legs. My breathing came in fast.

"I need to come. Please." She grabbed my hand on her thighs and squeezed. "Please."

"Soon." I got up and put her feet on my office chair, to keep her supported on my desk. My hands on my belt, I unbuckled it as I walked around my desk, my eyes all over her form. She looked disheveled, and while I'd been lost using my tongue, teeth, and fingers on her, she'd lifted her blouse and pulled down the cups of her bra. Her brown nipples stood erect and proud in the air as she played with her generous breasts. "What do we have here?"

Her head rested on the other edge of the desk, half hanging from it. I put my hands on each side of her.

"Hands off yourself, Lina."

She complied, and I dropped my head to lick one nipple, then suck on the other. Her breasts were too big for my mouth, as promised by the multiple times she'd enticed me with low-cut necklines, and they felt as perfect as I expected.

"Get my cock free." I closed my teeth on a puckered tip, softly rolling it.

Her arms over her head, her hands got busy with my buttons, the zipper, the underwear. She pulled my clothes down. One hand fondled my balls and the other wrapped around my shaft, and the relief of her touch rocked my insides.

I needed her lips.

My desk a complete mess, I rummaged through torn papers until I found her phone. I unlocked it using her face; the vibrator app was still open. My brain could barely make sense of the unfamiliar interface, especially when her thumb rubbed precum all over the crown.

"Shit." A tremor curved my back and made me pump into her hand. Never fully recovering, a slight pump of my hips into her hands, I squinted at the screen until I could make enough sense of it. I raised the vibration intensity from one to two thirds.

"Gabe!"

"Open your lips."

With great effort, I managed to push my cock gently into her mouth, her head still hanging over the edge of my desk.

"Suck me."

Her lips closed around me and she suctioned the head. I moaned, the sensation intense enough to cause a frisson to wave and crest up my backbone.

Too overwhelmed at first, my attention couldn't handle more than the wet heat of her mouth. I closed my eyes and fucked her face slowly, my mind long gone, all thoughts disintegrated. I kept my eyes closed, my hands on the desk to each side of her, my head heavy between my shoulders. Her moans intensified, mine singing right along hers.

Only when I knew I wouldn't come from her mouth alone did I open my eyes and grab her breasts. They bounced with our movements, with her writhing, and I anchored my hands to them. The vibration of her sounds transferred from her mouth to my cock; her arousal built and so did the intensity of the sensation. She lifted her legs like she'd come soon and the build up was too much to bear, and I rolled one nipple between index and thumb. I wrapped the other hand around her neck, wanting to feel the sounds through her throat and onto my skin.

Her body jerked and trembled, forcing me to slow down my hips even further.

"Fuck." I groaned. "Fuck!"

It seemed like her climax lasted forever. I lost more and more of my sense of time and space with each undulation and contraction of her body, and what it did to her mouth on my cock.

She pushed my hips back with a hand, and losing her mouth cost me ten years of my life.

She gasped. "Jesus, Gabe." She frowned, eyes still closed, and hiccuped. "Slow this thing down."

I gave her a break, putting the vibrator on the lowest setting, but not turning it off. Her phone still in my hand, I cast a studying glance all over her form. She was delectable. No tension seemed to exist in her body.

She'd melted for me.

My cock twitched. I grabbed it with my hand and pumped slowly, deciding my next move. This wasn't over.

"Want to come in my mouth, Gabriel?" Her voice had turned flirty. "Or all over my tits?"

I shook my head. "No. Where are the condoms?"

It took her a second to respond. Her eyes traveled all over my body, from my messy shirt, pants and boxers down to the middle of my thighs. Her hand wrapped around my cock again, hard and pulsing.

"You're going to get this in me?" she asked.

"You're all soft. I need to. I have to know how you feel."

I'd learned a thing or two, through my twenties, about how to find the balance between pleasure and pain.

She licked her lips. "Condoms are in my purse somewhere."

There was nothing elegant about how I made my way around the desk, my slacks almost to my knees and interrupting my steps. Too desperate to care, I found the condoms and put one on.

I gave Lina her phone as I opened the package. "Get the intensity to fifty percent."

"Gabe—"

"Lina. I need you to get close again. I want you squeezing my cock dry."

"I just— ung." She worked on her phone as I stood by her legs. "Done. Wow."

I checked the vibrator with my finger. "Higher."

"Done." She released a trembling sigh. "You know I can squeeze by my own volition, right?"

I smirked and put her joined ankles on my shoulder. "What would be the fun in that?" I bit on the side of her fleshy calf. "Now stop questioning me."

"Yes, sir."

I tapped her pussy a few times, in a preview of a punishing slap. "Now let me play with you."

"Yes, sir."

I held my shaft and entered her by a single inch, only the crown inside. "Aah. Perfect."

"Fuck." She squirmed, her hips pushing closer to me, like she wanted to force my dick in.

"Higher. Set it to the highest."

"Gabriel." Her voice came out breathy.

"Catalina. Do as I say. Now."

She whimpered as she tapped on her phone. She rocked her hips on my desk. "Holy shit."

I surrounded her legs with my arms to keep her in place. "Now keep quiet and take my cock like a good girl."

She nodded. I pushed inside, stretching her and living for each squeeze of her around my cock. We moaned in sync.

Sheathed in her, I kept the pressure of my hips forward, as deep as I could go. My heart beat so hard in my chest I had to close my eyes or I'd faint.

I bit my bottom lip for a distraction, not to come right away as I began a slow pump in and out of her, never fully leaving the warmth of her body. I kept my rhythm gentle, more for my sake than hers. Her body continued to roll in waves, and my chest caved in with the need to come.

"Play with your tits." My voice rasped through my throat, my breathing harsh.

Her hands were deep in her hair, her face lost in pleasure, and I groaned. She obeyed, and I thrust harder. Half a sob escaped her, like she couldn't take the intensity of everything for much longer.

"I need you to come again." I dug my teeth into her calf in a gentle bite. "Give me another orgasm, this time around my cock."

"I'm close," she breathed.

My eyebrows hurt I frowned so hard, my vision hazy. My body knew only one goal, to feel her clenching around me, helping me go over the edge.

I covered her hands over her breasts and squeezed. I unleashed my hips and fucked her hard.

Her head bobbled. Her body responded to me, letting me in, softening as I insisted she welcomed my relentless rhythm. A guttural sound built in her throat and she took her hands from under mine; she covered her mouth. Her second orgasm shot through her, a full body quiver that exploded in a long, muffled moan, and clenching muscles.

"Fuck. Lina. Yes, like that."

It took a minute for her pussy to stop squeezing me. My temple on her shin, I went back to fucking her hard. My own climax tantalized me, close, twisting and curling in my lower belly, and the tail end of my back.

I nibbled on her calf again and crossed over the edge. Two more pumps of my hips, and I emptied myself deep in her. I may have groaned, I wasn't sure. Everything exploded into ecstasy in my head, my chest, and even my consciousness quit me.

I floated for a second, my body loosening. I pulled away and staggered to my chair, barely managing to keep her ankles on my shoulder. I hung onto her legs as I recovered.

"This may be the best work you've ever done on this desk, Gabriel."

I chuckled and forced my eyes open. She rested on her elbows, looking down at me. A soft smile curled her lips.

"Did you turn the vibe off yet?"

"Yes. It was too much."

I slapped her calf in a reassuring manner. "We'll work on your stamina."

She laughed. "Lofty goals for only eight days, I see."

I chuckled and undid the knot in my tie, releasing her legs. We slowly worked on cleaning up and cleaning the mess we'd made;

somehow, my keyboard had ended up on the floor, and papers lay strewn all over.

Lofty goals, indeed, but not like she'd imagined. Because I had to find a way to keep this going. I couldn't let go. Not after the past couple of months, and what we'd just done on my desk.

Lina fit me, and there had to be a way to have it all. And I had eight days to figure it out.

Chapter 26

Lina

EIGHTEEN HOURS OF ABSOLUTE bliss later, I was sore and perfectly happy. Gabe was a sex god, as far as I was concerned, taking over and allowing me to quiet my mind for once. He didn't need me to make decisions or carefully evaluate the pros and cons of anything. With a sexy frown of concentration on his face, he simply took over and guided my body to the most orgasms I had ever had in less than a day.

We'd barely slept, but I felt energized. My body wasn't done fulfilling the promise we'd unwittingly fallen into the past few months, where we'd faked a romance that felt a little too real. I had crossed a line and my heart was involved, but the upcoming week wasn't about feelings. It was about releasing the sexual tension between us. I didn't think the romantic feelings I harbored would be helped much, but I hoped that would come with time.

Because I couldn't regret having Gabe undo a knot with his teeth, on a ribbon around my wrists tying me to his bedrest.

"Why are you so hot, Gabriel?" I asked him, using the Spanish pronunciation like I liked to do sometimes. "Everything you do is hot."

He chuckled and helped me sit up in bed. We sat, naked, my arms around my raised legs. His feet on the floor and his torso leaning to me, he smiled.

His eyes roamed over my face, and his fingertips were warm and soft on my skin when he put a strand of hair behind my ear. "If we didn't have all our business demands hanging over our heads, do you think you'd want to try with me? Making this real."

I blinked a few times. Maybe he was in a haze of post-climax optimism, but his words hinted that maybe he was crossing lines, too.

It's not only attraction for me, Lina.

Mellow hope wanted to flutter up my chest, but I pushed it down. The odds were against me, that this meant the same to Gabe as it did to me. That he'd crossed a line from attraction to real friendship; that he was falling for me, too. And I couldn't risk the vulnerability of asking, not yet.

But I wanted to get there, be brave, and ask.

"You're the first person in a long time, that would make me actually consider it."

His smile turned into a grin. "Good to know."

"You don't have to look so damn pleased, you know?" I arched an eyebrow.

He laughed. "Why not? I liked hearing it."

I shook my head and changed the subject. "Should we go get ready? We should be leaving in an hour to make it in time to the barbeque."

"Or maybe we should be late, as a sign of rebellion to your family."

"That's tempting."

"If you really want to go for it, I used to have a lip ring. Something tells me they'd hate that."

"What?!" I laughed.

"It was just a lip cuff, but I think your family would flip out anyway."

"Oh god. Do you still have it?"

"I stopped using them when I had to represent the Sotomayor Group in business meetings, but I could get another one. Maybe even get you your own, make sure to add some precious stones to it." His smirk became wolfish. "Lip rings can be a lot of fun to play with."

"Precious stones, huh? This is the first time you try to flex your deep pockets with me."

He raised an eyebrow and leaned closer. "I can show off if you like. Next time we can go to the lake house by helicopter, or I can schedule the family plane to go to a remote, private, balmy island, where we don't have to wear many clothes, if any at all."

That he would like to do all of that with me filled me with two twin waves, each twisting and coiling with each other, right against my breast bone. One carried all my longing, and the other my rising affection for him. The tide reached my throat and threatened to become tears.

I liked Gabe. I liked him a lot. So much that I wanted to believe the vision he painted for me.

"I'd accept a piece of jewelry. I'd wear it proudly," I said. "If it came from you."

His eyes softened on me. "On it. Let's go shower now, shall we? We'll find something to scandalize your family with."

———

Lina

Meat cooked on the grill, tended to by a chef, and finger foods were being passed around by support staff my parents had hired. We were financially comfortable, nowhere near as rich as Gabe, his family, and his friends, but my family clearly had a different relationship to money. The Sotomayors didn't seem to notice or care. Gabe's parents, Vi, Enrique, and Tío Miguel sat at the outdoor table with my dad and Lucía; they all chatted happily, while my mom and Tía Soledad made sure everyone was comfortable. Things were going well.

Gabe and I sat on a bench near an old apple tree in the yard, his arm around me. I had a drink in my hand that was the perfect mix of boozy and refreshing, and I sighed.

Gabe's fingers played lazily on the skin of my shoulder. "It's weird to see Enrique outside of the tournament."

"It's weird to see our families mingling together like this."

"Even after the day in the Cabin?"

"Yeah, I guess even so. After the weekend, their differences are even more stark."

"At least we made it in time."

I chuckled. "Only because I stopped you from doing what you wanted to do in the shower."

"Mmh." He squeezed me against him, his eyes playful. "It's fine. I still plan to do it at some point."

"You're surprising, Gabriel Sotomayor. You have this gentle, soft energy... then you show me this other side. The thing you whispered to me in the shower? Wow. Somehow the tattoo and fake piercing are not nearly as shocking, for a guy who can be so sweet."

"I'll take that as a compliment." He kissed my cheek, gentle and purposeful, like he hadn't for a while. This time, I let myself believe it was real. "So tell me. How do you feel about tattoos? I want to get more, especially if you like them."

"I like them."

"Would you get one with me?"

"My parents would die... which could be enticing, in the right circumstances."

"They don't have to know... unless you want them to know. Then we'll come to visit, both of us wearing our lip cuffs, and see how they react. Yours will bling and sparkle, it'll be impossible to ignore."

I laughed, but I didn't get to respond. An approaching figure interrupted our conversation.

Enrique left his dad's side and came to us. "Hey. Weird to see you around like this, Gabe. Not at a game, but at my uncle's house."

Gabe and I chuckled.

"We were talking about it earlier," Gabe said. "I thought I'd see you at my family's lake house last week."

Enrique shrugged. "Yeah, I had a meeting with a potential employer, or I would have been there."

I perked up. "Oh, really? In your industry?"

"Yeah. It's in a small farm wanting to focus on ethical practices."

"I hope it went well." Gabe squeezed my shoulder in a way that seemed encouraging.

"I think it did," Enrique said. "I'm hopeful. It'd be awesome to go straight from graduation to a job like that in my field."

Tío Miguel appeared out of nowhere. "I don't know why you're bothering with that when you have a perfectly good job waiting for you with us."

"Dad..." Enrique warned, his voice firm.

Gabe and I stood in unison; I needed to be at eye level with my uncle.

"I'm serious, son. You know we want you to take over."

"I don't want to work there—" Enrique said.

At the same time, I spoke up. "*I'm* trying to take over—"

"C'mon, Gabe." Tío Miguel ignored us both. "You're a smart man. You know what it takes to run a company. Tell my son here why he should come work for the company."

"With all due respect, but I won't." His voice matched the serious look of his face. "Lina is right here. It's disrespectful to say what you're saying, like she's not already doing the work you want your son to do."

The red undertone darkened in Tío Miguel's face. "That's not how things work. Just because you're dating my niece—"

"It's not because I'm dating her. It's because she's good at what she does and she deserves to be recognized for it by every-one, especially her own family. You're the one making a mistake, and that's both my personal and professional opinion."

I stared at Gabe. His words made my bones rattle. My heart seemed to lose its rhythm, a confused pace for a second, but things became clearer and clearer with each new drumming heartbeat. Little by little, with every new facet he showed me— from sweet to dominant to down to earth to protective boyfriend— he'd found a way into the bruised, closed-off organ in my chest. Whether he knew it or not, he'd claimed my heart.

Tío Miguel spluttered, and I didn't even pay attention.

Enrique patted his dad's shoulder "I don't want to work at the family company, Dad."

The older man glared at my cousin. "You will. I'm sure of it."

Enrique sighed. "I won't. But let's go sit by mom for now. You know she gets shy."

They left, and my eyes quickly returned to Gabe.

He turned me in his arms, his hands on the rounds above my hips. He squeezed. "You okay? I don't get how he can be so crass."

"Thank you. That meant a lot to me."

His face relaxed, his annoyance floating away on a breeze. He smiled. "What kind of boyfriend would I be, if I let him insult you that way?"

And then he kissed me, like he'd forgotten we were supposed to be faking this whole thing, just like I had.

Chapter 27

Lina

AFTER A WONDERFUL WEEKEND together with Gabe, I did something out of the ordinary. On Tuesday, on my way back to work after a meeting with a client, I took a detour and stopped at the Sotomayor offices unannounced. I entered the elevator and pushed the top-floor button, and prepared myself for the long way up.

What had pushed me to visit in the middle of the day was still in question, but I had an idea. It might have had to do with the few hours of sex that interrupted the work we tried to do on Sunday. It had been *fun* and I couldn't stop thinking about it. I wouldn't try to repeat the night at his office from the week before— though I wouldn't say no, if Gabe suggested it; a quickie in his office sounded wonderful— but I hadn't seen Gabe since the weekend. Only two days had passed, but since we didn't have much time left, priorities could be shifted for a short while. Coming to his office for a kiss in the middle of the day, one that didn't depend on having people around to excuse it, would be a great addition to the memories we were making.

The doors finally opened at my stop, and I stepped out of the elevator. I waved at Cynthia behind the reception desk and, with a grin on my face, I made my way in the general direction to Gabe's office.

"Hey!" I stopped at Solange's desk. As his assistant, we'd ended up chatting almost every time I visited. I offered her a cookie from the box I carried. "Is Gabe busy? He wasn't expecting me."

She took it but gave me a sad smile. "He is, sorry. He's in a meeting with São Paulo."

"Oh." I straightened and pushed my disappointment down. "Do you know if he'll be done soon?"

"He's scheduled to be done in half an hour, but then he has an internal meeting someone just booked in his calendar." She gave me an apologetic look. "He might come out of the office for a bit between calls, maybe? Or I can just give him a message?"

I stared at the box in my hands. Of course he was busy. Even if he made room for me most of the time, it didn't mean he would drop everything just because I showed up. He'd said no several times, and that wouldn't change just because we'd had a lovely weekend.

I sighed and gave Solange the box. "Just give him this the next time he gets a coffee. I'll text him later."

"For sure."

"Thank you, Solange. Take care."

I walked out of the place, my chest deflated. The whole way down the building, I bit back the self-recriminating voice in my head, telling me I'd messed up. There was nothing wrong with me visiting, just like Gabe couldn't help being busy when I showed up unannounced. This was the reality of our lives, for him to be even busier than I was. I had always known it, and shouldn't forget. I wouldn't let the impasse ruin the week.

———

Gabe: Solange told me you stopped by?

Lina: Yes. Sorry I didn't text ahead

Gabe: I was in meetings all day. Did you want to talk about something?

Lina: No, just wanted to see you. I don't know what I was thinking, of course you were busy

Gabe: That's sweet. I'm sorry I missed it. The cookies were delicious, thank you

Lina: It's fine. It's not like I can be surprised. Maybe I can see you tonight?

Gabe: Can't. I'm working late for a meeting with Tokyo. We're doing reviews with a few international offices and I can't move a lot of stuff around. I'm not even going to soccer this time. I also have a call with the team in New Delhi tomorrow, but maybe Thursday for soccer?

Lina: Sure, I'll be there.

Gabe: Sorry, Lina.

Lina: No, I get it. This is a good reminder, too.

Gabe: I have to go now. Text tomorrow?

Lina: talk tomorrow

Gabe: Good night.

———

Gabe

The Fall tournament over, the league had returned to the usual training schedule. For the first time since this whole thing began, I'd known that Lina would come to the game, and I'd been looking forward to it all day.

"Godspeed, Gabe!"

I ran through the field, sprinting toward the ball, a guy from the other team running next to me to mark me. We both chuckled at Lina's encouragement.

I caught the ball, played with the ball between my feet, managed a rainbow flick, kicked, and scored. Like a damn peacock, I showed off for my girlfriend. To fully make the point, I ran to her, standing at the edge of the field, and I stole a quick kiss from her.

The game resumed around me and I joined the play my team had begun, half my mind still on Lina. After a deliriously wonderful thirty-six hours, we'd spent most of Sunday working together in my condo. We'd researched our competition for the stadium deal, and began collecting it in an analysis spreadsheet that seemed quite promising. She went back home that night, and then we'd spent the next few days catching up with work. This Thursday was the first time we could see each other properly, instead of reducing our evenings to work through dinners together. And, instead of us continuing to explore each other's bodies and connecting in different ways, I was running behind a ball with a bunch of other guys.

The final whistle rang across the space, and I stood among my teammates catching my breath. My hands on my hips, I gazed around the people I spent four to eight hours a week with, and wondered if I could let it go. If I stopped playing, these could be hours I spent with Lina.

I still wasn't sure how I could make it work with her, and do it all.

A gentle hand rested on my back, and I turned to see Lina smiling at me.

"Good game. I brought your things." She held my bag forward, my water bottle on the other hand.

I kissed her cheek. "Thank you."

I dropped my bag to the floor and found my towel, which I gave to Lina. My shirt stuck to me, and I took it off quickly. I dried the excess sweat with it and dropped it to the floor, before reaching for my water bottle. Squeezing it, I sprayed water on my face and chest, and sighed.

"Do you do this on purpose?" Lina stared at me with a smirk and a glint in her eye.

"Do what on purpose?" I took the towel from her and dried up.

She waved a hand in front of my chest in a circle. "This. Splash water all over, so casual."

I smiled. "Oh. You like it, huh?"

"Why would I be here, otherwise?"

I stepped closer to her. "For my sparkling personality?"

She laughed, went up on the balls of her feet, and kissed me. "Put on your fresh shirt and let's go. I'm going to cook for you tonight. I took the liberty of getting groceries delivered to your building."

I put my fresh shirt on and, in the same movement, put my arms around her soft body.

I squeezed her to me and smiled. "What are you making?"

"It's a surprise." She put her hands on my shoulders.

Again, we were the only ones left in the field.

"Fine, I won't insist." I gazed around the space. Even if I gave up playing in the league, I'd continue to pay for it, so the league could continue to thrive.

"Why do you suddenly look sad?" Lina lifted a hand to my face.

I leaned into her palm. "I'm thinking of taking a break from soccer."

"Why?!" She frowned.

"I don't have enough time for it, I think."

I hadn't realized my face had shown my melancholic thoughts, and I wondered if she knew her face now showed me hers.

Her brow relaxed, and she looked at me with doleful eyes. "You love soccer so much, though, and it's good for you. It's the one thing balancing you out."

"You're good for me, too. You've given me some of it, when I manage to move meetings around."

"Yeah, but I'm not going to be around the same way after Sunday. After we break up, soccer can still be there for you."

"Right. Sunday."

She nodded. "I just need to stop thinking of Essie's smirk when she realizes I stopped coming and assumes we broke up."

"Stop thinking about that. I'm not thinking about Essie."

Though it was an interesting contrast, to think about what I was willing to do for Lina that I never considered for my ex.

"Okay. I'll stop. Eventually. But let's not talk about that yet. Not until the weekend, okay? We're supposed to be enjoying tonight."

Though I nodded and let her guide me to the parking lot, I couldn't say I agreed with her. As we walked out of the field, letting go of soccer was still an option. I had to talk to Jake and my parents, and make a few hard choices.

Chapter 28

Lina

"HOW'S THE STADIUM'S FINAL proposal coming along?" Tío Miguel asked me.

On Friday night, him, my dad, and I were in the small boardroom, finalizing a quarterly plan. I hadn't been sure how long it would take, so I'd told Gabe I'd text him after and see if we still had time to get together. The night before, we'd cooked, chatted, and had more incredible sex; it had been such a lovely evening that I couldn't wait to do it all over again.

I hoped we would, but I still likely had a couple of hours left in the office.

I took a sip from my coffee. "I sent you an email earlier. Gabe and I began a comparative analysis, and I started a draft earlier this week."

Tío nodded and appeared to scroll through his phone's screen. "Good. I'll find the email and send it to Enrique. I want him to take over part of it."

His words dropped a bucket of cold water on my shoulders, his implications dripping down my back and chilling me to the bone.

"Take over?" I managed to ask. I crossed my arms. "He can take over accounting and start where I did, if he changed his mind. The stadium project is mine."

Tío Miguel barely moved, only his eyes whipped to me. He frowned. "Relax. It's not like he will steal your boyfriend. He's just going to do the work part of it."

Air rushed in and out of my lungs. "This has nothing to do with Gabe. Enrique doesn't know anything about this project. He hasn't been around for ages! I made this deal happen, I know it inside and out. It's mine. If you want Enrique to come back don't use my baby to tempt him."

"Baby?" His voice rose. "If you want babies, marry Gabriel and make some. This is work! And my son needs to get his hands involved, if he's going to take over one day."

I didn't even glance at my dad, but I didn't need to. He was doing what he usually did: nothing. He watched his brother and his daughter get into a fight, again, and he waited to see when he needed to intervene and pacify. Again.

"Enrique can't take over," I said. "I have more experience than him! I like this. I want it. Enrique doesn't."

"Don't tell me what my son wants. He's my son!"

"He's told you he doesn't want this." I matched the volume of my voice to mi tío. "What will it take for you to believe him?

To take my ambitions seriously? How can you be so adamant to give him my job?!"

Tío Miguel stood and put both hands on the boardroom table. "We gave you this job. We let you run this project. We can change our minds and give it to someone else! It's always been Enrique, and you're silly if you didn't get that from the beginning."

His voice boomed in the space. If anyone was still around, they could certainly hear him. I responded in kind.

"Silly?! When are you going to stop treating me like this?" I stole a glance at my dad for the first time. Like I expected, he watched us fight but did nothing. I faced him. "When are you going to stop him from treating me like this?"

"Hija," he said, his voice gravelly. He stood as well. "C'mon. Let it go."

"Let it go?!" My voice turned shrill. I dropped my hands and fisted them at my side, my shoulders tight. "Seriously? I've given my life to this company, and you tell me to let it go? Let a cousin who doesn't care take over and ruin everything I'm trying to build?"

"Insolente!" Tío Miguel yelled. "*You're* building? Your dad and I built this company!"

"I helped! And I'm pushing this company forward, crafting its future right alongside you."

Tío Miguel scowled. "You were a summer hire who stayed for a while. That's all."

The pain of his words cut me. Blood left my face; my hands got cold. One thing was to suspect he felt this way about me, another was to have it thrown at my face.

I turned to my dad. "Is this what you think, too?"

My dad's eyes looked sad, and he opened his mouth to speak, but his brother interrupted him.

"You've been waiting. That's clear. You've been telling yourself a lie, thinking you were waiting to take over and hoping my son wouldn't return. Don't think I don't know that! But it's a lie. You're going to outgrow this. You found a good man, but even if you don't marry the young Sotomayor, it'll be someone else, and then your family will take all of your attention— as it should. And this company will disappear."

When I spoke, my voice came out thin. I hated it but, at this point, all I could do was use what little voice I had to not back down. To speak my mind, in front of these men who didn't care that I wanted to focus on the company. "You don't get it, do you? Enrique doesn't care. He's not coming back. Is it so hard to believe that I would want this? Really want this?"

"He's coming back!"

"He's not." I grumbled through my clenched teeth.

"Don't you want a family?" My dad asked.

My heart broke. The only reason I looked to the floor was so they couldn't see it shatter in my eyes.

"There's no point in trying to explain if you won't understand." I lifted my eyes at my dad. "If you made an effort to get to know me for who I am and not for who you think I should be, you could make my dreams come true. But you won't, because it means standing up to your older brother. This company will die, if no one shows up to take over. I'm the only one who wants to, but I don't have a dick, so I guess we all lose."

"How dare you!" Tío Miguel exclaimed, but I turned on my heels and ran to my office. I grabbed my bag and ran across the floor towards the stairs.

"Lina!" Dad called, but I ignored him.

I stomped down the stairs, my heart in my throat.

"Lina! Come back here!" Tío Miguel called from upstairs, but I ignored him, too.

I got in my car and drove away, tears clouding my eyes.

———

Gabe

Alone in my high-rise condo, I didn't have the time to cook dinner, but I started preparing a meal anyway. I should have ordered takeout or picked up food somewhere but, in a way, pretending like I could make room in my day helped. If I could spend time doing something so menial, I could believe that I could figure things out, and find a way to have it all. Even if everything this week pointed to the contrary, I couldn't ignore the way my heart craved to find work-life balance now, and not in two years. Nor could I erase the thoughts multiplying in each of my brain synapses, that I couldn't let Lina go. Yet dropping soccer was all I could think of, and it still didn't do enough for my daily agenda.

And this was without considering that Lina might not be on the same page that I was. She had told me she was ready to wait to climb over this hump in her career, before thinking about love. Then again, I'd told her the same...

A plan. I needed a plan, so I had something to offer. Then I would talk to her. And convince her not to break up.

Maybe a start would be to let her know I'd cook dinner for her, if she came to stay with me.

I grabbed my phone to shoot a quick text, only to find one of hers already there.

> **Lina**: Hey. Are you busy? Can I see you? I'm on my way to your place if you're there

A mix of excitement and worry swirled inside of me. This wasn't like Lina, and she was supposed to be in a late meeting, but the prospect of seeing her pumped into my heart in two extra beats.

> **Gabe**: Of course. I'm at home. Come straight up

I took ten minutes to finish dinner prep. I didn't know how long it would take Lina to make it to my place, or what to do with the butterflies in my stomach. In the end, I left the diced veggies in a bowl and put the meat back in the fridge. I was checking my emails on my phone when my doorbell rang.

There was only one thought when I opened the door to see her looking down and wriggling her hands on her bag.

Something happened.

My stomach dropped. With no words, I got closer to her, and put two fingers under her chin, quietly asking her to look up at me. At first she seemed to avoid my eyes, but I insisted.

She sighed and gazed up at me. It looked like she'd been crying.

I frowned. My mind darkened. I searched her face for a hint of what might have caused this look on her, but saw nothing. I placed a hand on her face; it seemed to make her sadder. Lead filled every cavity in my chest at the sight.

"Who was it? What did they do to you?" I asked.

She fought with the question for a few moments, not immediately answering. A mix of hurt and doubt marred her eyebrow. She pressed her lips tight.

I let a gust of air out my nose. "Come. Sit on the sofa; we'll talk."

She nodded and entered the condo, immediately making her way to the couch. She slumped and sighed.

"Tea okay?" I filled the electric kettle with water and set it to heat up. "I can give you coffee if you like, but my mom always offered me chamomile tea when I felt upset. I still have a box she gave me."

"That would be lovely, Gabe. Thanks."

We remained in silence, only the small sounds of getting her a cup and serving her tea filling up the space. I found her leaning back on the sofa cushions, like the time she'd almost fallen asleep, her head on the top edge of it.

I placed the cup on the coffee table in front of her; she followed the movement, her arms crossed over her belly. I sat next to her, giving her time and space, except for my hand. I ran my fingers through her hair.

Finally she settled her deep brown eyes on me.

"You look sad," I said.

"I fought with them. I told them how I feel."

I scooted closer, so I could put my arm around her. With the back of my free hand, I caressed her face.

"Your dad and Miguel. What did they say to make you sad?"

Her eyes didn't waver this time, but they filled with tears. "They pretty much told me they're counting down the days until I get pregnant and start popping out kids. They see me as a glorified intern and want Enrique to take over."

I winced. Her tears made me want to avenge her, sit her uncle and father down and rip them a new one. If they so much as had a single negative thing to say about Lina, I'd be sure to make them pay somehow. I'd be happy to do it, if Lina gave me permission, but not now. My focus now was on her.

I brought her closer to me with the arm around her shoulder. "If they don't understand you it's their fault. You're driven, you're ambitious. Your focus is on your work." Saying it out loud made my fears worse, reminding me why she might not want to make this thing between us real. "You've shown that to all of us. If they can't see it, it's their failure."

If I forgot what I knew, then that'd be my own fault, too.

A couple of tears fell from her eyes. She wiped them with hard hands. "Ugh. I don't like to cry. Especially in front of people."

"I'm not people."

She scoffed, but more tears fell from her lashes as she looked up at me. "No, you're not."

I wiped a tear from her face, as gentle as I could, in contrast with her gesture. "It's okay to cry."

Her face took on a pained expression, this time, and tears became waterfalls.

"It's okay. It's okay." I guided her to sit on my lap. I held her, her legs out to my side, and she rested her head on the crook of my shoulder. "You can cry. Let go, Lina. I've got you."

She leaned on me and didn't make a sound, as her tears wet a spot on my shirt. I surrounded her in my arms and let her cry and cry, nothing more than tiny hiccups of air coming out of her. I let her put her hurt into tears, and give them to me. Each of them got placed into a corner of my heart, fully aware that she wouldn't be crying with me if she hadn't learned to trust me over the past several weeks. Something told me no one had seen her cry in years and here she was, letting me hold her in my arms as she did.

"This isn't fake," I whispered. I knew she could think I only meant the friendship and comfort of the moment we shared, but I meant so much more. "This is real."

We stayed like that for a while, I wasn't sure how long. I caressed her back with a hand, or played with her hair, or went

327

back to holding her. She spent every tear at some point, the warm spot on my shirt now cooling down. She sighed deeply.

"I have a little story for you." I caressed her shoulder with my thumb. "Want to hear it?"

She nodded.

"My mom told me this many years ago," I began. "Chile is a very seismic country. There are earthquakes there almost every day. Everything is built to withstand them. You'd think structures have to be solid to be strong, right? That the firmer they are, the better. Well, turns out that's not the case. Buildings need to be flexible to withstand earthquakes. They crack and collapse if they're too rigid but, if they move and shift with the shaking ground, they do well. The energy dissipates in each wave that moves through concrete and steel, and sometimes it takes hours for a building to stop swaying after a quake. But they stop, and the buildings go on to stand proud among the mountains, full of life."

I sighed. "There's incredible strength in yielding at the right time, Lina. When things get hard, finding a place to surrender can save you." I kissed her forehead. "I'm glad I can be that place for you, tonight."

She shifted, her first movements slow. She placed a hand on my chest. "You're telling me you think I'm strong for crying with you."

"And that I'm honored I get to be the one to hold you." I took her chin again, lifting her face to me. Her eyes were red from crying, her hair messy, and she was still beautiful to me. "I want to be someone you feel safe being soft with."

She gave me a sad smile. "I think you could be, Gabe."

When I pressed my lips to hers in a gentle kiss, I put comfort in it. For her, and for me. Because I'd shown my heart to her there, but I wasn't sure if she'd seen it for what it was.

———

Lina

Gabe's words echoed in my heart as he took care of me. He fed me, made me another warm drink, and put things into the dishwasher.

He wiped the surfaces as I sat in the kitchen with another chamomile tea in front of me. I wasn't used to having men doing this kind of thing, and I loved that Gabe did it so readily. No fuss, no guilt-tripping. He simply took care of me. It made me fall a little bit more for him.

I wrapped my hands around my mug. Anticipatory grief sucked, and I wrestled with it. Gabe had said that he wanted to be someone I could be soft with, and just thinking of it filled me with warmth and gratitude and dreams. Even if these few days together led to nowhere, for a moment, I believed I could rely on someone. That alone was a gift. To know I didn't have to make rebar out of my veins, and harden my body into concrete... not with him, anyway.

"Are you staying tonight?" He folded the dish cloth he'd used to clean the stone tops, then washed his hands and dried them. "You haven't been sleeping here the last few nights, but I thought maybe you would tonight..."

He left the statement hanging and, when he looked at me, he didn't hide his hope.

The warmth in my chest expanded, before it cooled down with the words forming in my throat. "I didn't bring anything I need. I just took my purse when I left the office and came straight here. I don't have pajamas or make up remover or— anything, really."

"If you don't want to use my clothes and stuff, I'm happy to order things for you. We can get things delivered fast with just a few taps. Let me treat you."

What I heard was, *let me keep taking care of you.*

I smiled. "Okay. I'd love to stay."

He grinned, and surrounded the island to give me another kiss.

Ugh, he was a little too good to be true, but I'd started to be okay with that. More than that, I'd started to love it.

He gave me his phone with an app open. I'd never seen it, but it seemed like an online shopping store of a brand I'd never seen before. I bit my lip when the screen shone with no prices on the items. After I made a few selections, I gave him his phone back.

"You didn't get PJs?" His eyes lifted from the screen to study me.

"Can I use some of your clothes? Do you have a 2XL shirt, maybe?"

I eyed him, like I hadn't learnt by now the shape of him. I didn't think that was his size, but it didn't mean he didn't have a shirt like that.

"I'm pretty sure we can find something."

He casually added a five hundred dollar tip and closed the app. "Your things should be here in a couple of hours."

My family was fine, but not *that* kind of fine. I raised my eyebrows.

"What app is that?"

"One of Javier's projects. My mom helps him run it. It hires people in vulnerable situations. They earn a flat fee for the service plus tip. All the items are new and bought with money donated to the organization. It's pretty neat."

"That sounds wonderful."

He frowned. "Do you want to watch something on the TV while I send a few emails? If it bothers you, I won't get on my computer, but there are a couple of things I should really look into."

"I don't want to work tonight, but I understand if you need to. I did promise my stuff wouldn't get in the way of what you have to do."

He pursed his lips and crossed his arms; we stood close enough that the gesture brought us to touch in a few places.

"I don't think we're the same people who made those promises," he said.

I bit the inside of my lip again. "Have things really changed? We're both still swamped with work and responsibilities."

"Is there a world where we could make it work, anyway?"

"Is this enough for you?" I placed a hand on his folded arms. "A few stolen moments and working together every evening?"

"It would only be like this for a few years."

We gazed at each other for a long moment. I conjured images of a future together, one where the things we did to pretend became the template for something real. I frowned, torn, my stomach tightening while my heart took flight. In just a few words, Gabe let me know he'd be in, if we could agree on the how.

Going for it meant having someone who saw me, held me, and cared for me. Someone kind, safe, and driven like me. Someone whose family showed me what we could build together, and how close that would be to my every dream. It also meant risking my future, if my dad took it as a sign that I was ready to get married and give him grandchildren.

Something must have shown on my face, because Gabe lifted a hand to my cheek. "Sorry. You're tired. We can talk about it sometime this weekend."

A scoff escaped me. "On the weekend we said we'd break up?"

He didn't respond except for a smirk curling his lips.

Lina

We went to sleep a little after we received the things Gabe had ordered for me. Wearing a shirt from his college years, I got into bed with him next to me. I went to sleep in the comfort of his warmth under the covers.

Light barely made it behind the blackout curtains when Gabe woke me up with tender kisses on my face. He brought me closer to him and wrapped me in his arms, both on our sides and face to face, and he never stopped the gentle pecks on every corner he could reach. The movement of our bodies started slow, undulations helping us rub against each other, waking our bodies up. Soon our breaths mingled together and our touch became more purposeful, reverent, and still sweet.

He brought one of my legs over his hip, aligning our centers. Small shudders traveled through his body when I touched him, and I pressed closer to him, seeking more.

He kissed me with adoration. I kissed him back, giving him another piece of me. He undressed me with revering hands, I caressed him like I treasured him. Seemed my body knew that I cherished him before the rest of me did.

Both fully naked, he put on a condom and kneeled between my legs. He dropped his body to mine in a series of slow movements, his hands caught in passing over my skin, as if drawn to cataloging each roll and dip and soft expanse of flesh. Minutes or eons later, he rested between my legs and kissed me again.

I crossed my ankles behind him and hugged his neck, keeping him close. He rocked against me and I tasted his lips.

Gabe entered me in stages, pushing in a little bit at a time, a small roll of his hips with each deepening move. My breath caught in my throat and I pulled him closer, needing him to fill me up. He groaned and drove in until he couldn't go any further. I sighed in pleasure.

The rhythm we set fit perfectly like everything else. I met every pump of his hips with mine, both of us shifting, sliding, pressing, rubbing, tilting in sync. Arousal built with every pass of the head on my insides, and every tease of his pelvis on my heated flesh, adding to the waves of affection that sprung from my heart. By the time we came, warmth filled me up with as much intensity as the lovemaking had rocked my nerve endings.

He retreated but remained between my legs, his head on the soft round of my belly as we caught our breath. He kissed it.

My awareness sported a new thread, gold and silver twirling together, stitching the parts of me that didn't want to let Gabe go.

"Think about us, Lina. Think if there's a way we can have it all."

I ran my fingers through his hair and did just that.

Chapter 29

Gabe

FOR A MAN WHO liked to take control in bed, I'd certainly given it all up making love to Lina that morning. I could still hear the tiny sounds she made as we moved together, so soft against my ear, yet with enough power to scorch every nerve that fired up in response. It wouldn't surprise me if some critical brain structure had already changed as a result of my time with Lina, both in general and this morning in particular. I'd surrendered, and I planned to not let it be for nothing.

We'd fallen asleep again afterwards, naked and in each other's arms. I'd forgotten to set an alarm, a first for me, and woke up a little too late to enjoy a lazy couple of hours with Lina. Instead, I gave her my phone again to order breakfast while I took a shower, then she did the same while I prepped a few docs I'd need later in the day.

I had a very important conversation with my parents ahead of me, and I wanted to be prepared.

So I'd kissed Lina before she got in her car and I got in mine, and I went to get some other relevant information from my office. Half an hour after that, I entered my parents' estate with nerves rolling in my stomach.

Just like that evening all those weeks ago, I entered the home through the unlocked kitchen. Unlike that time, I found my parents sitting on the patio having drinks, the table set for four.

"Gabriel!" Mom got up and came to meet me. Her hug was as perfect as always. "¡Qué bueno verte!"

"Tú también." I squeezed her extra hard, then did the same with my dad. "Is Vi joining us?"

"For food in a bit. ¿Quieres un aperitivo?"

My dad got me homemade pisco sour and we sat down at the table. My folders screamed at me from the empty spot next to me.

"How's Lina?" Mom asked. "How are things going there?"

I bit the inside of my lip. "She's… good. We are… it's complicated."

Dad frowned. "Are things not going well? I thought everything was wonderful, after seeing you two at the lake house!"

I opened my mouth to reply, before two thoughts clashed and they pushed a scoff out of my mouth. "You guys seriously don't beat around the bush, huh? You catch a whiff of a problem and sniff it out immediately, don't you?"

I smiled at my parents, and they smiled back.

"You know us," Dad said. "We want to know everything about our children."

"And I'm pretty sure you love it." Mom patted my hand twice.

"I do, yeah. Actually I was hoping we could talk about Lina."

"Lina?" Dad frowned. "I thought you wanted to talk about work. That that's why you brought paperwork with you."

Instead of my nerves going up, they went down. I trusted my parents that much.

"I want to talk about both, in a way. When I got together with her, I knew my chances of making it work would be low. You both know how much work there is in my position, and with the transition coming up... the logical thing would be to break up. I just... I really, really don't want to."

My parents exchanged a look, but gazed back at me a second later, as usual letting me get everything out of my chest before they started with questions or advice.

"The thing is, Lina is as busy as I am, and we were on the same page when we first... got together. We knew we really didn't have a life where we could be together and continue with everything the same. She has goals that matter as much to her as mine matter to me. She might not want to sacrifice them— I don't *want* her to sacrifice them. But if I don't know how to help her figure that out, if she were even willing... I don't know how to do that for myself, either."

I took a deep gulp of air. "I need to find ways to make more time for myself, and the only thing I can think of is giving up soccer. I think I might have to ask Jake to help me with a few things, but I want to know if you think that will put me at risk with the board, because I can't risk that."

It was only after I'd finished, most of the air gone from my lungs, that I noticed I'd pressed the palm of my hands against my thighs, pushed, and kept pushing. Enough was up in the air that I'd needed to ground myself somehow, and my legs had been where I'd moored myself.

I released the tension in my shoulders and rubbed my hands on the rough fabric of my jeans.

I pursed my lips. "I don't know what to do. I don't want to break up with Lina, but I also don't want to fail you."

My parents frowned simultaneously.

Dad spoke first. "Fail us? What are you talking about?"

"The transition to CEO, Dad. You want to retire and I need to convince the board to let me take over. I don't take that lightly. The stadium deal is going to do a lot for me that way, but I still have to prove I deserve the role. I'm not going to risk any of it, not your dream of early retirement nor me getting the CEO role like we all want. I just don't know how to do it all. If I drop soccer and I rearrange a few of my responsibilities, maybe I can—"

I made to grab the folders I'd left on the empty chair next to me, but my dad waved a hand to stop me.

"Wait, Gabe. No. First of all, you can't fail us. We're all together in this. We're all here to help you in the transition; it's a team effort."

"But if I want to be good for the role and earn the promotion— if I want to be able to walk in your shoes and deserve it— I need to learn how to manage it all, like you did."

I pressed my lips together, the vibrations from my vocal chords traveling from my throat down to my lungs, leaving an electrical charge in their path. Anything could flip the switch, and it would be hard to breathe.

"Oh, hijo." My mom brought her hand to me again, her love and warmth blanketing the section of skin where she touched me.

"You think I manage it all?" Dad's eyes searched mine.

"I know you do. You did everything I'm trying to do and more. You had a wife and two kids while you built this up. I *have* to figure this out, too."

"It's never been me alone, Gabe. Now I have your mom, you, Vi, Jake, and our whole team."

"And what about back then? It was you and mom alone. I know the toll it had on you both. I know you were stretched thin."

I didn't need to remind them of those times. If I had one salient memory, I was sure they had many more.

"We were managing a much smaller company back then, and don't be mistaken, hard work is part of success, but it's not all of it. Plenty of people work just as hard and don't get the same opportunities we did." Dad leaned forward, elbows on the table and hands linked. "We have a lot of privilege and we had a lot of luck. Let us use it to help you. You're putting too much pressure on yourself. That time was hard, but I don't need to pass that on as part of your inheritance. I don't want you to feel like you need to sacrifice your happiness for anything, not even the company."

"We had each other, Gabe." Mom squeezed my arm. "If you can have that with Lina, then we're happy you're trying to figure it out. You could never disappoint us for trying to have that."

"But your retirement..."

"I'm still young, hijo. Working an extra year or two is perfectly fine, if it means you have a chance at finding something good with someone special. Those years were hard but, you know what made it possible?" He took my mom's hand, and gave her an adoring look I'd seen him give her many times through the years. My mom smiled back at him with the same kind of love. "Having your mom by my side."

Fondness for my parents rippled through me, a comforting tide moving across every corner of my being. They continued to gaze at each other with deep affection, and it echoed in my DNA, each gene they'd given me recognizing what mattered. Love mattered. Oak-sized and mature like theirs, or a tender sprout from an acorn, fighting to take root in the ground, like what I felt for Lina.

Mom turned to me, her eyes sparkling. "Our family as a whole— we don't have to work. Each one of us could live off the interest we get for our investments alone, and live a grand life. Yet none of us chooses to do so. Why? Because we all get some-thing out of the work we do. I love that I get to run foundations and social assistance projects, and disrupt conversations at the club, when I say we should all be giving more money away." She smirked.

"And I love to funnel money to her," my dad laughed. "And do things right, rewriting the narrative for companies like ours. You have that, too, Gabe— don't lose sight of that. You couldn't fail us, okay? Jake and I and the rest of the team will help. We will make it work— We. Together. So don't break up with Lina... not for this."

My hand still hovered over the folders, my fingertips barely touching the hardened plastic cover.

I smiled as I pulled away from them. My eyes skipped back and forth between my parents. "I have always looked up to the two of you. If I can be half as good as you are, I'll have achieved every dream I've had. I love you both, so much."

"And we love you." Mom squeezed my arm one last time. "If Lina makes you happy, then I hope you make her happy, too."

"I'll try my hardest to get her to stick with me. You're itching to adopt more of my people, aren't you?"

My parents laughed, and I grinned, and with their love blowing wind at my back, I finally had permission to give my love for Lina a chance.

Lina

The emotional rollercoaster of the last eighteen hours had left me exhausted. From devastation after the fight with my dad and uncle, to getting to know true comfort, to feeling so cherished that I got a bit emotional when I thought about it... My heart still beat a little erratically.

I entered my home trying to make as little noise as possible. It would be best for my mood to avoid seeing my dad, and try to nap in my room instead. Once the fragile feeling making tunnels in my muscles disappeared, I'd ask him to make a decision about my future in the company. No point in returning to work, if it would lead me nowhere.

For a moment, imagining the week ahead as preparation to leave made me breathless. I wouldn't give them more than that. I'd have to reach out to my network and see if anyone was hiring, but then I'd have my future open to me.

My heart beat fast as I went up the stairs, the force of it echoing at the base of my throat. Would it be okay to ask Gabe for job leads? I didn't want to work for him; I didn't want anything to come in the way of us potentially getting together. But he knew people, and if I ended up needing a new job, I was pretty sure he'd be happy to help.

Hence why I didn't want to have anything come up between us. He was an incredible man and if I may not get my family company, I wanted to at least get the guy.

The door to my room was open. I froze a few steps from it, my hand hanging in front of me. No noise came from inside and, a few moments later, my body thawed and I pushed the door open with two fingers.

My dad stood next to my bed, facing a side table.

"Dad?"

His shoulders went up to his ears; he didn't turn to me right away and, when he finally did, his eyes looked sheepish.

"Oh, bueno. Hola, hija. I thought you would be away for a bit longer." He rubbed his lips together. "Were you with Gabriel?"

I nodded. He did too.

I entered my room and stood in the middle of the space; the distance between my dad and I remained wide. "Please don't make a fuss about me staying with him."

Dad chuckled, and the gesture somehow made him look several years younger. "I won't. Not Gabriel. I like him."

"Then don't rush to marry me off. Gabriel is amazing, but we're nowhere near thinking about a wedding yet."

"Yet? No, I— well." He stared at the floor and took a few breaths. "As happy as we— I would be— if you two decided to— Mmh. Lo que pasa es... well."

He sighed and turned to collect an envelope I hadn't seen. He took a few steps my way and offered it to me. His eyes didn't quite meet mine.

"I'm not good at words, sometimes," he said. "Especially in English. And I really want to explain myself to you."

I hesitated, more out of surprise than anything.

He insisted, pushing his arm closer to me. "Please. Read it. I'm better at writing things down."

I took the envelope from him and held it in my hands. *Catalina*, it said.

I stared back at him, a hard knot in my throat.

My dad rubbed his lips together again. "I'll be outside by the tree, if you want me after you read it. Or you can find me later... whatever you prefer."

I nodded and waited until he'd left, the door closed behind him, to release the tension in my shoulders. It left me with a shaky breath.

I sat on my reading chair and opened the unsealed envelope. My dad's script met me and my eyes teared up almost instantly.

Hija mía,

I wish I were better speaking up and sharing my thoughts clearly when needed. Ask your mom, I have written a few letters to her in the past when my words failed me. But I hope that, just like she has in the past, you will accept this attempt instead.

You are one of the joys of my life, Lina. We waited so long for you, and I'm grateful everyday that we had you. I am proud that you are following my steps and want to take over this company I founded. It may be wrong, but I think of it as one of my life accomplishments, that you want to keep it going. If you didn't know that you absolutely have my shares in the company, then that is my failing. I should have said so a long time ago, but I sometimes have trouble making a stand. I was raised to listen to Miguel on everything; setting up this company was the one thing

I did on my own... and not for long. His attitude has been a necessary part to our success, and I usually let him take the lead.

When Miguel goes on and on with his rants, I tune him out. When you join him and argue with him, I panic. Your mom says I'm like an ostrich and hide my head in the sand at the smallest hint of trouble. I know she's right, and I'm sorry for what it's done to you. You deserve better from your father. I will try to do better. But don't let my cowardice scare you, I've always been on your side. I'll do my best to show you, moving forward. And it will be my pleasure to see Enrique go on to chase his dreams, while I support you as you chase yours. Your uncle will have to accept it.

You can have it all, hija. You can have this company, a partner, and children. Or none of it, I suppose. Whatever you choose, you can have. If I insist on you having a family of your own it's because I want you to know joy like I've known, with your mom and you in my life. But as long as you're happy, I will be happy to cheer you on. Whatever that looks like for you. Even if I keep on having trouble speaking these words to you, know I feel each of them in my heart.

Please forgive your old man for his old school ways, and

know that I love you most of all.

Tu papi

Tears had fallen down my face for as long as I had been reading the letter, but seeing how he'd signed it added power to the wave of emotion cresting inside of me. He used to ask me to call him papi, growing up. I'd stopped sometime as a teen, and seeing the word on paper again, in his writing, healed half the papercuts I'd learned to live with.

I let myself cry, alone this time, but it felt different. Gabe's hug from the night before had filled some tank inside of me, where I didn't feel as alone with my tears. After reading my dad's letter, it was easier to believe I could count on my father's support, as well. It changed my outlook for the future by a hundred eighty degrees, all over again.

And I loved the promise it carried with it.

After, when I went outside to find my dad, we hugged for a long time, and neither of us said a word.

Chapter 30

Gabe: are you at home right now?

Lina: yes. Just got up from a nap. Why?

Gabe: I know it's been only a few hours, but can I take you out?

Lina: I'd enjoy that

Gabe: I'll be there in an hour

———

Lina

I DIDN'T KNOW WHAT to expect from Gabe's texts. Was this goodbye, in his eyes? But I prepared for the night like it would be my chance. At the lake, I'd told him if he wanted his person to be with him even though he had very little time to give, he had to ask. Give them the choice. And yet, as I'd fallen asleep for a much needed nap, it had been easy to decide I'd freely take as much as he could give; he didn't even have to utter the words.

The doorbell hadn't finished ringing when I opened the door. His finger was still on the button, and it lingered there as a nervous smile appeared on his face.

"Hi." I held a jacket in my hand, and I squeezed the fabric to quiet my trembling fingers.

At first he didn't respond. His hand moved from the doorbell to the space between us, and he offered it to me.

"Ready?" he asked.

I gave him my hand and he led me to his car, where his driver waited for us. We settled in the back seat, and soon Josué took us away from my parents' home and into city traffic.

"Where are we going?"

He grabbed my hand again. "You'll see. We're not far."

It took us several minutes to get there, but Gabe kept quiet, so I didn't ask again.

The car finally stopped by an open shopping market known in the city for its picturesque storefronts.

"Go get a coffee or something, okay?" Gabe told Josué. "Use the company card. I'll text you when we're done, and thanks again for doing this on a Saturday night."

"This is what you pay me for, Gabe."

"But when was the last time I asked you to do this on a weekend?"

"Still."

"Coffee and a snack, then."

Josué chuckled, and Gabe got out of the car to help me do the same. Once I'd put my jacket on, he put his hand on my lower back and guided me into the pedestrian-only streets connecting the many shops in the area.

"We won't have to walk for long," he said to my ear.

It hadn't been necessary for him to speak quietly to me that way; even though this area was quite busy during the day and I would have had trouble hearing him over the bustling noise, on a Saturday evening the place was mostly empty. Most stores had closed, except for a couple of coffee shops, where a few couples chatted in a cozy, intimate setting.

He didn't stop at any of them, though. I sighed and followed Gabe through the cobblestone street, a cold breeze in the air. We held hands, and he used the connection to guide me to a store with dark green walls and a big sign in golden letters that read, *La Belle Fleur*.

Gabe knocked on the door, despite the sign indicating it was closed.

I frowned. "Are you sure this is where you meant to take me?"

He gazed at me and nodded, just as the lights turned on inside and someone opened the door.

He smiled at me before turning to the petite woman that appeared in front of us.

"Hi," Gabe said. "I'm Gabriel Sotomayor, I called earlier today. I talked to Martina on the phone."

"Hi, yes. That was me. Come on in."

The woman opened the door for us and we stepped into the space. Flowers and vases filled every corner of the store, colors exploding in multiple textures against every shade of green imaginable. Shelves created surfaces for more blossoms, exotic and classic ones alike, layering flowers into a lush display. Even the counter was covered in flowers in pretty vases, leaving only the center of the room open to us.

I turned in a circle, admiring the effect. Some of these flowers were meant to be outside during the day but, at night, they all came together into the shop and made it breathtaking.

"I'll be in the back room, if you need me." Martina smiled at us, and left us alone.

I turned to Gabe. "I must admit my curiosity is piqued. What are we doing here?"

He smiled as he stepped closer to me. He looked me straight in the eye. "Do you think they're pretty?"

"Yes." I squinted at him. "That's never been my problem with flowers. They're gorgeous, of course."

I didn't think he'd forgotten our conversation about flowers before, so I bit my tongue not to remind him. He'd get to it soon.

"What would you say if I told you I would get every single flower here for you, if you wanted? That you can pick anything you want."

"I'd say you know they make me sad."

He nodded. "Yes. So how about something more permanent?"

He took a velvet box from his pocket and presented it to me.

I stopped breathing, my eyes glued to the small rectangular case.

"It's not a ring, Lina. You can breathe again."

My lungs restarted into a soft chuckle, and I stared at him, my hands clasped tight in front of me.

He smirked. "You said you weren't waiting for a ring at the end of this, remember?"

"I remember." I blinked a few times.

He opened the box. "But I did say I might get you a commemorative brooch."

A beautiful vintage gold flower rested in the velvet case. The stem curved slightly, and two delicately carved leaves wrapped around it. Several layers of petals surrounded the center disc, with small diamonds suggesting dew drops. The disc itself was made of a single deep yellow crystal, each internal facet glimmering in the light. A striking golden dahlia. My gasp was quiet, but audible.

He chuckled and took it out of its container. "To be honest, when I bought it I did so hoping it would make you laugh. A gasp works well, though, because now I hope you like it enough to keep. Maybe even use it."

"Are you kidding? It's gorgeous! Can you help me put it on my lapel?"

He handled the piece of jewelry on the thick wool of my jacket, his concentration frown in place.

"When I picked it," he said, securing the brooch and contemplating the results, "I thought it was a way to give you permanent flowers. This one wouldn't make you sad. It will never die. So maybe you would look at it and remember me fondly."

The flower on my lapel had a beautiful patina; the crystals on it shone. A knot threatened to form in my throat but I fought it. Gabe had given me no signs to say this was goodbye or something different. With his good-guy, cinnamon roll personality— so salient in most contexts, except when it counted— I wouldn't be surprised if he hadn't considered changing the rules of our arrangement. Besides, he was stretched thin at work, and I'd understand if he wanted to prioritize that and his family.

But I had to try.

I lifted my eyes to him. He stared back at me, ready for my gaze. My heart began a race in my chest, the rhythm of each beat a drum against my breastbone.

Opening up was hard for me. It wouldn't have been a real option for me, if Gabe hadn't already shown me he'd keep my courage safe.

"I kept the flower," I blurted. The knot in my throat disappeared, but nerves took over my stomach. "The one from the wedding. I was always going to remember you fondly."

I bit my bottom lip. He soothed it with his thumb again, like he did before, like he couldn't take me causing myself even a hint of pain.

He smiled. "You kept it?"

"So maybe this one— this one can mean something else."

His eyes twinkled. "What could it mean?"

"Something permanent, maybe." Determined, I steeled myself and showed him the most tender part of myself. "I don't want to break up, Gabe."

His smile stretched slowly, the corner of his lips tilting in a delicious slant.

"I see." His fingers fanned on the side of my face, and his thumb pulled slightly down from my bottom lip. His eyes locked on my mouth. "You're a woman who goes for what you want."

"Yes."

Could he feel my breath, the simple word on his thumb?

Most of all, what would his answer be?

"I tried to go for what I want, too. I brought you here to show you I'd give you every flower if you wanted, hoping you'd want a special one instead."

"What I want right now is to know what you want." I curled my hands in the folds of his jacket, like he'd go away and I'd need to stop him.

"You." His hand moved to cradle my neck, fingers digging into my skin as he pressed his lips to mine. "I want you, Lina. I brought you here to beg you to stay with me."

"Beg?" A shockwave built inside of me, from the ground, up my legs, and to my hands; I pulled him to me with the power of it. "Fuck's sake, you don't have to beg!"

And I kissed him. Kissed him hard, kissed him soft, kissed him like I could keep him forever. He wrapped his arms around me and brought me tight against him, his mouth following my lead for once. My hands traveled up his chest to his shoulders.

I hooked my arms around his neck and lifted myself to the tips of my toes, only so I could kiss him even more. Dizziness took over my head, lightness in my chest, and maybe I needed to take a deep breath, but for the first time, I understood women of old who could faint when feelings took over.

"Lina—" his chuckle was at least halfway to a moan. "We'll make time. We have time."

"I'll wait, Gabe. You said this stage will last a couple of years for you. You don't have to ask— I'm offering."

"No— I mean, that's amazing." He shook his head as if he was as overwhelmed as I was, and a soft chuckle came out of him. "Wow. I didn't know I needed you to want it as much as I did until now but— I meant we need to talk, and we have time for that. I just needed to know you want to have it all with me, too."

"I want it all with you."

His grin filled the whole flower shop with light. "Then we'll have it all."

I echoed his joy with a smile just as wide, just as full of hope.

"C'mon," he said. "Let's go to my place. We have things to talk about. We'll change the rules. We'll figure it out."

After one last kiss, we let Martina close behind us.

Stepping out into the cool night air, the vintage flower on my lapel, I held Gabe's hand with no intention of ever letting go.

Chapter 31

Lina

SEVERAL WEEKS AFTER OUR conversation at La Belle Fleur and later in Gabe's condo, I closed the folder in front of me, which contained all the information I'd worked so hard on for several weeks.

I gazed around the small boardroom on the top floor of the company building, letting my eyes connect with my dad, uncle, and the rest of management.

"It's decided, then." I made my voice sound confident; it pleased me to feel my vocal cords and even my whole chest offered no resistance to my goal. "This is the final plan for the shortlist proposal."

If I gave myself permission to be extra, I would decorate the folder with gold foil and preserve it in a shadowbox. Nothing less for the document that solidified that the stadium deal would be mine, and an opportunity for my father to mentor me as the future director of Martínez and Associates.

I stole a final glance at my uncle. The look on Tío Miguel's face, so full of contained rage— the dark purple of blood flowing to his brown face, a deep frown, and tight lips— gave me immense pleasure. Best of all? My dad kept quiet, but did not placate *me*. I bit the inside of my lip not to let out an evil snicker.

A knock on the door distracted me. My assistant hovered there, waiting for my attention.

"Gabriel Sotomayor is here."

I grinned. Of course he was. He'd helped me with the final proposal, shaping the stadium deal and turning it into the section of our careers we got to share. A project we were both incredibly proud of. One we were confident would give him the CEO title officially, too.

Funnily enough, this project was only a small part of everything we shared. We'd really, really found a way to have it all.

"Please tell him I'll be right out, thanks," I said. "We're almost done here."

We wrapped up the meeting, and I didn't even try to hide the joy exploding in my chest. Maybe that was why, when I entered my office to find Gabe standing in the middle of it, facing toward me and talking on the phone, I ignored the device and half-tackled him into a hug.

"Yeah, move that meeti—fffff— agh." From the sound of his interrupted message, his lungs may have malfunctioned as I walked right into him and squeezed. He surrounded me with his free arm to keep me in place, confirming what I'd known:

he'd loved my hello. "Sorry, I just— anyway. Please move that meeting to the afternoon, Solange."

I rested my head on the nook of his neck. The warm smell of his cologne filled my senses and I sighed in pleasure.

"Right, yeah," he said to the phone. "Mh-hm. Okay."

I loved hearing the vibration of his voice in his chest, but I lifted my head regardless. Peppering kisses on his jaw, neck, and face was a favorite thing of mine, too.

He seemed to enjoy my lips on him this way, because he shifted his head to give me better access, while still talking on his cell. "Well, yeah. That's something Jake is going to oversee now, so can you discuss it with his assistant?"

I briefly considered closing my door and getting on my knees, but the last time I'd done that he'd made me pay afterwards. Even though I didn't have all the details for what we'd be doing that night, I knew enough to know it wasn't the right time to do that.

For a treat, I allowed my hands to get under his blazer and grab his side rolls through his tailored shirt, then continue the journey to his ass. I squeezed and brought his hips forward to rub against my softness.

"Ungh." The sound had been low in his throat, but I heard it, and I laughed. "That's it. Yep. That's it— Solange."

The chuckle that came out of me had a similar range as his bassy *ungh*.

"Gotta go now," he continued. "Ah-hah. Sure. Okay, bye. You too, bye."

He'd already pulled the phone away from his ear as he said the last few words, and now tapped on it with his hand half-way around me. With both arms now, he brought me closer and, in the same move, gave me a hard kiss.

"You're evil," he said. "We need another talk, it seems. You know I have a hard time thinking when you're all over me like this."

I grinned. "It's not like you didn't like it. Even though it can... get hard."

He smirked, raised an eyebrow, and rubbed his semi on me. "And it's not like you don't like it when I give you a stern talking to."

"Oh, noooo." I made my tone as fake as possible. "Are you going to punish me later? I thought we wouldn't have time for it tonight."

The smirk turned cheeky on his lips. He took a step back from me and rearranged his shirt; his blazer. The phone went directly to his pocket. "We don't have time for it tonight, but there's always the weekend. I'm thinking you really need a reprimand."

With a smile on my face, I rounded the corner of my desk and focused on turning off my laptop and gathering my things.

"Are you finally going to reveal the plan for tonight, then?" I grabbed my bag and made sure I wasn't forgetting anything. "My overnight things are in my closet, if you can help me get it?"

Gabe went for it. "We're going to see that band you wanted to see live."

My hands froze halfway to closing my purse. I lifted my eyes to him. "You mean... no, you don't mean *Cruz Al Sur*? They're not playing here tonight."

When he turned back to me, his eyes crinkled at the corners with his joy. "We're getting dinner on the plane. We can change before landing and the car will take us to the show. Then we'll stay in a hotel, before flying back tomorrow morning. I'll have to work while having breakfast, probably, but..." he shrugged. "I wanted to treat you."

My insides liquified, the movement intense enough to count as a small tide. My heart jumped to my throat. "Gabe—"

Unable to speak, I stood still for a moment. Gabe's smile widened further, the sight amazing on his face and thawing me out of my shock. He lifted a hand to me, and I practically ran around my desk to hold it.

I stepped right in front of him, our fingers interlocked, and I gazed up at him. "Thank you."

"We said we'd make time for special nights, didn't we?"

I nodded. "We said we'd do more than work together in our pajamas."

"Exactly. Especially on a minor anniversary."

"A... what?" I pushed away from him with my free hand on his chest. "What anniversary?"

He dropped a soft kiss on my lips. "Happy three months together, Lina."

To the surprise of us both— judging by the way he blinked twice, eyebrows high on his forehead— I scoffed.

"We've been together for a bit over *five* months, Gabriel."

The gesture on his face didn't change as he let a gust of air out. "No."

"No? What do you mean, no?"

"Can't believe you're counting since we—" he stole a glance out the door, to verify our privacy, but seemed to change his mind in the process. "No, Lina. We got together when I gave you the brooch."

The same brooch I had in its velvet box in my bag, to wear later that night.

I slapped his chest in a playful blow. "*Of course* I count it since— you know. Since things happened while preparing the contract for the stadium project."

"But that wasn't... on *purpose*. After the brooch it was on *purpose*. We both meant it and—"

"Gabe."

"Lina."

We engaged in a stare off for a long moment, before he broke and laughed.

"We are ridiculous, after all, aren't we?" He pulled from my hand. "We have to go. We can keep arguing on the plane."

I pulled back and made him kiss me once more. "Good thing you're so cute."

He laughed and I followed him.

Even though this could become an ongoing discussion between us, it didn't scare me. Because whether we'd been together for three or five plus months, one thing was certain: what mattered were the years we had in front of us.

Something told me they'd be good. And I couldn't wait to make it all true.

Epilogue 1

Gabe

THAT YEAR, THE CONSTRUCTION Cares gala had the most attendees I'd ever seen. Unlike my first few years participating and bringing my friends with me, this time I also brought my fiancée.

The whole gang had attended this year, as well as my parents. My friends and their person, this time including my sister in the group as Jake's partner— things had finally cleared up there a few months before— socialized with some of the people we met here annually.

To think that I used to seek Lina out for a yearly check-in the same way, before everything had changed for us. Awe moved through my chest, warm and airy, and lifted me up, because I hadn't had to wait years to have her in my life every day. She slept next to me every night, and she was the first thing I saw every morning. Between her and my newly appointed CEO position, my chest swelled with the same kind of joy I saw in my parents' eyes when they looked at me.

I squeezed Lina's hand, the one carrying a jewel she liked to say was way too big for her. She secretly liked it, I thought.

"I should have chosen a different dress." She put a hand on her solar plexus, where a new tattoo healed under the fabric. "Or moved my ink appointment for another time."

The hall this year had been decorated with an Andean theme, heavy on the Quechua fabric designs and Diaguita ceramics. My mom had helped organize the gala this year, and she'd made sure to ethically source and celebrate every piece, which had been borrowed and which would be returned to their people afterwards. I cast my eyes over one of the ceramic pieces displayed nearby, and took in the elegant geometric shapes.

I leaned closer to Lina and whispered into her ear, half my attention still on the red, black, and white painted bowl. "That's the issue with getting tattoos. Once you start, you never stop."

"You're one to talk. I can see your latest peeking out your sleeve cuff."

I grinned at her. "But that just proves my point! When we first got together, all I had was my shoulder done. Now I have a full sleeve and a thigh one."

"The thigh one is my favorite," she sighed. "Though I really like how it looks when your tattoo peeks out of your shirt."

I stepped closer to her and smirked. "Oh? Tell me, how much do you like it?"

She stared at me with a playful look. She undid my tuxedo jacket's button, finding the muffin tops she so loved to squeeze.

"Get tattoos all over, Gabriel. Please. That's how much I like them."

I wrapped my arms around her, her hands still on my sides. "Okay. Just because you like them so much."

"Though at least part of it is because I still delight in the look Tío Miguel had when he saw you shirtless at the lake house."

I laughed. "That was such a high moment in my life."

"Third only to the face he made when my dad announced he was giving me his shares, which is the second best moment."

I lifted my hands to her face and smiled. "And which one is the best moment?"

I had a pretty good idea what her reply would be.

She grinned. "The moment you asked me to make this all permanent. This time with a ring I'm pretty sure people can see from the International Space Station."

The music in the hall changed from soft classical in the background, to more active classical. The kiss we shared in that moment was awkward, with both of us grinning, but it was perfect, anyway.

She smiled against my lips. "I wish that was a sign that they finally added a dancing portion to the night. Instead, it's time to do some bidding."

I let go of her and buttoned my jacket again. "We could dance anyway. If you think you can move your arm around despite the weight of that rock on your finger?"

"You seriously overdid it, Gabe. What if I hurt someone with this thing?"

"I'll pay their medical bills in cash. Not to worry. I don't give you as much jewelry as I thought I might, so let me show off once in a while, okay?"

She faked a sigh. "Okay."

"I have to make it worth it, making your family a little too happy that you're getting married. You're so old at almost thirty-three, they were about to have an apoplexy."

"What?" She laughed. "I didn't want to give them the joy of it. That's why I needed to make you wait."

"Then why did you say yes?"

She hugged me, her arms underneath my jacket, wrecking it again. "Because I love you too much for it to matter more than you and I, together."

"You and I, together. I like how you said that."

"Forever, okay?"

I nodded. "And always real."

"C'mon." She took my hand and led me back to our table. "Let's go spend some of our money and change a few people's lives. What do you think?"

"I think I'm pretty happy you changed mine."

The smile she gave me promised me many more, for the rest of our lives. And I couldn't wait to see each one of them.

***

THE END

Do you want to get a peek at Gabe and Lina finally taking some time off, and getting spicy at a private island? Then

sign up for my newsletter and get the second epilogue! Visit leonorsoliz.com/yfn-2nd-ep and get yours!

Thank you

I'D LIKE TO THANK my husband and our little family, for all the support (particularly in patience, time, and labor) you've given me. I don't think I'd be publishing my stories without you. The fact that this feels like a family endeavor is so special to me.

I also want to thank my online friends, whether we talk on Discord, Booktok, or Bookstagram, each one of you helps me to keep going when things get hard. And thank you to Chantel and Beth, for giving this book a read and helping me make it what it is, with your comments and swoons.

Thank you to my IRL friends and my coven, for listening whether I need to vent or celebrate, and do it with me.

I am incredibly fortunate to have you all in my life.

About the Author

LEONOR WROTE HER FIRST Meet Cute at eight years old and never really stopped. After many years of practicing and dreaming, she took the plunge and wrote a full-length romance novel. Then she wrote some more.

Her stories are written for comfort: love as it can be. Writing love for today means diverse characters with emotional depth and wisdom. Her characters are doing the work, folks.

Leonor is a Latina living in Canada, working as a therapist during the day and fitting as much writing to her life as she can. She's also a multi-crafter, trying her hand at watercolor, jewelry, and anything else that strikes her fancy.

You can connect with me on:

www.leonorsoliz.com

hello@leonorsoliz.com

TikTok: https://www.tiktok.com/@leonor.soliz.author

Facebook: https://www.facebook.com/leonorsolizz

Instagram: https://www.instagram.com/leonor.soliz/

Twitter: https://twitter.com/leonorsolizz

Upcoming Series by the Author

COZY LATINE BILLIONAIRES

The story of two Latine siblings and their best friends, and all four of them find their person. Ethical billionaires, found families, and some of the best tropes around.

Check it out here

LAGUNA ISLAND

Several interconnected stories with one thing in common: their love for this slice of heaven by the sea.

Check it out here

Also by the Author

HOLLYWOOD LOVE

One of the most famous actors in the world meets a new and upcoming Latina filmmaker, and it changes their lives and the lives of the two closest to them.

Check it out here

Printed in the USA
CPSIA information can be obtained
at www.ICGtesting.com
LVHW091630130624
783067LV00003B/200

9 781738 056200